One Sunday at a Time:

Book Two of the Forever Divas Series

One Sunday at a Time:

Book Two of the Forever Divas Series

E.N. Joy

www.urbanbooks.net

Urban Books, LLC
300 Farmingdale Road, NY-Route 109
Farmingdale, NY 11735

One Sunday at a Time: Book Two of the Forever
Divas Series

ISBN 13: 978-1-62286-454-6
ISBN 10: 1-62286-454-9

First Mass Market Printing May 2017
First Trade Paperback Printing April 2016
Printed in the United States of America

10 9 8 7 6 5 4 3 2 1

*This is a work of fiction. Any references or sim-
ilarities to actual events, real people, living or
dead, or to real locales are intended to give
the novel a sense of reality. Any similarity in
other names, characters, places, and incidents is
entirely coincidental.*

Distributed by Kensington Publishing Corp.
Submit orders to:
Customer Service
400 Hahn Road
Westminster, MD 21157-4627
Phone: 1-800-733-3000
Fax: 1-800-659-2436

One Sunday at a Time:

Book Two of the Forever Divas Series

by

E.N. Joy

Dedication

This book is dedicated to all the women out there who feel like they have so much going on in their life that they are about to lose control. Know that losing control is a good thing . . . when you plan on letting God take control.

Acknowledgments

I would like to acknowledge Stacy Johnson-Leonard, Shawn Hamilton, K.k. Burks, Tonya Woodfolk, Qiana Drennen, and Jocelyn Boffman Green. You didn't know me from Eve or Adam—I've yet to meet all of you in person—yet you became my unofficial street and social media team by supporting me and advocating for me and my work simply on the strength of your belief in what I do. That alone speaks volumes as to why I write. Thank you for sharing my work and introducing me to readers around the world who otherwise would have no idea who E. N. Joy is. Lovers of the written word like yourselves truly make an author feel like a rock star. Thank you!

OTHER BOOKS BY E. N. JOY:

Me, Myself and Him
She Who Finds a Husband
Been There, Prayed That
Love, Honor or Stray
Trying to Stay Saved
I Can Do Better All By Myself
And You Call Yourself a Christian
The Perfect Christian
The Sunday Only Christian
Ordained by the Streets
"A Woman's Revenge"
(Anthology: *Best Served Cold*)
I Ain't Me No More
More Than I Can Bear
You Get What You Pray For
When All Is Said and Prayed
Behind Every Good Woman (eBook only)
She's No Angel (eBook series)
Angel on the Front Pew (eBook series)
California Angel (eBook series)
Flower in My Hair
Even Sinners Have Souls
(Edited by E. N. Joy)

Prologue

"You can't leave me!" Deborah yelled at Lynox, spittle flying from her mouth. She looked like a madwoman. She felt like a madwoman. Her hair was in disarray, and perspiration had beaded up on her forehead. It was a wonder she didn't have foam caked up in the corners of her mouth. She was acting rabid, like the victim in a science fiction horror movie who had failed to escape the vicious plague that was attacking all of Earth.

She needed help; that was no longer the million-dollar question. The question now was, why hadn't she gotten the help she so desperately needed, or rather, why hadn't she continued getting the help she'd once been receiving? For a minute there she had felt that she'd been doing so well that she didn't need any help. There had always been the possibility that if she fell back into her slump again, she could just pick up where she'd left off in her treatment. Not only had some of her old traits reared their ugly heads, but she was far worse off now than she had ever been before. What had started off as a manageable snowball was now an avalanche. If Lynox didn't get out of the way, he'd be buried alive underneath it.

"I can leave you, I am leaving you, and I'm taking the kids with me," was Lynox's reply to his wife's statement.

So now not only was her husband leaving her, but he was also taking their two sons with him? The rage that welled up in Deborah's being was uncontrollable. That didn't come as any surprise. She'd lost jurisdiction over her emotions a long time ago. At first, when her life had seemed to be getting hectic, she had managed somewhat. She'd hidden the darkness under the beam of an invisible flashlight. Outsiders couldn't see the darkness or the object projecting the false lighting. But then, emotionally, it had felt as if one thing was piling on top of the other. Anger issues. Depression. Anxiety. The need to be in control. Compulsion for order. There had been times, after researching the term, when she'd even thought she might be bipolar. Heck, maybe she had been experiencing a little bit of all of them, which was a recipe for disaster. With her husband standing in front of her, a suitcase in hand, and threatening to leave her, it looked like the recipe had been followed to a tee, and now the timer on the oven was sounding. It was done. Over. Finished. Kaput.

"Why are you doing this?" Deborah cried out. "Why are you hurting me?" Deborah stood there, blocking the closed bedroom door. She'd already told Lynox that he was leaving over her dead body. Those hadn't merely been desperate words flung out of her mouth. She'd meant it.

"I was hurting you when I was pampering and pacifying you, instead of making you go do something about it," Lynox told her.

"So now what?" Deborah raised her arms and then allowed them to fall to her sides. "You call this helping me?"

Lynox shook his head. "No. I call this giving you the opportunity to help yourself." Lynox slowly walked toward his wife. It pained him so much to see her like this. He didn't understand how a person's emotions and behavior could shift so erratically. Why was it that he and Deborah could experience the best night in the world, but then Deborah would wake up mad at the world? Or how could one little thing that threw her off schedule or was out of order send her on a rampage?

Although Deborah loved her job as a literary agent and an editor, it was hard for Lynox to tell sometimes. Getting steady, good-paying projects was every freelance editor's dream. But as an agent, sometimes Deborah could get overwhelmed by submissions or needy authors. So when all her projects collided or piled on top of one another, she often operated out of fear of not getting done what she already had on her plate before another healthy portion was served up. When Deborah was working on one project, her mind would already be on the next one, and the one after that. God forbid Lynox or the children needed her to do something for them. She'd bite their heads off just for asking.

For Deborah, there were instances when she felt pangs of guilt for feeling as though she'd put her job before her family. She'd be regretful, which would make her feel like less than a good wife and mother, sending her into a bout of depression. Everything about her life was like a double-edged sword, and now she was cutting up. Lynox had already received one wound too many. It was time for him to go, but Deborah wasn't going to allow that without putting up a fight.

"I promise I'll be better," Deborah pleaded, looking into her man's eyes. "I'll do whatever you want me to do." Deborah bounced up and down like a child begging her parent to buy her something from the ice-cream truck.

Lynox rested his hands on Deborah's shoulders. The gesture was both to comfort her and to make her stop bouncing. He could see that his leaving was eating her up. He was afraid. He really didn't know what his wife would do after he walked out that door, but he was more afraid of what might happen if he didn't.

"Don't you get it, baby? I don't want you to do whatever *I* want you to do. I want you to do what you need to do. You need help, and unless you feel that you need help and you get that help for yourself, things won't get better."

Lynox was right. The way Deborah stared into his eyes with no rebuttal was silent proof that she agreed. Still, if she did get help, she wanted him to be there by her side during the process.

"I will be getting help for myself because I want to," Deborah said. "But I'd be lying if I said that I wasn't doing it for the family too. I know if I'm better, then you guys will be better," she said. Made sense too, because when she wasn't happy, nobody was happy. Her misery seemed to eject from her pores, bringing everyone in the house down or forcing them to walk on eggshells. Even her nine-month-old son was whiny and cranky when Deborah was having a bad day or just a bad moment even.

"I will support you," Lynox said. "For the sake of our children and our marriage, I will support you."

Deborah exhaled a gasp of hot air. "Oh, yes. God, thank you!" Deborah threw her arms around Lynox and cried. This time hers were tears of joy and relief. She gripped his shirt, holding on to him as if she never wanted to let go. She didn't want to let go.

"But I'll just be doing it from another address."

Instantly, Deborah's demeanor changed. She stiffened, and her tears of joy seemed to stop midway down her cheeks. She pulled back from Lynox but still gripped his shirt. "You're dying to go out there and be with her, aren't you?" Deborah glared at Lynox. "That's what your leaving is really about."

"Be with who, Deborah?" Lynox noticed that Deborah's eyes were turning wild. "No. You know what? I'm not even about to do this with you. Not again." Lynox removed Deborah's hands from his shirt and walked over to the door. He turned to face Deborah. "Call me when you get some help . . . for real this time." He opened the door, his back now to Deborah.

He should have thought twice about turning his back on Deborah. The Beats Pill speaker crashing against the door, missing Lynox's head by inches, was proof of that. Lynox held the doorknob. He gripped it tightly, causing the palm of his hand to turn red. The veins in his hand were pulsating. He squeezed his eyes shut so hard that he got an instant headache. It was like déjà vu all over again from only a couple of months ago. He had to get out of there before things got physical, like they had the last time. He still carried far too much regret from that night to pile on more. He opened his eyes and took two steps out the door.

"You took vows. You said you would be with me until death do us part," Deborah shouted at Lynox's back.

Deborah's words stopped Lynox in his tracks. He turned around and faced his wife. "The death of what, though, Debbie? The death of being in love? The death of trust? Given how our marriage is disintegrating, the death of one of us? How many things have to die, things that are supposed to be the foundation of our marriage, before the marriage itself dies?"

Deborah had no reply for her husband. Sure, the vows they'd each read from the Bible and exchanged included the words "till death do us part." But Lynox was right. Their vows didn't specifically say that this death was the physical death of the husband or the wife. So many things had already died, some that probably couldn't even be resuscitated. Deborah was willing to ride this thing out, though, until the wheels fell off. That was easy for her to say, considering that she was the one wearing them down until they did.

How had things gotten this bad? They were at the point of no return. And now she feared that once Lynox walked out that door, he wouldn't return. She wouldn't be able to live with herself knowing that she was the cause of her marriage being over, the cause of her family being split. She couldn't live like that. She couldn't live without Lynox. She couldn't live without her family together as one. She couldn't live. She wouldn't. So allowing Lynox to walk out that door and go on with his life, leaving her on her own to bear such devastation, wasn't an option. So Deborah did what she had to do to stop the pain before it ever hit.

Chapter 1

A few months prior . . .

"Would you know what crazy looked like if you saw it?" Deborah said as she sat on her therapist's couch. It was a different therapist than the one she'd seen regularly almost two years ago.

Prior to her arriving for her first visit with this particular therapist, Deborah had, once again, pictured the stereotypical couch in a shrink's office. Her old therapist had had a leather one. She figured almost every therapist would offer his or her patients a couch. She'd also pictured herself being the stereotypical patient, lying on a couch and pouring out her life story to a stranger. The previous therapist had never even got a quarter of Deborah's life story before she stopped seeing her.

So here Deborah was once again, taking another stab at it. She'd share her deepest and darkest moments with someone who wouldn't judge her. Well, he might judge her, but it would go against all his professional ethics to do so verbally . . . to her face. No, he'd save it for pillow talk with his significant other. Deborah was okay with that. What she wasn't okay with was lying down on the couch on which now she sat. It looked like a tweed couch someone had salvaged from the curb on trash pickup day. It gave Deborah the heebee-jeebies. Her skin crawled as she imagined all the unseen bedbugs that might be getting comfortable on her clothing. On top of whatever the outrageous therapy bill might be, there would be an exterminating bill.

All this better be worth it, she thought. She had said she would never get to the point in her life where she had to see a therapist again, and now she felt so foolish, having done exactly that. She felt like a failure, like her past treatments, efforts, and prayers had all been in vain. Here she was, back at square one, after she'd come so far. That was one of the reasons she had decided to try a new therapist. She didn't want the old one to think that she was a loser who couldn't keep it together. And that was the same reason why she hadn't told her husband anything about this appointment. "Don't Ask, Don't Tell." Sure that policy had once been meant for the military and not for marriages, but if the shoe fit . . .

Deborah had chosen this therapist because she'd heard he was one of the best psychiatrists in town. Word in the industry was that if he couldn't help put all the nuts and bolts in place, then the patient was pretty much broken for life. God, Deborah hoped she could be fixed. Walking around broken, whether physically or mentally, amounted to less than a good quality of life.

This MD had been officially back to practicing for only a few months, but he had been highly recommended by one of the sisters at Deborah's church, New Day Temple of Faith. As a matter of fact, it was her fellow church member's praise report and testimony about what he'd done to help her situation with her ex-husband and his birth mother that had penetrated Deborah's spirit and given her the impetus to seek him out.

"Why would you ask that? If I'd know what crazy looked like if I saw it?" Dr. Vanderdale asked Deborah as he sat behind his old wooden desk. It looked as though it, once upon a time, might have been sitting on the curb, right next to the couch. When he had decided to start practicing again, he had had his old office furniture brought out of storage, rather than buying new items to furnish his office. It made him feel like he'd never stopped practicing. He'd had it all professionally cleaned, dusted, and polished, though. "Do you think you are crazy?"

"Isn't that why people like me come to see people like you?" Deborah asked legitimately. She had done her research when initially trying to find a therapist. She had needed to know what the difference was between a clinical therapist, a psychiatrist, a counselor, and a psychologist. When all was said and done, she hadn't been able to grasp 100 percent how one could help her more than the other, and so she'd gone for the one who could write prescriptions. Because she had been about a day away from trying to find a street drug to get her mind right.

"Growing up, I was always told that people who go see shrinks also get a monthly check," Deborah said.

Dr. Vanderdale squinted his eyes and shifted his head slightly to the side to signify that he wasn't quite sure he understood what Deborah was trying to say.

"You know, a Social Security check?" Deborah determined by the expression on Dr. Vanderdale's face that he still didn't get it. "Mental disability check." Deborah took her index finger and twirled it at her temple. "You know . . . cuckoo."

Dr. Vanderdale nodded his understanding. "Ahh, I get it." He chuckled. "I know there is a stigma attached to seeking therapy, especially in the African American community."

Deborah gave Dr. Vanderdale the side eye. "And you would know this because . . ." Given Dr. Vanderdale's blond hair, which had some gray peeking out, pale face, and green eyes, Deborah couldn't imagine this man knew anything about what went on in the African American community. Not giving Dr. Vanderdale the opportunity to respond, Deborah added, "Oh, I get it. Knowing that was part of your professional research and studies. If you are going to try to help African American patients, I suppose you would need to know a little bit about them."

"That too, I suppose," Dr. Vanderdale said, "but mainly because I've worked with quite a number of African Americans in the past. On top of that, I have two African American granddaughters."

Just then everything clicked in Deborah's head. "Oh, yes, that's right. Paige's girls."

Dr. Vanderdale was the former father-in-law of Paige, the church member who had referred Deborah. Even though his son, who had once been married to Paige, had passed away, Paige still remained close with the family. Her oldest daughter was from a previous relationship with a black man, while her youngest daughter had been fathered by Dr. Vanderdale's son. The Vanderdales made no distinctions between the two. They were both their grandchildren, no matter what.

Dr. Vanderdale nodded his head. "Yes, Adele and Norma are Grandpa's little princesses." His face lit up, like that of any proud grandpa. He turned the five-by-seven picture he had sitting on his desk in Deborah's direction so that she could get a good look.

The girls were two of the sweetest kids at the church. They made Deborah want to try for a little girl. But, heck, she could hardly handle the two boys she had. Deborah looked at the picture and admired the creamy, light caramel complexion of Norma, the youngest girl, and the deep chocolate complexion of, Adele, the older one. With that brown hair somewhere between curly and kinky that both girls had, those brown eyes, and those pudgy noses, they had clearly been swallowed up by Paige's genes.

"They look just like their mother," Deborah said, shaking her head at how they were Paige's identical mini me's.

"Right." Dr. Vanderdale turned the picture back in his own direction. He smiled as he stared at the little girls. "They look exactly like their mother, who, it goes without saying, is black." Dr. Vanderdale chuckled, then said, "I remember when Adele was first born. My housekeeper,

Miss Nettie, who is also black, said, 'No way is she going to get a pass. She doesn't even pass the brown paper bag test.'"

He stopped laughing. "I had no idea what she meant by that, so I asked, and she explained it. I was appalled to learn that back in the day, some blacks weren't admitted into clubs if they were darker than a brown paper bag. I felt so ashamed. Here I'd been working with African Americans practically all my life and had never bothered to learn anything about their culture and their oppression as a people, other than what had been portrayed on television or what they'd shared with me. And then I had the nerve to be the grandfather of black children. Not only did I go back to college and enrolled in some African American studies courses, but I also did my own research. I asked questions. Had sittings with some elders and soaked in everything they shared with me."

Deborah was amazed. "Wow. I commend you."

"No need to commend me. This is something I should have done when I decided to work with and try to help anyone outside of my own race. Different cultures operate differently. I was doing myself, my patients, and my staff a disservice by not knowing the depth and the history of who they were."

Deborah's shoulders tightened. She shifted her body, trying to find comfort, to no avail. Her eyes were cast downward.

"What was that?" Dr. Vanderdale asked, jotting something on the tablet that rested on the desk in front of him.

"What?" Deborah shrugged her shoulders.

"You tensed up and cut off eye contact with me."

Realizing she had, Deborah purposely loosened up and looked the doctor square in the eyes. She was well aware that she looked like a kid who claimed she didn't steal the cookie from the cookie jar but who had crumbs all around her mouth. Apparently, the doctor was well aware too, at least according to the expression on his face. But Deborah decided if the doctor didn't say anything else about it, then she wouldn't, either.

"Can I offer you a bottled water? Coffee or something?" Dr. Vanderdale asked, pushing his chair away from his desk and then standing. Deborah was new to his roster of clients. He hadn't yet gotten a chance to feel her out or gain her trust. He wasn't going to push. Not yet.

Deborah was on the fence, but not regarding her thirst. She questioned whether or not she wanted a therapist who didn't call her on her stuff. Otherwise, how else would he or she really get to the bottom of things? But at the same time, did she really want to get to the bottom of things? The therapist she'd seen before had merely scratched the surface. A scratch could be dealt with. And Deborah had dealt with it, thanks to what she called her "happy pills." The pills had helped with her anxiety, her quick temper, her depression, and mood swings. In a nutshell, those were all the things the old therapist had diagnosed Deborah with. If pills were what it would take to keep Deborah from popping off, then she'd gladly pop them instead. And she had up until learning that she was pregnant with her second child.

After only a few months of being on the meds, Deborah could see where the pills were benefiting her. Between the pills and talking with her therapist, she had functioned in a manner that was pleasing to her and to those around her. Especially her son, who once had had to bear the brunt of Deborah's behavior, thanks to him being the only one around who she could take things out on. But then came Lynox. Even though now she realized that as her husband, he was the best thing that could have ever happened to her, back when she had reconnected with him, he had been her main stress trigger. It had all been unbeknownst to him, though.

As an aspiring author with a huge ego to match his larger-than-life aura, Lynox had reached out to Deborah to possibly edit and then agent his manuscript. Her reputation had proceeded her not only in their small town of Malvonia, Ohio, but in the literary world as well. After a game of cat and mouse, Deborah finally gave in to Lynox's advances. Even after she found out that he was the leftovers of a church member named Helen, she still continued seeing him. But then her first love came back into the picture. Ballin' out of control, literally, as a high-paid athlete who played professional basketball in Chile, he talked Deborah into thinking they could pick up where they'd left off prior to him leaving the country.

Wanting to right a haunting wrong, one that had tormented Deborah for years, and praying that the grass would be greener and that God would give her and her ex a baby to replace the one she'd aborted years ago, she sacrificed her present with Lynox for a future with her ex. Sure enough, Deborah got pregnant. She wanted to believe God had planted the baby she'd aborted in her womb again. All would be well. But there were no words for the devastation Deborah experienced when she learned that halfway around the world her baby daddy already had a wife and a kid. That alone would have been enough to drive any woman insane.

Realizing she was never going to be any more than the secret side chick, Deborah headed back to Malvonia and picked up her life again, and Lynox too. This time it was Deborah who had to do the pursuing, but eventually she became Lynox's girl . . . again. Unfortunately, though, she didn't have time to tell Lynox about her child before he revealed that his deal breaker in a relationship was a woman who already had children. He wasn't a ready-made family kind of guy. Instead of coming clean automatically with Lynox, Deborah had this bright idea to get him to fall in love with her first so that when she did tell him she had a child, he would be in too deep to even care. Hiding her son and dealing with the judgment of her mother and pastor ultimately pushed Deborah to her maximum limit.

Deborah realized she was on a razor's edge when her pastor reported her to children's services. Pastor Margie had overheard what she considered Deborah verbally abusing her son. Pastor Margie had also happened to record the incident with her cell phone. It was when Deborah heard herself, in her own voice, treating her son like a dog in the street that she knew she needed help. She got help. Therapy and happy pills made for a perfect combination to improve her mental state. Then, in spite of finding out that she had a son from a previous relationship, Lynox proposed to her. They married, and just three months ago she gave birth to their own son together. Even though upon finding out she was with child, Deborah had to stop taking the pills, marital bliss and a blessed pregnancy kept her on cloud nine . . . or so she thought.

In the midst of everything, her therapy visits became far and few between, then dwindled right down to no visits at all. Joy still filled her spirit, though, even after giving birth to her youngest son, Tatum. But then, when he hit his two-month-old mark, Deborah started falling into a familiar slump. This didn't go unnoticed by Lynox, who suggested that she consider calling her therapist.

"Maybe you should go back to counseling at least," he suggested to his wife.

"Why?" Deborah snapped. "So he can put me back on dope to cope? What? You can't deal with the real me?"

"The real me," Deborah now whispered under her breath.

"Pardon me," Dr. Vanderdale said as he returned to his desk with two water bottles. He held one in front of Deborah.

"I didn't say I wanted water," Deborah told him.

Dr. Vanderdale grinned. "Mrs. Chase, you're going to find that with me, there is a lot you are not going to have to say. I'll just know. Even when you don't think I know, trust me, I do." He winked and then opened his own bottle of water and took a sip. He then placed the cap back on the bottle and said, "But I think it would make for a much better process if you would come out and say things on your own."

Deborah remained silent.

"The real you."

"Huh? What?" Deborah asked.

"When I was walking back to my desk, I heard you mumble under your breath. You said, 'The real me.' That's why you clammed up a moment ago. Right?"

Deborah's eyes nearly jumped out of their sockets. *Darn, this man is good*, Deborah thought. Still, she chose not to respond.

"Like I said, Mrs. Chase—"

"Can you call me Deborah please?" she interrupted. Mrs. Chase sounded so professional. She didn't want to constantly be reminded that she was receiving professional help. She'd rather it seem more like she was simply talking to a friend. "All my friends call me Deborah."

Dr. Vanderdale smiled. "Certainly." He fol-
ded his hands in front of him, intertwining his
fingers. "Like I said, Deborah, it will make the
process much easier if you tell me things and
don't make me guess. That makes me feel like
a psychic you are paying two dollars and nine-
ty-nine cents a minute to speak with and gives
me the impression that you are trying to test
me by making me do all the talking to see if I
get it right."

Deborah chuckled. A part of her had kind of
sort of been doing just that. And she practically
was paying this man $2.99 per minute, if not
more. Thank God she had top-notch health
insurance that was covering 90 percent of her
sessions.

"I do know some things based on the forms
and questions I had you answer online prior to
your appointment. I printed everything out and
read your file last night. But I prefer not to rely
on what you put on paper. I'd rather hear it from
you."

"Understood." Deborah nodded her understanding.

"Then can we address your clamming up a
moment ago?"

Deborah took a deep breath. It was clear this
man was not going to move on until Deborah

spelled it out for him. "I've never wanted my husband to experience the real me, to know what I refer to as the dark side of me. The ugly side of me. The side of me that pops off. That cusses and says hurtful things simply because I'm hurting. The depressed me." Deborah spoke it like a true champ, owning up to it. But inside she wanted to cry for having to admit that this who she was. She'd managed to hide it from everyone around her. No matter which one of those emotions she was experiencing, she had always known how to paint on a smile. But lately, she hadn't been so skillful at it. Out in public, yeah, she'd still been able to hide any depression, pain, hurt, and anxiety she might have been experiencing within, but at home, it had become harder and harder to be a fake. "I don't even want to know that person, let alone introduce her to the one person whose opinion of me I truly care about."

Dr. Vanderdale didn't interject anything, since Deborah seemed to be on a roll. He listened.

"So it struck a nerve when you said that you'd be doing your grandchildren a disservice by not knowing the depth and the history of who they are." Deborah paused.

Dr. Vanderdale figured this was the time for him to speak. "Why did that hit a nerve?"

"Because even though I might have known who I was marrying, I made sure my husband didn't know who he was marrying. I made sure, deliberately, that he never knew the depth of me. That he never knew what was underneath the phony smiles, or even which smiles were phony."

"So he didn't know about you previously seeing a therapist and being on medication?"

"He did, but not the extent of it all," Deborah confessed. "He even thought that he had something to do with me having to get on meds." Deborah briefly explained to Dr. Vanderdale the situation regarding Lynox not wanting a ready-made family. She relayed some of the side comments he'd periodically made, not knowing Deborah had a child. "He knew that all the cartwheels I had to do in order to hide my son from him became too much for me. He even apologized." Deborah stared off into space and thought back to the day she had shared with Lynox the fact that she'd been seeing a therapist and taking pills.

"Forget about those pills," Lynox had said. "Those are temporary. The same way a person never forgets how to ride a bike or how to love, they never forget who they truly are inside. Or as you church folks would say, who God called you to be." Lynox had pointed to Deborah's heart.

"She's in there, and with God's help and mine and your son's, you aren't going to need a pill to be that person. You got that?"

A tear slid down Deborah's face as she replayed Lynox's words in her head. He'd had so much faith in her mental healing. She truly felt as though she was letting him down by even being in this doctor's office. "I failed him. He thought I'd get better, and I've only gotten worse, only he doesn't know it. And it's been killing me, trying to keep the beast at bay."

Dr. Vanderdale raised an eyebrow as he began to write. "Beast? You think you're a beast?"

"I can act like one. I even went as far as to cut up in church one time, although no one witnessed it, except for the person who I was cutting up at. I knew I was getting out of control then. Usually, I'm good on Sundays, at church anyhow. But I learned that it's much easier to be a Christian at church than it is at home. At home we have our walls of Jericho. The walls hide our sin and actions from the public, of course, but not from God."

Dr. Vanderdale looked at his tablet, where he had written a few things down. He then looked back up at Deborah. "You said you're good on Sundays at church. What about when you're not at church?"

Deborah closed her eyes and exhaled. "Sundays are the worst days for my depression. I don't know what it is about Sundays, but when I open my eyes to daylight, it feels so dark. Sometimes merely thinking about having to get out of bed and go to church makes it worse. Who wants to see all those happy, joyful, praising folks when I'm feeling miserable inside? During service I find myself rolling my eyes and sucking my teeth, thinking that half of them are acting just as phony as me. That underneath all that 'Hallelujah' and 'Praise the Lord' is a sad and depressed person too. Lately, I don't want to go to church more times than I do."

"Then why do you go?" Dr. Vanderdale asked so that he could analyze Deborah's response. "You don't have to go."

"I do if I want to keep the title of Christian. How can I call myself a Christian if I won't even go to the house of the Lord to fellowship with other Christians? Plus, don't get me wrong, but church isn't a bad place. I love the people. I love the atmosphere, and what I love most is the possibility. The possibility that one Sunday I'm going to walk out of there and really be a changed person. They say the church is a spiritual hospital for the sick, so I go on a wing and a prayer of getting healed. So you see, I do have to go."

"Deborah, you do know that God can heal you right in your own living room, right?" Dr. Vanderdale wasn't trying to discourage Deborah from attending church at all. His wife and his former daughter-in-law both attended New Day. He'd witnessed himself the change in his wife's life when she started fellowshipping at New Day. But this wasn't about his wife. It was about Deborah. "God is everywhere."

A lightbulb went off in Deborah's head. "Yeah, you're right."

Dr. Vanderdale saw a glimmer of hope in Deborah's eyes. "I'm not saying that you shouldn't go to church, seeking a healing, but as a Christian, you must know that God is omnipresent. His miracles, signs, wonders, and blessings are not confined to the church walls."

Listening to Dr. Vanderdale made Deborah glad she'd chosen his practice from which to receive her treatment. He wasn't a Holy Roller who felt that the only way she could be healed was through the laying on of hands and prayer. But at the same time, he wasn't afraid to speak on God or include Him in the healing process. That was a plus for Deborah.

Once upon a time she'd visited a Christian counselor, and the woman had been gung ho about making everything about Jesus's healing stripes and not about how Deborah could participate in the healing process. The fact that Deborah was even taking medication at the time hadn't sat well with this counselor, and she had had no problem expressing this. That had turned Deborah off a tad. It had also confused her with her therapist, who had also been a Christian and who had prescribed the pills, contradicting the counselor, who had felt Deborah didn't need them. As far as Deborah was concerned, though, the verdict was still out. Maybe the pills had been nothing more than a temporary fix, and maybe not. Maybe it had all been in Deborah's head, and the pills had worked only because Deborah had so desperately wanted some type of help. Heck, they could have been sugar pills, for all she knew. But that was neither here nor there. What mattered was what would work for her now.

"I know that God is everywhere," Deborah assured Dr. Vanderdale. "When you first said that, it reminded me of something that took place a few years ago."

"It must have reminded you of something good. I saw the way your eyes lit up."

"Yes." Deborah nodded. "Years ago I got an abortion. The guilt and shame of it was one of the things that was painful, making me hurt.

That's not the good part, of course," Deborah explained. "The good part is something I'll never forget, which was getting delivered from that pain and shame right on my living room floor." Deborah's eyes filled with tears of joy. "It was so amazing." A tear slid down her face. "I wish God would purge and deliver me from all the other mess that's plaguing me as well. All the other mess that is tearing up my mind and making me cra . . ." Deborah's words trailed off.

The fact that Deborah was about to say a certain word didn't go unnoticed by Dr. Vanderdale. Even though he had a PhD, that didn't necessarily mean it took one to know what his patient was about to say. "Go ahead, Deborah. Finish your thought."

Deborah was quiet for a moment and thought before she spoke. "When we first started this session, I asked you a question, and then you asked me one in return."

"Uh-huh," Dr. Vanderdale said, recalling the beginning of the session.

"Well, to answer your question, yes. Yes, I do think I'm crazy." With that, Deborah roughly wiped away the tears spilling from her eyes. She then stood up. "And I'm crazy for being here." Who was Deborah kidding? She'd seen a Christian therapist and a Christian counselor who had totally different views on her healing.

Well, if everyone served the same God, why was He telling them different things about the same person? And what could God tell this new therapist that would be any different? Like Dr. Vanderdale had said, God was omnipresent, and knowing He was the greatest healer of all, Deborah decided she wouldn't waste another minute of her time or Dr. Vanderdale's and would go home and let God meet her right where she was.

"Wha...what do you mean, you are crazy for being here?" Dr. Vanderdale stood, hiding the terror in his eyes at the possibility of Deborah walking out his office door.

"Who are we kidding? I'm sure you're an excellent doctor, one of the best, if not *the* best, from what I've been told. That's one reason why I chose to come to you. But if God can't fix me, what makes you think you can?" Deborah grabbed her purse from the chair next to her. "I'm sorry for wasting your time. Just bill me for whatever the insurance company doesn't cover." And on that note, she exited the office.

"Mrs. Chase! Deborah, wait!" Dr. Vanderdale called out. It was too late, though. The door slammed in his face. He slowly sat back down at his desk as he sighed. He stared down at the notes he'd written down concerning Deborah

during her brief time in his office. Like he'd told
Deborah before, there was so much he could tell
about her even without her speaking about
it. And from what he could tell, she was in
trouble, and she needed help before it was too
late . . . and before somebody got hurt. More
than likely, it would be her.

Chapter 2

"Baby, great. You're home," Lynox said as he planted a kiss onto his wife's lips as soon as she walked in the door. "Here." He handed her their three-month-old baby boy. He then raced over toward the stairs and grabbed his roller case that he transported his books in.

"Is there a fire or something?" Deborah asked, kissing her son on the forehead and then rocking him. "Where's Tyson?" Deborah looked around for her school-aged son, who was in kindergarten.

"Next door, with the Perkins," Lynox said as he whizzed back to the front door, where Deborah stood with the baby in her arms. "Charles bought CJ a new game or something. Benji came over to see if Tyson wanted to break it in with him. I let him go over about a half hour ago. You might want to check on him in a little bit. You know Tyson can be a handful.

We don't want to ruin a good relationship with our neighbors. You know Charles makes the best homemade sangria ever." He winked at Deborah.

Deborah was glad to see that Lynox had loosened up as far as allowing Tyson to go play with his best friend, CJ. CJ was a year older than Tyson. He was in first grade. But Tyson was very mature for his age. He'd been speaking in full sentences and holding complete conversations for quite some time now. Because he was tall for his age, people thought he was older than what he really was, so they treated him as such, and he adapted. Folks were surprised that a kindergartner could communicate better than some first and second graders. Because of how advanced Tyson was, he went to kindergarten the first half of the day and to first grade the second half.

CJ was a smart kid too. He was also nice, quiet, and calm, the polar opposite of Tyson, who was always overly excited about everything and bouncing off the walls. Tyson did, however, respect his parents as well as other adults. It was CJ's parents, Charles and Benji—his two dads—that Lynox had been leery about. Charles was CJ's biological father, having divorced his wife, CJ's mother, three years ago. He now lived with his life partner, Benji.

It had been a year ago when Deborah and Lynox's new neighbors had come over and introduced themselves. It had taken Lynox and Deborah a minute to catch on to the fact that the two gentlemen with the little guy in tow were a couple. They'd looked like two regular, manly white dudes. Neither of them had been feminine in any apparent way. Lynox or Deborah would have never known the real deal had CJ not referred to both of them as Dad. That was when Lynox and Deborah had shot each other peculiar looks. Those looks hadn't gone unnoticed by their neighbors. Embarrassed that she and Lynox were outed by their obvious reaction, Deborah had had to apologize to the couple immediately.

"I'm so sorry," Deborah had said, truly apologetic.

"It's okay," Charles had said. "We get that look all the time."

"Well, you shouldn't," Deborah said. "Especially not from someone like myself, who is a Christian."

This time it was Charles and Benji who shot one another a look.

Deborah chuckled while nodding. "Oh, I get it. You've had your share of the abomination, hell, and damnation sermons when it comes to your lifestyle, huh?"

"And how." Benji laughed.

"Don't worry. I don't have a heaven or a hell to put you in," Deborah said. She looked at her husband. "Right, Lynox?"

Lynox hadn't yet wiped off the look on his face from when he realized his new neighbors were a gay couple. His mind had been stuck on the finding that both men were the boy's dads. One could have been the biological father and the other the stepfather, but that wasn't the case. "Huh? What? Oh, yeah, right," he said, not really sure what he was agreeing to.

"In addition to that," Deborah continued, "it's not about what I think of your lifestyle. It's about what God says. What you do is between you and Him. But I must warn you." Deborah pointed a finger at the men. "Whenever the opportunity to minister to you arises, I will take it." She laughed, and her neighbors joined her. "But not just because you're . . . you know." She looked down at CJ and then back at the men. She didn't finish the thought, because she wasn't sure what words they used to describe their relationship around their son. "I don't discriminate in my ministering of God's word. Ask the young girl down the street who recently moved in with her boyfriend." Deborah used her fingers to make quotation marks when she said the word

One Sunday at a Time   37

boyfriend. "I don't do it to judge, because I once lived in sin as well. Just fornicating, even with another woman's hus—"

"Uh, honey," Lynox interrupted and shook his head. He knew Deborah was about to give her testimony of how she was the last person who could pick up a stone and throw it at anybody. She'd fornicated. She'd participated in an adulterous relationship. She'd told lies. She'd had an abortion. She was as big a sinner as the next. She'd say the only thing that made her different was that she wasn't living in sin anymore. But Lynox felt that was a bit much to share with people they'd known only a minute . . . literally. "TMI," Lynox told Deborah. "Besides . . ." He nodded at CJ, who was standing in between his two fathers, looking as confused as all get-out.

"Oh, oh. I'm so sorry." Deborah put her hand over her mouth. "I hope you don't get the wrong idea about me." She pointed to Lynox. "About us. I really do love everybody. I don't love what everybody does, but then again, God doesn't love everything I do, yet He still loves me. It's my job as a Christian to love everyone with the love of Christ." Deborah would have continued on with her religious mumbo jumbo if Lynox hadn't pulled her in for a hug. She was rambling, trying too hard to prove to her neighbors that she wasn't one to judge, but at the same time letting them know she believed God's Word concerning every situation, including homosexuality.

"We are so glad you stopped over to introduce yourselves." Lynox extended his hand for a handshake.

Benji looked down at Lynox's hand. He then held out a limp hand for Lynox to shake, while putting his other hand on his hip. The look on Lynox's face was a true Kodak moment. He wasn't sure if he should shake Benji's hand or tell Deborah to whip out her file and polish and give this dude a manicure.

After basking in the look of horror on Lynox's face for only so much longer, Benji burst out laughing, and Charles joined him. "Gotcha." Benji changed his limp hand into the shape of a gun.

Everyone laughed.

"Yeah, you got me," Lynox admitted.

Benji extended his hand for a real handshake. Lynox and Benji shook hands, then Lynox and Charles.

"It's nice meeting you both," Lynox said.

"Same here," Charles said.

"And you too," Benji said to Deborah. "I think." He had a puzzled look on his face.

Once again they all laughed.

Later on that night Lynox and Deborah had engaged in pillow talk. Lynox had informed her that he didn't have anything against their new neighbors, but that he wasn't sure he could take them up on the offer they'd made prior to departing, which was that Tyson could come over anytime he wanted to play with CJ and have sleepovers.

"And why not?" Deborah had asked. "CJ seems nice, and so does his par . . . so do Charles and Benji." Deborah would try her best to show the love of Christ to everyone she met, but it was hard for her to come to terms with CJ having two men as his custodial parents.

"I'm sure CJ is a great kid. Charles and Benji were some cool cats. Nice sense of humor." Lynox paused, looking straight ahead.

"But . . ." Deborah was going to force him to give his reasoning.

"But they're gay. I don't want my son to see that lifestyle and think it's okay. Or even worse." This time a hard swallow came after Lynox's pause.

Even though Lynox didn't say a word, Deborah knew her husband well enough to know what he was thinking. "Shame on you." Deborah softly slapped Lynox's hands. "Just because a man is gay doesn't mean he likes little boys, and you should repent right now for thinking it."

"I'd be fearful of someone abusing Tyson no matter if they're gay or not . . . man or woman."

"Yeah, being fearful and being outright suspicious are two different things."

"And how do you know?"

Deborah shifted her body to face her husband. "Do you think our neighbors are the first gay people I've ever met? Please! Besides, I am the agent of the bestselling memoir *Woke Up Like This*. It chronicles the life of a man who woke up one day and decided that was the day he would admit to the world that he was gay. The admission included his wife and kids."

"So he woke up like that, huh?" Lynox shrugged. "I guess he throws the theory out the window of being born gay. Heck, who knew you could just wake up gay one day?" Lynox threw his hands in the air.

Deborah chuckled. "Look, knucklehead, I'm not one of those people who you'll ever find debating about whether a person can be born gay. All I know is that we can *all* be born again. Now, God bless you and good night."

That had been the end of the conversation and any misconceptions Lynox had about his neighbors. Deborah was right; Charles and Benji were living in sin just as much as the girl down the street who was fornicating with her boyfriend. Heck, just as much as he was whenever he told a little white lie here and there. The Bible didn't excuse little white lies versus big ones. Sin was sin, as Deborah liked to say. They were all sinners and needed Jesus.

But right now, as Lynox raced out the door, he needed Jesus to restore time. He was running late, thanks to Deborah not coming home until right before he needed to walk out the door. He wasn't used to trying to get himself ready and taking care of the kids at the same time. He had always had Deborah there to do the latter.

As the early November chill smacked him across the face, Lynox realized that he had forgotten something. "Shoot. My jacket."

"Where are you going, anyway?" Deborah asked him as she watched him race back inside, go to the closet, and pull out a jacket.

Slipping into his black leather jacket, Lynox replied, "You know I have that book club meeting over at the Book Suite in Columbus."

"Oh, that's right." Deborah thumped herself upside the head, a minor punishment for her forgetfulness. This only justified her getting up and leaving right in the middle of her session with Dr. Vanderdale. Had she not, Lynox would have been a no-show at his meeting.

On her drive home from Dr. Vanderdale's office, Deborah had had the notion to turn her car around several times and go back, but she hadn't. Her getting home right in the nick of time for Lynox to leave was confirmation that she'd made the right decision.

"Where were you?" Lynox looked down as he zipped his jacket.

"I uh, just, uh, lost track of time. I'm so sorry," Deborah answered, without actually answering.

"It's fine." He planted another kiss on his wife's lips. "Don't make me dinner. I'm sure there will be plenty for me to gnaw on at the meeting. These book clubs be going all out for your boy." Lynox proudly popped his collar.

"Oh, my humble husband." Deborah shook her head. "Get on out of here." She play spanked him on the behind.

Lynox kissed her on the lips yet again. He hadn't even been married to Deborah for two years. This was still the honeymoon stage, as far as he was concerned. Next, he kissed his baby boy on the forehead. He was about to exit, but then he turned back one last time. "And don't forget, this weekend Reo Laroque and his wife, Klarke, invited us over to their place. They're celebrating Reo's fifteenth year as an author and his fifteenth book release."

Reo Laroque, like Lynox, was a very well-known *New York Times* bestselling author of sensual tales. He was actually one of the reasons Lynox had started to write. They both wrote for the same publisher, but for different imprints, so they were still pretty much label mates. Lynox had felt so honored the first time he got to actually meet Reo at BookExpo America in New York, at a reception hosted by their publishing house. Since then, Reo had become like a mentor to Lynox. At the time they first met, even though Columbus, Ohio, was Reo's hometown, which was only a hop, skip, and a jump from Lynox in Malvonia, Reo had been living on the West Coast. They would communicate through e-mail and social media and would even hop on the phone to chat every now and then. But Reo had moved back to his hometown, so recently the two had been able to connect in person a couple of times. A genuine friendship was starting to develop between them.

"I won't forget about Reo's celebration," Deborah assured him.

"Like you didn't forget my meeting today?" Lynox said sarcastically.

"Man, get on out of here." Deborah shooed him away with her foot as she laughed. He raced out, and she closed the door behind him, then looked down at her baby boy. "Mommy forgot about this weekend with the Laroques. But shhh." She put her index finger up to her lips. "Don't tell Daddy."

The baby cooed. This made Deborah smile. But as she thought about all the work, meetings, and duties that were ahead of her, she couldn't help but wonder how long that smile would last.

Chapter 3

"I need you to stop and pick up my dry cleaning if you can," Lynox called out from the walk-in closet that was off of his and Deborah's private bathroom.

Deborah stood at the sink, rubbing Noxzema on her face. Today was the first day in a while that she didn't have a single errand to run. Lynox had a workshop to teach on The Ohio State University campus that would take up his entire day, and Tyson was off to school. When Tatum was awake, he required tending to, but he slept the majority of the time still. So Deborah had her day planned out. In addition to giving Tatum her undivided attention when he needed it, she was going to do some editing and would squeeze in writing her own book, which she'd been working on for years. It was just that she was always so busy putting her two cents into other people's work that she always had to put her own story on the back burner. She'd promised herself that today would be the day when she at least warmed it up—devoted some consecrated time to her own creative endeavor. But now here came Lynox, throwing a monkey wrench into her plans.

"You drive right past the cleaners, don't you?" Deborah asked.

"Yeah, but I'm not going to have time to stop, and I need the suit for the Laroques' event tonight."

"Babe," Deborah said in a forced sugary voice. She was trying to keep her cool. But she was the type of person who had everything planned out down to the minute. Getting off track was not something she could easily deal with. It gave her anxiety to just think about falling behind schedule or failing to do everything on her to-do list that needed to be done. "If you knew you needed the suit tonight, why did you wait until the last minute?"

"I know, I know. I need to handle my business more." Lynox was only saying what he knew his wife was about to say. He agreed that he needed to do better when it came to handling his affairs and staying organized. But no matter how hard he tried, he'd never measure up to Deborah, who was the queen of taking care of business and being organized.

Deborah sighed. She knew it was useless to have this conversation with her husband. Regardless of what was said, she'd end up doing whatever it was he'd asked her to do, anyhow. "Leave the ticket. Even though Mr. Chong knows us by name and face, he does not deviate from his wife's rule about not giving folks their items unless they produce a ticket," Deborah said. "Wish more men would listen to their wives." Deborah cleared her throat and screwed the lid back on the Noxzema.

"Point taken," Lynox said, exiting the closet.

"Good." Deborah rolled her eyes and began to rinse the white facial cleanser off her face.

"You're so cute when you're mad." Lynox walked over and hit Deborah on the butt. "Can I get some before I go?" he whispered in her ear.

"Two seconds ago I would have said yes, but now in the time it takes to give you some, I have to go to the dry cleaners." Deborah was going to make sure Lynox regretted the day he asked her to run that errand for him, especially as much as that boy loved him some sex with his wife. Sometimes he'd write sex scenes in his books that were so hot and heavy, he'd have to seek out his wife to take care of the desires that had arisen in him.

Deborah didn't complain, not out loud, anyway. But usually her day was so full and busy that she barely had energy to snore, let alone perform her wifely duties. She could *so* relate to that scene in the movie *Sex and the City* where the redhead's husband wanted to change positions in the middle of sex, and she told him, "Let's just get it over with." It was like that sometimes.

Men didn't realize that, yeah, they might work hard at their career, but usually women worked hard at their career *and* at taking care of the family. Moms were usually the ones at the parent-teacher conferences and PTO meetings. Moms were usually the ones who volunteered for school field trips. Moms were usually the ones who had to take the kids to some kind of practice and pick them up or even sit there to cheer the kids on. Moms usually did the cooking, the cleaning, and the homework. Dressed the kids, did the kids' hair, and everything else. And on top of that, the mom still had her own career and work to do. Then, when all that was said and done, she was supposed to have the energy to work in the bed too. It was hard to muster up the strength sometimes.

"It will take only five minutes," Lynox said seductively, nibbling on her earlobe.

"With the baby, it will take me at least a half hour," Deborah said. "The dry cleaners you use may only be a five-minute drive from here, but you have to take into consideration that I have to get the baby all packed up. I have to get him buckled into the car. I have to drive to the cleaners. I have to get him unbuckled and out the car, and then I have to go into the cleaners, get your clothes, and go back and buckle the baby again. Drive home, then unbuckle the baby yet again. So you see how much easier it would be for you, all by yourself, to go pick up the dry cleaning, versus me going through all those steps to do it?" Deborah then breathed, because she'd managed to say all of that in one breath.

Lynox looked into his wife's eyes through the mirror. He no longer had lust in his eyes. "I meant it would take only five minutes for me to make love to you, but never mind." Lynox removed his hands from Deborah, then exited the bathroom with his head held low.

Deborah threw her head back and let out a quiet "Ugh." Why did he have to go and mess up her mood? Now not only was she uptight about breaking her day up to run the errand, but she was also feeling as if she was letting her husband down. Her superwoman cape had her initials engraved on it. Not living up to the meaning of the cape meant that she was a failure. She was expected to do it all, so she had to do what was expected. She'd be feeling vexed all day long if she didn't. That would take away the productivity from Deborah's day. It would stifle her creativity. She'd be too focused on what she hadn't accomplished, versus what she could accomplish.

Deborah wiped the last of the Noxzema off with her facecloth. She then picked up a tea towel and pat her face dry. She looked at herself in the mirror and said, "Well, superwoman, duty calls." With that, she slipped out of her robe, revealing the matching nightie underneath it. She then exited the bathroom, met Lynox in the bedroom, where he was getting dressed, then proceeded to get it over with.

Deborah was on cloud nine as she stood among some of the literary industry greats. She'd spotted another local agent, Joylynn M. Ross. She was chatting it up with Dr. Maxine Thompson, one of the best book doctors in the business, hailing all the way from sunny California. That woman could take the most dreadful book and turn it into a masterpiece. Author Brandi Johnson was there, Tysha, Author

Maurice "First" Tonia, Vanessa Miller, Colette Harrell, and the one and only Nikita Lynnette Nichols, who hailed from Chi-Town. Deborah thought she was going to have a literary orgasm, she was so starstruck. But what really blew her mind was that everyone she looked up to seemed equally pleased to meet her.

"Your reputation truly precedes you," Dr. Thompson said to Deborah after Deborah introduced herself to the legendary editor. She had figured that instead of staring at Dr. Thompson from across the room like a crazed fan or waiting for someone else to introduce them, she'd take it upon herself to make the introduction.

"The same goes for you," Deborah replied. "It's an honor, Dr. Thompson." She nodded.

"Please, call me Maxine."

"Honey, I see you met the woman who almost stole your husband," Lynox said, approaching Deborah and wrapping his hand around her waist.

"Pardon me?" Deborah said, a little caught off guard by her husband's comment.

"Well, if you hadn't agreed to take on my project, Dr. Thompson was next on my list to query." Lynox winked at Dr. Thompson.

Deborah relaxed, and Dr. Thompson blushed.

"I'm jealous," Dr. Thompson said to Deborah. "Not only did you land one of the top-selling male African American authors in the business, but you got him to put a ring on it too."

"Pow," Deborah said, holding her hand up for her diamond wedding set to be admired.

The three laughed.

"I am honored that I was at least second on your list," Dr. Thompson said to Lynox. "But I can most certainly understand why Mrs. Chase here was your first."

After a few more words were exchanged by the trio, everyone's attention turned toward the clanging sound coming from the wide carpeted staircase at the center of the Laroques' great room, the place in which the event was being held.

The seven-thousand-square-foot home in New Albany, a suburb of Columbus, Ohio's capital city, was one to be envied. Upon entering the home through the dark orange–stained Asian double doors, guests were greeted by a huge foyer that was the size of a living room in the average home. For this particular night, a makeshift coat check had been situated to the right of the foyer, while an open bar had been set up to the left. The center area had been left open to provide space for all the guests. After making the trek across the shiny hardwood floors, the guests were swallowed up by the vaulted-ceiling great room. Lynox had been to book events in hotel ballrooms that were no larger than the Laroques' great room.

Tonight's color scheme was a beautiful, bright, and vibrant blend of turquoise, royal purple, and silver. The silver chandelier that hung at the entrance to the great room looked as though it had been installed specifically for the celebration. Long, colorful strings attached to the balloons hanging in the air just below the ceiling tickled the tops of the taller guests' heads. There was a sitting area smack in the middle of the room. There was a total of four love seats and couches arranged around an oblong table with a fitted turquoise tablecloth on it. The centerpiece was a tall vase filled with marbles and stones that matched the color scheme.

Servers carried around trays of Reo's favorite appetizers, and back in the left corner of the room was a table with a huge cake with a replica of Reo's latest book cover on it. A banner that read CONGRATULATIONS hung overhead, and more balloons were anchored to the table. There were about ten tall, round tables around the room for guests to stand at and converse. The only chairs were the ones that had been placed in the right rear corner of the room. There were about twenty-five chairs before a podium with a microphone. The place looked spectacular. It was celebratory, yet chic. And to top things off, a live band had set up and was playing in the upper balcony that overlooked the great room.

"Can I have your attention everyone?"

All eyes went on Reo's lovely wife, Klarke, as the band played its last note. She stood on the second step of the staircase, with a glass of champagne in one hand and a fork in the other. She'd clanked the fork against the glass to get everyone's attention. She stood and waited with patience and poise as the chatter quieted down and guests began to migrate over to where she was standing.

"Let's give it up for our live entertainment." She looked upward and pointed her hand toward the balcony. "George Bostic and the Garment of Praise, all the way from Toledo, Ohio, ladies and gentlemen."

Members of the neo soul group took their bows during the applause, and then all the attention went back to Klarke. It was probably safe to say, though, that some eyes had never left her.

She was a bombshell. Since she looked not a day over thirty-five, no one would even believe she was closer to fifty. Originally from Toledo,

Ohio, but having recently moved from the state of Nevada, Klarke now made New Albany her home with her husband and his sixteen-year-old daughter from a previous relationship. Klarke had two adult children of her own from a previous relationship. The two shared a son together, but he was out of state, attending college on a full academic scholarship.

"Tonight we celebrate fifteen years and the fifteenth book release of the wonderfully talented, sexy, amazing, and most creative man I've ever met on the face of the earth."

Guests laughed when they spotted Reo signaling with his hand for Klarke to keep the compliments coming.

"I'll stop there, because this could get too personal." Klarke winked at her husband, and oohs and aahs filled the room as some fellows elbowed one another and winked at the message behind the words of the wife of the guest of honor. "But if any of you have ever picked up a copy of one of his books, you know that he is a master at what he does and truly deserves to be celebrated."

Applause halted Klarke's words. Once it died down, she continued.

"And tonight that is exactly what we are here to do. Not only to celebrate my husband and his

books, but also to celebrate the release of his
fifteenth book. Is that crazy or what?"

Once again there was applause.

"So without further ado," Klarke said, "I present to you the one, the only national, international, and *New York Times* bestselling author
Reo Laroque."

There was thunderous applause as Reo
hugged his wife and planted a sensual kiss on
her lips, all while looking her in the eyes. Just
that short interaction between Reo and Klarke
told a story. One could see the struggle, the fight,
the pain, and the sacrifice they'd been through to
be together. A novella had just been told, all in a
touch, all in a look, all in a kiss.

Once Reo was able to tear his eyes away from
his wife, he addressed the crowd. "If you all don't
mind following me over to the podium with the
mic," Reo said, "I'd truly appreciate it. I don't
want to lose my voice and not be able to give a
reading from my work tonight." Reo led the way
as the crowd migrated to the chairs that sat in
front of the podium.

He then stepped up to the mic. "First off, I
want to thank God for so much more than this
night," Reo began. "I want to thank Him for my
beautiful wife, whose catering and event-planning company is actually responsible for the

decorations, the food, and everything." Reo
raised both arms and turned his upper body
from left to right. "Taylor Made Event Planning.
Go to their Web site and book them for your next
event."

Everyone chuckled at the plug Reo was giving
his wife's company.

Klarke gave him a thumbs-up, winked, and
then mouthed, "Way to go, honey."

"But seriously," Reo continued, "tonight
would not have been possible without my wife
and children. They are truly the motivation
behind my doing what I do."

Reo shared a few more acknowledgments
before he told his guests a little bit about his
new title and then read a brief excerpt from
it. His written words were as captivating and
engulfing when read out loud as they were on
paper. Afterward, he spent the next hour at the
book table, autographing copies while the band
continued to play its mellow tunes. By the time
he was finished, both Deborah and Lynox were
about ready to head home. Actually, they'd been
ready about twenty minutes ago, but they didn't
want to leave without saying good-bye to the
guest of honor.

"Well, Reo, my man, it's been real," Lynox
said as he and Deborah approached Reo. Klarke

was by his side. "Congratulations on all your success. It's well deserved."

Reo pulled Lynox in for a manly hug. "Brother, I appreciate it, and that's such a compliment coming from you."

"Aw, man, go on with that," Lynox said, shooing off Reo's compliment with his hand.

"I'm serious. I was thinking, and we don't have to go all into it right now, but maybe you and I can work on a book together. You know, a joint collaboration or something."

Lynox practically had to pick his jaw up off the floor. Never could he have imagined in a million years Reo Laroque wanting to share space on a book cover with him. Lynox was indeed at the top of his game in the book business, but Reo was the trailblazer.

"Wow, honey. That's awesome," Deborah said to Lynox, resting her hand on his shoulder. She knew how much her husband admired Reo and how hearing those words must have made him feel.

Lynox was still speechless. His mouth hung open, but no words came out. He stood there, slightly shaking his head in disbelief. "I . . . I don't know what to say."

"Don't say anything right now, anyway," Reo said. "Just think about it."

"I'm in awe myself," Klarke admitted. "So many writers have come to my husband, wanting him to participate in this anthology or that project with some other author. He's always declined. Now here he is, the one asking someone else to do what he wouldn't do."

"That's because when you get in the ring with someone," Reo said, "you want to make sure they are of your same caliber. In Lynox's case, working with him would challenge me as a writer. I'd have to try to keep up with him." He laughed.

"I must say I'm honored," Lynox said. "I don't have to think about it. It was an immediate yes from the moment you asked. It's just that the word was stuck in my throat."

The foursome chuckled.

"I'll get with my agent," Reo said.

"And your agent can get with mine," Lynox said, turning to Deborah, who, of course, was Lynox's literary agent.

"And we'll hash it out with the publishers," Deborah said, chiming in.

"Good enough," Reo agreed. He looked at Deborah. "Thanks, you guys, so much for coming. It was a pleasure having you here, and I look forward to working with you." He turned to Lynox at this point and added, "With both of you."

"Same here," Lynox said. He shook Reo's hand.

"And, Deborah, since our men will be working together, perhaps that will give us some time to hang out," Klarke said.

"I'd love that." Deborah didn't really have a lot of girlfriends. Outside of church, she didn't associate with any other females. She had never imagined making new friends at this point in her life, but Klarke really seemed like cool people and like someone who would be nice to hang out with. So Deborah figured, *Why not take her up on the offer*? If nothing else, perhaps Klarke could give her some tips on how to lose the last ten pounds of baby weight she'd been struggling to shed. As tight as Klarke's body was, she had to be doing some type of exercise and/or diet regimen. "Sounds like a plan to me," Deborah added.

"I'm so glad my idol decided to give up the fast life in Nevada to move back to the Midwest," Lynox said, patting Reo on his shoulder.

"And it's good to be back home, my brotha," Reo said, giving Lynox some dap.

"Pardon me," a man with a camera interrupted. "Can I get a picture of the two of you together over by the podium?" He looked from Reo to Lynox.

Lynox looked at Reo. "Hey, this is all about you, but I'm game if you are."

"Let's do this. The two hottest male authors in the game right now, if we don't count that darn Carl Weber. This is a once-in-a-lifetime photo op."

"You know it," Reo agreed.

Lynox turned to Deborah. "This will be real quick, hon, and then we can head out. Okay?" In his excitement, Lynox didn't even wait on a reply.

The two men gave each other a brotherly handshake and then headed off, with the cameraman leading the way.

"Modest, aren't they?" Klarke joked as she and Deborah stared at them as they walked away. She then turned to face Deborah. "I meant what I said about us getting together. Now, I'm not one to simply talk about connecting. I really want to hang out and do some girl stuff. I know you have little ones, but I don't want to hear one thing about not having a sitter. My sixteen-year-old loves kids and babysits for everyone in the neighborhood. She's raising money to pay for her driving lessons."

Deborah shot Klarke a puzzled look.

Klarke didn't even have to ask Deborah why she was looking like that. It wasn't a first. "Yes, honey. My money is *my* money. My husband's money is *his* money . . . not our children's. The only thing the law says we have to provide them is food, clothing, and a roof over their heads. I'm sorry, but both Reo and I have worked hard to get where we are in life. And even though we could easily write a check to cover the cost of the driving classes, I think we are serving our child better by letting her work for it."

Deborah put her hands up in defense. "Trust me. You do not have to explain a thing to me. I was watching one of those reality wife shows, and a woman's child was about to go off to college, and she didn't even know how to do a load of laundry. Really? Where they do that at?"

"In Beverly Hills, apparently," Klarke said, rolling her eyes. "I saw that episode too. But we can't lump them all together. That one other wife who has a really rich husband in the music industry . . . Remember that she helped set her daughter up in her very first apartment, but from thereafter, the daughter had to take care of herself?"

"Yes. And it was in New York, of all places. That's one of the most expensive places to live."

"But we could die tomorrow, and then what are our babies going to do if they are dependent on us?"

"Like I said, I completely get it."

"So, how about you contribute to my daughter's driver's education fund by allowing her to watch your little ones while we go out for coffee or something?"

"You know, my youngest baby really *is* just a baby," Deborah said. "Only a little over three months."

Klarke looked Deborah up and down from head to toe. "Girl, you just dropped a load and already looking snatched? All right now!"

"Thank you," Deborah said. She truly did appreciate the compliment but knew that if she didn't have on those Spanx, there was no way Klarke would be saying something like that to her. She had to admit that tonight she was snatched in her size eight clothes. But since having Tatum, getting back into her size eights had been a struggle. She could zip up her size eight jeans only after ten minutes of tucking all her extra skin down into them. Deborah knew firsthand that a size eight in clothes and a size eight buck naked were two very different visuals.

In her clothing, Deborah could pull it off. She knew how to stand with her neck straight, her shoulders up, and how to suck her gut in. Then there were the Spanx and the waist trainers, which played a huge role in her appearance as well. But once she came out of all her clothes and let it all hang out . . . and she actually breathed . . . it was a sight to behold.

A size eight at age forty wasn't the same as a size eight at thirty. And the extra skin, which wouldn't go away no matter how many crunches she did, really messed with her self-esteem. If only she wasn't afraid to go under the knife, she'd get a tummy tuck in a heartbeat. This extra skin wasn't anything liposuction could fix. It needed to be cut off. She couldn't wear Spanx twenty-four hours a day, and what woman didn't want to feel good about herself twenty-four hours a day? Oh, well, at least at this party, among all these beautiful women, even the belle of the ball was giving Deborah her props. Apparently, not only was Deborah good at hiding how she really felt, but she was also good at hiding how her body really looked.

"You are welcome," Klarke said. "But, anyway, my daughter has a partner who helps her out with babysitting, so your baby will be fine." Klarke leaned in and whispered, "Shelia, our house manager, does a wonderful job with kids too."

"House manager?" Deborah said to the woman making her daughter earn her own money to pay for driver's education.

"That's a fancy term for *housekeeper*."

The women laughed.

Deborah shook her head. "Spoil the mother, not the child, huh?"

"Hey, I said our kids need to learn how to take care of themselves. But Mommy, on the other hand, has paid her dues." Klarke held her hand up, and Deborah gave her a high five.

"I am not mad at you," Deborah said. "Sometimes I feel like I need help."

"Then get you some. Don't be ashamed to get some help, girlfriend. It doesn't make you any less of a wife or any less of a mother. We women are always trying to be superwoman and do it all. Take care of the house, take care of the kids, the man, and all while working jobs ourselves."

"I promise you that you just stole the words that were in my head this morning," Deborah said, loving the fact that this sista could relate. "God forbid you work from home, like I do," Deborah continued. "Folks think you can stop whatever you are doing to take them to the store, to do this, or to do that."

"Right. If you were clocking in at a nine-to-five, would folks really expect you to leave your desk and go ask your boss if you can take them to go drop their car off at the mechanic?"

"Say that again. I've been editing and agenting for years, and some folks still can't grasp that what I do is my job and not a hobby."

"Still doesn't keep us from stopping in the middle of our work to look out for somebody else, though," Klarke said. "We're so worried about others' expectations of us, on top of the ones we place on ourselves."

Just thinking about those instances when she was trying to meet everyone else's expectations on top of her own made Deborah begin to hyperventilate slightly. "It becomes so overwhelming sometimes." She stared off into space, taking deep breaths and then letting them out.

"Calm down." Klarke laughed, then rested her hand on Deborah's shoulder. "You look like you are about to go crazy just thinking about it." Klarke's laughter faded as she raised an eyebrow, partly wondering if Deborah was okay or was pulling a Fred Sanford act.

Deborah noticed the expression on Klarke's face and quickly regained her composure. She began to laugh it off. "I'm only playing. You know how it is." Deborah was embarrassed that she'd allowed herself to get all riled up like that. If only she and Lynox had left when she'd wanted to, she wouldn't be concerned about being exposed now. But no. Lynox had to go be Hollywood and smile for the camera.

Deborah anxiously began to look around for Lynox. She spotted him giving the photographer his business card. The photographer must have requested it so that he would get the spelling of Lynox's name correct when he published the photo. "Well, it looks like they're wrapping up." She turned back to Klarke. "Again, thank you so much for having us."

"You are welcome." Deborah went to pull away, but Klarke still had a nice grip on her hand. "Next week. I mean it. I'm going to text you the day and time for us to get together." She released Deborah's hand. "And from the looks of things, you need some downtime, anyway, to relax." She shot Deborah a knowing look. But what exactly did she know?

Deborah paused before speaking. "What do you mean?" Even though it wasn't her intent to sound defensive, she did.

Klarke was slightly taken aback by Deborah's sudden shift in demeanor. Just a second ago they were vibing and relating. Now Deborah was practically snapping her head off. "Well, nothing. I just—"

"Honey, you ready?" Lynox interrupted, putting his arm around Deborah's shoulders.

She didn't realize it when she wormed out of his embrace. "Yes, sure. I'll go get our coats from the coat check." Deborah stalked off.

Lynox glanced over at Klarke with a puzzled look on his face. "Everything okay?"

Klarke shrugged, her eyelids fluttering in confusion. "Yeah, as far as I know."

Since Klarke was shrugging it off, so was Lynox. He complimented Klarke on such a lovely evening before he went after his wife. Hopefully, on the drive home she'd tell him what was going on. It didn't matter what her mouth said. By the way she'd reacted, it was clear that something was wrong. And if he was being honest with himself, something had been wrong for the past month or so. The challenge would be figuring out how to make it right.

Chapter 4

"Did you enjoy yourself?" Lynox asked Deborah as they pulled away from the Laroque residence.

"Yeah, I did, actually," Deborah said dryly, then proceeded to scroll down her Facebook News Feed on her cell phone.

There were a few more seconds of silence before Lynox spoke again. "Then what was that?"

Deborah looked up from her phone. "What was what?" Her head wobbled on her neck; then she turned her attention back to her phone.

"That, back there." Lynox nodded in the direction of Reo and Klarke's home.

Deborah was confused. "What do you mean? Didn't I look like I was enjoying myself the entire time? The Laroques are amazing. Their home is amazing, the guest list, food, entertainment . . . What was there not to enjoy? Not to mention he invited you to collaborate with him on a project." Deborah turned to face Lynox. "Honey, this was the evening of all evenings. How could you question whether I enjoyed myself or not?" She turned her attention back to her phone, this time exiting her social media account and checking for any missed texts. "Did I miss something? Did you not enjoy yourself? You seemed to be having a splendid time as well."

"I very much enjoyed myself," Lynox said, keeping his eyes on the road. "I posed the question only because of the way you snatched yourself out of my arms and stormed off to the coat check. I thought maybe you and Klarke might have had some sort of disagreement or something. But when I talked to her, she was as clueless as I was."

Deborah's head snapped up from the cell phone as she stuffed it in her purse. Her eyes daggered into Lynox. "What do you mean, when you talked to Klarke? About what? About who? Me?" Deborah became very agitated. "You talking to another woman about me?" The mere thought of Lynox engaging in a conversation about her behind her back made her blood boil. If he wasn't speaking about her to her mama, his mama, or a sister, she had a problem with that.

"No, nothing like that." Lynox removed his right hand from the steering wheel and patted the air. "Calm down, honey. Calm down. It wasn't anything like that."

Watching Lynox's hand fall, as if she was a child who needed hand signals to be instructed on how to behave, only teed Deborah off that much more. She felt as though he was also trying to silence her. That angered her as much as if he'd told her to shut up, like he was her superior, the boss of her, or something.

Deborah stared at his hand gesture, her anger rising more. Before she realized it, she'd slapped Lynox's hand and shouted, "I don't need you shushing me and telling me how to behave. And on top of that, I don't need my husband talking about me to some other woman. That's like relationship one-oh-one. Talking to a person of the opposite sex about issues with your spouse opens the door for the devil to go to work." Deborah turned and looked out the passenger window, all the while mumbling under her breath. "How you gon' talk about me with another female? You got me mixed up. You wanna know something about me? You come to me, not some other broad." It didn't help any that the woman he'd talked about her to was beautiful. In Deborah's mind, that was all the more reason for Lynox to find an excuse to converse with Klarke. It only made it that much worse that he had used Deborah as an excuse.

While all those thoughts and fears were running through Deborah's mind, Lynox's mind was still back at Deborah slapping his hand. Now who was the one treating the other like a child?

"I'm not Tyson, Deborah," Lynox said as calmly as he could.

This was the first time Deborah had ever done anything like that to him. He wasn't sure if she was joking or trying to give an example of a "bossy act," something akin to how he had patted the air with his hand. Perhaps that was her payback. Whatever it was, it didn't sit well in his spirit, and because of that, he needed to express that to his wife so that it would never happen again.

Deborah snapped her head around. "And what's that supposed to mean?" She rolled her eyes. "I'm not blind. I can see that you aren't Tyson."

"It means you have every right to smack your child's hand, but I'm your husband. We don't do that."

Lynox was not about to try to check her when he was the one who had started it. Deborah had been scrolling down her News Feed, minding her own business, when he decided to start picking. "Negro, please." Deborah shooed her hand and let out a harrumph. "You know darn well I didn't mean it like that."

"I don't know what you meant," Lynox said as he pulled onto the highway, heading to their house. "To be real one hundred with you, I haven't been able to read you for the past few weeks."

"Well, like that Facebook group you're in says, 'Don't read me. Read a book.'" Deborah sucked her teeth and rolled her eyes.

Lynox squinted his eyes, in thought. He couldn't recall ever mentioning to Deborah that he was in that group. "How did you know I was in that group? I don't recall you being a member." He looked over at his wife a couple of times in between keeping his eyes on the road.

Deborah kept silent, as if she hadn't even heard a word he'd said. She felt so busted. She should have kept quiet while she was ahead.

"So what are you doing now? Trolling my Facebook information?" Lynox asked.

Again, Deborah remained silent. How could she tell her husband that right after having the baby, and not having lost all the baby fat, she'd started to feel a little insecure? She'd been the most confident and secure woman he'd known. But going from a tight size eight pre-pregnancy to not being able get a big toe in her eights at first had not been easy for Deborah. Whether she was biased or not, Lynox was one fine specimen of a gentleman. The entire atmosphere in a room shifted once he entered it. Women were drawn to him, even without knowing he was the man behind the pen that had created so many sensual novels. Learning that about him was only a plus to females. Women often wondered if Lynox was anything in bed like the wild, sexual characters he wrote about. After all, there was a saying that authors often wrote mostly about what they knew.

Women at book events had tried Deborah before. She had attended many, not only as the supporting wife, but as his editor and agent. Even with her sitting there right by his side, some tricks had had no problem leaving on the signing table a pair of lace red thongs, a fetish one of his main characters had. Deborah had always remained calm and professional, knowing that the women were mocking the book and that Lynox had to play along with it in order to please his fans. Besides that, Deborah had never felt intimidated. She herself was a beauty, and she had always made sure she was dressed her best whenever she was next to her man. That was when she'd been a for real size eight, one that Lynox was used to wrapping his arms around, and not the woman who was stuffing all her extra skin into a size eight. Nowadays, with all the excess meat and flab rolling out of the top of her jeans, she could hardly hide her envy of some of the pop bottle figures that approached Lynox's table.

There was one little hot number in particular who had shown up at a book signing last month.

"Hi. I'm Montea. We're Facebook friends," she'd said, her hot tamale–red lipstick matching her formfitting red dress and her cleavage hanging out.

It was at that moment that something had been triggered in Deborah's mind. If Lynox was "friends" with women like this on Facebook, and they were local, she couldn't help but wonder if something more than innocent Facebook posts were being exchanged. That night, after Lynox was sound asleep in bed, calling hogs, Deborah had quietly got out the bed, undetected, and had gone to their home office, located in the basement. Instead of making her way over to her own desk, she'd gone to Lynox's. She stood over his computer; its screen was black. She wiggled the mouse around, but nothing happened. Next, she hit a random button on the keyboard, which brought his computer to life.

With much anxiety, Deborah sat down and began checking out any open programs on Lynox's screen. Just as she had suspected, he had at least three apps open. She'd been on top of him about making sure he completely signed off the Internet because it was causing them to go over their monthly data usage. Clearly, she had not gotten through to him. And it was a good thing too. With his apps already open and logged into, she didn't have to spend numerous hours trying to figure out passwords.

"There is a God, indeed," Deborah mumbled under her breath. That declaration alone had put a thought in Deborah's mind . . . a scripture and a thought. The Word said that God would not allow her to be ignorant of Satan's devices. That meant that if she believed God's word, then she wouldn't need to worry or go looking for any wrongdoing being done to her, that it would fall right into her lap . . . almost from heaven. Well, as far as she was concerned, she hadn't really gone looking. She'd simply clicked a button or two, and—*bam*—there it was, right there in her lap. She'd take this as a sign from God that something was going on that she needed to know about.

It was midnight when Deborah first got on the computer. Her heart beat fast from the fear of her husband catching her on his computer. That didn't stop her, though. Her adrenaline pumped as she invaded his virtual privacy. It was almost five o'clock in the morning the next time she looked at the time on the computer. Time had gotten away from her quick, fast, and in a hurry, and she still hadn't really found anything concrete that would lead her to believe Lynox was up to no good. There were quite a few flirtatious in-box messages Lynox had received from several women. Lynox had replied to them, and Deborah felt, out of respect for his marriage, he should have simply deleted them without acknowledging them. He'd received messages such as You are so freaking hot, or Your smile is so beautiful. I can only imagine what tricks you can do with those lips. Lynox had replied with a simple Thank you, but Deborah felt that was two words too many. To her, he was creating dialogue, because it took two to tango.

She searched for another hour before she heard Lynox above her, moving about. She didn't want him to come down and see her on his computer. The early morning hours were when his creativity was at its peak, so she knew it would be only a matter of time before his feet came padding down the steps. Again, in the past hour she'd found nothing truly suspect, but she'd taken notes and created a file folder with things she had found, something she'd learned from a book she'd read titled *A Woman's Revenge*, written by three Christian fiction authors.

But what she hadn't learned from the book was how to react when cold busted for being a snooper. And as she rode in the passenger seat on the way home from the Laroques', it was safe to say that she'd been cold busted.

"You've been following my footprints on Facebook," Lynox told Deborah as they drove down the highway. "You know what groups I'm in and everything."

Deborah didn't say a word. She simply held her head up, as if she had every right to know his virtual whereabouts.

"Do you know the pages I like? My friends?"

And the profile pictures of other women you like, Deborah thought in her head and kept it there. Being insecure truly wasn't a character-istic that she wanted to broadcast, as if she was proud of it.

"Have you trolled my Facebook friends' pages as well?" Lynox didn't sound any too pleased.

Again, Deborah remained silent. But for Lynox, that was all she wrote. Her silence was as good as a confession to him. He smelled something, and if it was roses, they were roses that had been left in stagnant water and now had a stench about them. He had to nip these flowers in the bud and throw them out.

"What are you doing?" Deborah asked Lynox as he slowed down and began changing lanes.

He went all the way from the far left lane to the far right one. A sound, what Deborah would call a road fart when she was a kid, let her know that they were pulling over to the berm. The tires rolling across the uneven pavement made a funny sound. "Why are you stopping on this dark highway for an eighteen-wheeler to come smash us to bits and pieces, leaving our kids without a mother or a father?"

"Stop it," Lynox said after putting the car in park. "Don't play with me, Deborah. Something is going on, and we are going to stay parked right here until you tell me what it is." The mere thought that Deborah was snooping around in his affairs made Lynox furious inside, and he felt hurt. Mistrust was not something he wanted as a part of their marriage. "One minute it sounds like you are trying to accuse me of wanting to get with Klarke, a woman I hardly know, and the next minute I'm cheating with women on Facebook."

"I didn't say anything about you cheating with women on Facebook," Deborah answered in her own defense.

"You might not have said it, but actions speak louder than words. First, you mention a group I'm in, which you would have no idea about unless you were digging around, specifically trying to figure out my activity. The only reason why you'd be digging around is that you suspected something. Then, when I ask you about it, you don't say anything. So if you have something on your mind, I'ma need you to say something." And with that said, Lynox paused, waiting for Deborah to reply.

Deborah bit her tongue. She felt silly and stupid all rolled into one big flour tortilla. Why was she overreacting? What had started all of this in the first place? What had been so serious that she and her husband were getting into it, instead of having a peaceful drive home after attending such a well put together event? Why was she allowing voices in her head to feed her negative thoughts and words, which ultimately influenced her behavior? This mistrust thing, especially, was a beast and was quite draining.

"So you're not going to talk?" Lynox asked. "This is some bull," he said, facing forward and placing his hands on the steering wheel. "You are acting real crazy right about now. And you know I don't do crazy." He put the car in drive. "You know for a fact that I got rid of one crazy broad in my past, so if you don't think I'll do it again, you've got another think coming."

Lynox was not prepared for the slap that Deborah planted on his cheek, nor did he see it coming.

"Darn it, Deborah!" Lynox balled his fist out of instinct. Veins popped out on his head. He gritted his teeth. The shaking and the visible tension in his hand made it look as though he was battling with an entity to keep it from forcing him to strike his wife. Tears of anger formed in Lynox's eyes as he shook his head at Deborah.

Deborah sat stunned, in shock and in fear. She couldn't believe that she had struck her husband. That was domestic violence. She didn't condone a man hitting a woman or a woman hitting a man. She had never imagined in a million years that she'd be involved in an abusive relationship, let alone that she would be the abuser. She honestly couldn't blame Lynox if he hit her back, and that was exactly where her fear lay. But even with fear being so prevalent, she was still angry. Why did he have to bring up past relationships, especially right now? She was already feeling inferior to other women.

Deborah's eyes danced back and forth as she noted the anger in her husband's eyes and the anger his balled fist symbolized. A part of her wanted to brace for the impact, but she didn't. Deborah knew the man she had married. She knew the things he was capable of, and hitting a woman was not one of them.

Too bad for Lynox that he was just finding out exactly who it was he had married and what she was capable of doing. This was not the same woman he'd met a few years ago. That woman was bold, direct, and confident, yet never arrogant or offensive. She loved the Lord, and if she messed up, her spirit grieved as much as she grieved the Holy Spirit, and she'd do everything in her power to make it right. But now this woman next to him was becoming more and more unrecognizable by the second, so where was the God in her, which Lynox had once recognized?

Lynox didn't attend church nearly as much as Deborah. He relied on that scripture that said something about the wife being sanctified for the husband. So he left the majority of the whole "seeking God" thing and the fellowshipping in the house of the Lord to his wife. Well, it looked like that was no longer going to work for them. Deborah was barely able to stay sanctified herself. They didn't need money and they didn't need material things to have a strong and thriving marriage, but they definitely needed God. And if Lynox couldn't find Him in his wife, then he supposed it was time that he go seek God for himself.

Lynox was grateful in this moment that his wife had been covering him in prayer, because that was the only thing that had kept him from losing control. But he honestly didn't know how long the strength would last. He needed to refuel after tonight's incident, so he made up his mind that he was going to be the first one through the church doors come morning.

He needed to have a little talk with Jesus. Up until now, church had been something he had engaged in whenever he woke up on Sunday morning and felt like going. His walk with Christ would no longer be like a stroll in the park; it would no longer be walking hand in hand on the bright, sunny days only. It had been fairly easy to give God praise when things were going well, but the real test for Lynox would be whether or not he could continue to praise and walk with God when it was raining and things weren't looking so bright. In this case, it wasn't about a little drizzle or a heavy rain that was passing by. A storm was brewing, which was evident by the sound of the roaring thunder. But just wait until the lightning struck.

Chapter 5

The next morning her ringing cell phone woke Deborah. Well, actually, she was already awake when the phone rang. She had woken up when she heard Lynox get out of bed and go to the bathroom. She hadn't gotten out of bed herself, though. She'd lain there and feigned sleep. What was she supposed to do after such a dramatic night? Wake up and say in a singsongy voice, "Good morning, honey," as if nothing had happened? Not happening, so she had just lain there, paralyzed like a scared possum, and listened to her husband mill about.

She'd heard the water running and him sifting through clothes in their walk-in closet. She'd heard the dresser drawer slam one time. He must have been retrieving a pair of socks. She'd heard another drawer slam. A T-shirt. She'd remained still, replaying in her head all her regrets from last night. If only she could take it all back, hit the REWIND button, and have some sort of do over. Even if she couldn't erase all her erratic actions, if she could only change one thing, it would be that she had not let the sun go down on her wrath. Or was it Lynox's wrath? After all, he'd been the one storming around this morning with a chip on his shoulder, slamming the bathroom door, the drawers in the bathroom, the medicine cabinet door, the closet door, and then finally the front door. He'd done so much slamming and stomping, Deborah was almost certain she'd heard his dress shoes abusing the walkway that led to the driveway, where his car happened to be parked.

He'd done all that without saying a single word to Deborah. Well, actually, he'd said four.

"You going to church?" Those were the words he'd asked Deborah before he stormed out of their bedroom. She'd simply ignored him, as she hadn't been certain if it was an invite for her to go with him or if he was trying to figure out if she was going at all. And if she was going, she'd reasoned, he would have opted not to go himself.

What Deborah had wanted to say was, "Negro, how you gon' ask me am I going to church after you done showered, shaved, got dressed, and are on your way out the door?" But things were already heated between the two of them. She hadn't want the situation to catch fire.

A part of Deborah had kept nagging at her to get out of that bed and carry her tail on to church. After all, this was the day that the Lord had made. She should be rejoicing and be glad in it. Instead she was mad in it. Mad in her bed. Besides, had she gone to church this morning, it would have only been because it was what she felt was the Christian thing to do. How could she call herself a Christian if she didn't go to church? However, she'd never really read anywhere that going to church was one of the requirements of being allowed to call one's self a Christian. There had been times when she did look forward to Sunday service. As of late, though, church had started to feel more and more like a requirement, rather than something she looked forward to doing. In the past few weeks, just thinking about having to get up out of bed and go to church had practically ruined her Saturday evenings.

She hadn't experienced that feeling of loathing in the face of having to get up and go somewhere since she worked in corporate America. Back then it was her Sunday evenings that were ruined, as she dreaded having to get up and go to work on Monday morning.

Several months ago New Day had started an 8:00 a.m. service. Deborah loved going to that service because she could get church over with early and have the rest of her day to do what she pleased. The early morning service wasn't as long as the late morning service, either. There was no way service could go over, because they had to make sure the church was cleared out and ready for the next service. Undisputedly, the later service was easier to attend, since she had to get the boys ready, but it was worth the sacrifice to attend the early morning one every blue moon.

Typically, it was only she and the boys who went to church. Every now and then Lynox would attend, if he woke up feeling chipper and full of life. Usually, it was after something good had happened, like him making the best sellers' list or something. He had attended enough to know everybody at church, and everybody knew him. Everyone was aware that he traveled a lot for his book signings, so when he was absent, they never knew if he was out of town or if he had opted to sleep in and get his Sunday lesson from the Word Network or from one of the church DVDs Deborah had purchased from the church bookstore. So it had absolutely surprised Deborah when she realized that today Lynox was heading to church. Nothing good had happened the night before to make him want to go give thanks.

That was why at first she hadn't been sure if he was getting up and going to church, or getting up to pack his bags and leave her. That was how angry she had made him last night. When she'd peeked from under the covers and looked through the open bathroom door, she'd seen that he was wearing a suit when he finally exited the closet. Surely, he wasn't going to get all jazzy just to go to a Motel 6. But he'd removed all doubt about where he was heading when he asked her if she was going to church.

Deborah had declined his invitation, if that was what it was, even though church might have been exactly where she needed to be with her man this morning. Either way she looked at it, she wouldn't have been there for God, which was the real reason why anyone should want to go. She would have been there praying that the sermon moved Lynox to forgive her and forget last night. It would have been all about her and her wants and needs, not about giving God glory just because He was God.

Deborah pulled the comforter over her head. She wasn't sure if she was trying to hide from her miserable thoughts about last night or from the annoying ringing of her cell phone. After a couple more rings, the phone stopped. She pulled the covers back down to her chest and stared at the ceiling. That was when it hit her that it could have been Lynox calling her. Maybe on his drive to church he had had a change of heart and wanted to make amends with her. Deborah shot up in bed to get the phone so that she could check her missed call. Before she could even pick the phone up, it started ringing again. Deborah hurriedly reached for it and tumbled right out of the bed and onto the floor. That didn't stop her from snatching the phone from the nightstand and taking it down with her.

"Hello," Deborah said, out of breath, as she sat on the floor and leaned up against the nightstand.

"Well, I called to see if I needed to get the boys ready for church, but from the sounds of it, you and the hubby got anything but Jesus on y'all's mind."

Deborah let out a sigh when she heard her mother's voice on the other end of the phone. "Oh, hey, Ma." She couldn't have hidden the disappointment in her tone even if she'd wanted to.

"Well, don't sound so excited to talk with me," Mrs. Lewis said.

"It's not that. It's just—"

"Oh, spare me the details."

Deborah let out a sigh, pulled herself up off the floor, and sat down on the bed. "Mom, please. Lynox isn't even here. He already left for church."

"Oh." She sounded a little surprised. "And you didn't go?"

"No. I, uh . . ." Deborah didn't want to lie to her mother. But, on the other hand, she didn't want to tell her what had transpired between her and Lynox, either. Deborah was a strong believer in the notion that a married couple should not share their issues with friends or family. Outsiders tended to stir the pot and offer what they personally would or wouldn't do. But to each his own. Not everyone handled things the same way as others. What worked for one person might very well be the thing that brought the house of cards down for another. "I was still in bed when he left."

"Overslept, huh?" her mother said, making a false assumption, and Deborah let her.

"So how are the boys?" Deborah quickly changed the subject.

"You know Grandma's babies don't ever give her any trouble."

Deborah could hear her mother planting a kiss on the baby, presumably. She imagined her mother had him right there in her arms.

Although Tyson stayed with his grandmother all the time, it wasn't until just recently that she had started keeping Tatum. She had a thing about keeping babies before they were three months old. They were way too new and small for her comfort.

"So what time are you coming to get them?" Mrs. Lewis asked.

Deborah chuckled under her breath. They might not be giving Grandma any trouble, but Grandma was ready for them to go. "I'm going to text Lynox and have him pick them up on his way home from church. Is that okay?" If Deborah didn't have to get out of that bed anytime soon, she wouldn't.

"Sounds good to me. I'll make sure they're all packed up and ready to go."

"Thanks, Ma. I'll talk to you later." Deborah ended the call and sat there for a moment. Her body was weak. Her sadness and depression were heavy. It would take a minute for her to muster up the strength to peel herself off the bed. Of course, while she sat there, her mind turned to thoughts of her and Lynox's fight. She put her head down and shook it. She couldn't believe things had gotten physical. Well, *she* had gotten physical, anyway.

She'd wanted to tell Lynox that she was sorry. But apologizing equated to admitting to her ugly acts. That was too hard. Often people didn't apologize for their wrongdoings, because they felt they hadn't done anything wrong. Confirming that wrongdoing was too painful. Denial was far more comfortable. And no matter how hard Deborah tried, she couldn't gather up enough courage to allow the words "I'm sorry" to escape her mouth. As a matter of fact, not a single word had been spoken between the two since they had continued their car ride home last night. Deborah was surprised that Lynox had not opted to sleep on the couch or in the guest room. If she had to bet, she'd put five on the fact that he slept with one eye open last night. He'd called her crazy, and she'd given him good reason to. Yet she'd snapped when the word came from his mouth and drifted into her ears.

Crazy.

She'd once heard that crazy people absolutely detested being called crazy, that officially being labeled that made them go, well, crazy. That was pretty much what had happened in Deborah's case. She'd been questioning for some time whether she was flat-out crazy, whether any doctor or pill in the world could help her. So to hear Lynox say the word had really hit a nerve. She might have physically slapped Lynox with her hand, but he'd mentally slapped her with that word. And to bring up his past relationship with a chick who he thought had put the *c* in *crazy* had really got Deborah's panties in a bunch. Lynox hadn't had to say a name. Deborah was certain that when he mentioned getting rid of a crazy woman from his past, he'd been referring to Helen.

Lynox being under the same roof as Helen during church had never been a concern of Deborah's. But Lynox bringing Helen up last night had triggered something in Deborah's mind. Why did he have to remind her that Helen had been with him first? Now, all of a sudden, she couldn't get the thought of those two being together out of her mind. Why had Lynox alluded to Helen? Had he been thinking of her as of late?

Helen volunteered in children's church sometimes. Deborah typically signed the boys in and out of children's church. On some occasions, when Lynox did attend church, Deborah would let him get the boys after service, while she spent a little extra time fellowshipping in the sanctuary. Had anything occurred between the two ex-lovers during those times?

Deborah and Helen had apologized to one another and had forgiven each other for all the

ugly things that had transpired between the two
of them. But had Helen been sincere, or had she
been playing Deborah all along? Had she made
Deborah think that they were cool, that she
wasn't a threat, so that she could pull a sneaky
move and try to steal Deborah's man?

All these questions circling in Deborah's mind
wouldn't let her get back in that bed and rest
even if she wanted to. She and Lynox were on
the outs right now, and that made it all the easier
for Helen to slink in. Huh! Not under Deborah's
watch.

Deborah looked over at her cell phone. She
picked it up and placed a call. "Mom," she said
when her mother answered the phone. "Change
of plans. Get the boys ready. We're going to
church, after all."

"Sister Chase, it's good to see you in the house
of the Lord this beautiful Sunday morning."

"Yeah, yeah, yeah, blah, blah, blah," was absolutely what Deborah had on her heart to say to
the cheerful usher who stood outside the closed
sanctuary doors and greeted her. But instead,
she got her flesh under control, smiled, and said,
"Good morning." She went to open one of the
doors, but the usher continued to block it.

"Elder Ross has already started prayer. You know pastor doesn't like any movement or walking around during prayer or when a prophesy is being given."

I know church rules. I been in church long enough to know that, Deborah thought, fussing in her head. *Who do you think you are, giving me the rundown, when I have been a member of this church and have known Pastor for quite some time, while you was still sliding down poles over at the Dollhouse Strip Club?* Ooh, if only Deborah could say with her mouth what she was thinking in her head. Her spirit woman was already being convicted for just thinking it. She could only imagine the type of conviction that would fall on her if she actually said the words out loud. So she opted to say nothing. *Just nod and smile, Deborah. Nod and smile.*

Deborah wished she had gone with her first instinct and had not even taken the baby to the nursery and Tyson to children's church. But she had wanted to lay eyes on Helen and perhaps do a little inquiring, and of course, she'd needed the boys in tow to do that. She would have looked ridiculous if she'd gone to children's church without any children.

She 100 percent intended only to inquire this time. No laying on of hands, which was how things had turned out the last time she'd called herself going to have a little chat with Helen. As luck would have it, this Sunday Helen wasn't even volunteering in children's church. It wasn't her week, which was what Deborah had been told when she dropped Tyson off. Deborah couldn't get out of there quick enough after getting Tyson all signed in. With each click of her heels down the hall to the church vestibule and then to the sanctuary doors, Deborah had envisioned Helen spotting Lynox alone in the sanctuary, sans wife, and then making her move on him for old times' sakes. Ordinarily, Lynox would be strong, able to fight off the clutches of Satan, but this morning he was vulnerable and weak. Deborah didn't know if he could withstand the force of Helen's sex appeal.

As she impatiently waited outside the sanctuary doors, Deborah could feel her heartbeat picking up. Her blood chilled throughout her body. These were all signs she'd experienced prior to her panic attacks. She was only becoming more and more anxious as Elder Ross continued his prayer.

Somebody needed to speak to Pastor Margie about when Elder Ross was called upon to pray. Deborah wasn't wearing a watch, and she hadn't checked the time on her cell phone, but she knew good and well that she had been standing outside the sanctuary, waiting for Elder Ross to finish praying, for at least ten minutes. His prayer had started off slow and smooth. He'd done the normal prayer over the church, the pastor, the leaders, the ministry, and so on. Then he had got all loud and boisterous and had started the "Somebody in here needs prayer for this, and somebody in here needs prayer for that" stuff. Then he had got to speaking in tongues.

"It don't take all that," Deborah said under her breath as she waited impatiently.

Every couple of minutes the usher would crack open the door and peek inside. She'd then turn and smile at Deborah, with a "Not quite yet" look on her face. If that usher knew what was good for her, the next time she cracked open that door, she'd let Deborah in. The usher might have about fifty pounds on Deborah, but she was going through her.

Finally, there was clapping and shouts of "Amen," as if Elder Ross had closed out the prayer. The usher checked to make sure they were sealing Elder Ross's prayer in a praise clap, then opened the door wide to let Deborah in. By then a couple more latecomers had shown up, and they all entered the sanctuary.

Inside there were ushers waiting to direct them to seats, as well as to hand them the church announcements. Minister Motley was making her way to the pulpit in order to read scripture.

Deborah held her hand up when one of the ushers attempted to give a copy of the announcements to her. "That's okay. I'm sure my husband has one," she said. "By the way, do you, by any chance, know where Lynox is seated?" Deborah could tell by the usher's expression that she didn't have a clue. "That's okay. I'm sure I'll find him."

The rows of seats appeared to be filled to capacity as Deborah made her way down the center aisle. She looked up and down, from left to right, hoping to spot Lynox. She was his wife. She needed to be there in the sanctuary with him, by his side, blessing the Lord for even giving her someone who could put up with her mess. If only she had womaned up and apologized to him last night, she probably wouldn't even be going through this right now. Why did she always have to be right instead of righteous? Here she'd pushed the man so far away that he felt it would take Jesus Himself to talk him into allowing her back into his good graces. If that was the case, Deborah would be right there when the conversation took place.

"Good morning, Sis," someone greeted as Deborah walked by.

"Morning," Deborah threw over her shoulder, clueless about whom she was even giving that halfhearted greeting to. She did that a couple more times before she was about five rows from the pulpit. Still there was no sign of Lynox at all. "Dang," Deborah said as she bit down on her lip.

Some members were seated, while others were still standing. The scripture had been read, but praise and worship was next, so some had decided that they might as well remain standing. Between the praise team—especially if Sister Paige was singing a solo—and the musicians, they wouldn't have been able to stay in their seats, anyway. Of course, all this up and down was making it hard for Deborah to get a clear view down each row.

Deborah was at the third pew when she realized that she might as well take a seat before she ended up at the altar. "Pardon me," she said as she scooted down to a vacant seat, still looking around for Lynox.

"Come on, everybody. Put your hands together, and let's bless the Lord," the praise and worship leader said as the musicians played behind him.

Deborah began clapping only because she'd been instructed to, and not because she was really focused on praising the Lord. Praise songs weren't designed to be like secular music. With praise music, more than just the beat was supposed to pull the listener in. It was about the words that were being ministered. When it came to praise music, one shouted out, "That's my song," because the words rang true to one's spirit, and not because one could bounce to it, although there was nothing wrong with getting a little Holy Ghost bounce on, especially if it was a good old-fashioned Kirk Franklin or Tye Tribbett song.

But not one word being sung was registering with Deborah. She was distracted by not knowing where Lynox was. The feeling of distraction in church, unfortunately, wasn't new to Deborah. It was just that usually she was better at concealing how her mind was drifting off, how she was wondering about other things, such as what she was going to prepare for dinner after church, which manuscript she would start editing next, whether or not she was going to do the laundry today or tomorrow, and whether there was a PTO meeting that week or not. Such mental distractions somehow so easily tore her from what was going on in the Lord's house. Her mind was so hard to keep under control sometimes, and as last night had proven, so was her mouth . . . and now her hands.

"He deserves a real hand praise, not a mechanical one."

Deborah looked to see if, by any chance, the praise and worship leader was looking dead at her when he said those words. If he was talking to her, it was his right to do so. That flimsy and robotic hand praise she was giving the Lord while she was scanning the sanctuary was shameful. She began to clap her hands harder. In case the praise and worship leader had been addressing her, she didn't want his throwing of shade to be in vain.

Within a minute or so, Deborah was clapping her hands and singing the words along with praise and worship. Her clap slowed and her vocals were behind a count when she finally spotted someone she had been looking for. *Helen.* She was sitting in the second seat from the end of the row that was two rows behind Deborah. She was on her feet, clapping and singing along as if her life depended on it, unlike Deborah, who was just moving her lips, hoping no one noticed she wasn't singing the right words.

Standing next to Helen was her teenage son. He was clapping and swaying, leaving the singing to his mother. But he genuinely looked to be giving God the glory. Deborah prayed that her boys would someday worship God in spirit and in truth. Even if sometimes she did feel as if she was going to church only out of routine, she at least hoped that raising her boys in the way that they should go would be beneficial.

With the thought that she had to be an example for her own children, Deborah decided to turn back around and make a genuine effort at giving God some praise from her heart. As Deborah went to turn her head and face forward, she saw him, Lynox. She might as well have jumped into a pit of fire, because that was how hot she was. There he was, sitting down. He was clapping his hands, but he was not standing like almost everyone else. That was not what had Deborah on fire, though. It was who he was sitting by. Helen!

Chapter 6

The ratchet thing to do would have been for Deborah to go snatch Helen up and mop the sanctuary with her. Oh, that would have definitely given folks something to talk about. One thing was for sure: Deborah wouldn't have to worry about people disliking her for her over-the-top actions. Reality television had proven that the most ratchet, *fightingness*, least classy, meanest, and most hateful person on the show became the fan favorite, got the highest paycheck, and eventually ended up with a spin-off and a starring role on Broadway. Society had spoken. Ratchet was the new black.

With Helen's son on one side of her and Lynox on the other, they looked like the happy little family. Would that be what Lynox's family portrait looked like soon? The thought alone made Deborah nearly lose her breath.

"Breathe, girl. Breathe," Deborah said to herself in a low voice as she turned back to face the altar.

Back when Deborah used to see her counselor, they used to practice these breathing exercises. Whenever Deborah felt as if she was about to go from zero to ten, she would take deep breaths in and then exhale in order to calm down. Deborah closed her eyes. She inhaled and exhaled. Those on the outside looking in probably thought that she was in worship.

Deborah did a couple of sets of the breathing in and breathing out. She opened her eyes. She was no longer upset at Helen. Why should she be? She wasn't married to Helen. Helen had no commitment and had made no promises to Deborah. She should have never been mad at Helen in the first place. It was Lynox who was showing complete disrespect by sitting next to a woman with whom he'd been intimate in the past and whom Deborah could take or leave. So even though the breathing technique had helped her to release her anger at Helen, she was madder than ever. Only now her anger was directed at Lynox.

Deborah decided to try another exercise her counselor had taught her. She'd count away her anger. "Ten, nine, eight, seven . . ." But by the time she got to one, she still wanted to go snatch her man up and ask him what the heck he was doing, sitting next to that tramp.

Deborah wanted to kick herself for even think-ing for one minute that Helen had changed. Once a tramp, always a tramp. And all that mess Lynox was talking about Helen being crazy and him kicking her to the curb was just a front. It was nothing more than a lie he was telling so that Deborah wouldn't suspect anything.

"Ugh!" Deborah said, balling her fist and punching downward.

"That's right, Sister. Knock that devil out," the woman next to Deborah said.

Deborah looked at the woman as the words to the song being sung registered. It was a song about going into the enemy's camp, knocking the devil out, and taking back all the stuff he'd stolen. Deborah realized that the woman next to her must have thought that Deborah was acting out the words to the song. Deborah simply smiled and then faced forward. After a couple of seconds she looked over at Lynox again. He was now standing and getting all into the song.

"That music sure is loud," he had complained sometimes when he attended church with Deborah.

It didn't seem to be bothering him now. Maybe the sweet nothings Helen had whispered in his ear prior to the music starting had softened the blows of the notes.

Deborah shook her head and turned back around. She grabbed her purse and her Bible bag and slid down her row and out to the aisle while everyone was still standing and clapping. Lynox obviously hadn't seen her coming, and now he wouldn't see her going.

As Deborah speed walked down the center aisle, she couldn't see any faces, just blurs. That was how fast she was moving. The fact that her eyes were filled with tears didn't help.

"It's gon' be all right, Sister," one of the ushers said to Deborah as she burst through the sanctuary doors.

It was just her, alone on the other side of the closed sanctuary doors, consumed by anger. She was breathing heavily, and tears were streaming down her face. "God, what is wrong with me?" she cried out, briskly wiping the tears away. Why was she so quick to anger about every little thing?

After catching her breath, she ran out of the church and to her car. She got in her car and began driving. Every now and then she'd beat on the steering wheel. Next, she would cuss, and then she would cry. One time, while sitting at a red light, she even busted out into a laughing fit. Her emotions and her thoughts were jumping all over the place. Breathing hadn't helped.

Counting hadn't helped. Suddenly, Deborah thought she knew the one thing that would help.

Even though the church was a fifteen-minute drive from Deborah's home, she got there in eight, breaking all kinds of traffic laws. Either way it went, she was going to break the law if she didn't do something to put her mind at ease soon. She was going to break the law by driving back to that church and wearing somebody out, or she was going to get a speeding ticket while driving home. Fortunately, neither happened.

Deborah entered her house and ran straight into her private bathroom. She opened the medicine cabinet, picked up bottles, looked at them, and then set them back down. "Shoot," she said after she'd gone through every pill bottle in the cabinet without finding what she was looking for.

Deborah looked around, in thought. She then began pulling open the bathroom drawers. She rummaged around in each and every one of them and still came up empty-handed. After letting out an expletive, she opened up the cabinet under her side of their dual sinks. Within three seconds the nice orderly contents had been pushed and shoved all over the place. Under usual circumstances, she would not have been able to proceed with her search before putting everything back in its place. Even if the house was burning down and Deborah knocked a book off a shelf while she was running out the door, she'd have to go back and pick it up. Watching the house burn down to the ground would have been more aggravating if she knew a book was out of place. Such disorder would have ordinarily driven Deborah insane, but she was already headed down that road. She'd make a U-turn and clean up her mess after she found what she was looking for.

Just when she was about to give up on her side of the sinks and go check to see if maybe she'd misplaced it on Lynox's side, she finally saw it. She'd found what she was looking for.

"Yes," Deborah said, clutching the pill bottle in her hand. She double-checked the label. "My happy pills." She kissed the bottle and pulled it against her chest like it was a long-lost lover. She had to count on two hands how many times she'd carried that very same bottle over to the trash can to dispose of it. She would never need them again, she had always told herself. The times she'd contemplated throwing them away she'd been happy, genuinely happy . . . and without the aid of a pill. And with a handsome husband like Lynox to help her through life and her two amazingly beautiful children, she couldn't have imagined that she'd ever find herself in a miserable slump again, one where she would need medication to pull herself out.

She'd prayed to God constantly to keep her mind, and He had. Well, at least she had thought He had, but now she felt as if she was losing it. And it was the fear of this very moment that had made Deborah change her mind each time she went to throw away the pills. The fear that one day she just might need those pills.

With the bottle in hand, Deborah walked over to her sink. She opened the bottle and poured one pill into her hand, turned on the water, then threw the pill down her throat and chased it with water. "Ah," she said, feeling better already, knowing that soon enough that pill would kick in and relax her. She looked at herself in the mirror. She thought for a moment and then said aloud, "Maybe I better take two." She read the instructions on the bottle. It had been a while since she'd used them. The bottle said that she needed to take only one. But she felt as if her mind was spinning out of control far more than it had been when the pills were first prescribed. Therefore, she felt two would really do the job of getting her right . . . fast! Then maybe she could pitch the bottle for real this time. She'd take full advantage of the effects of the two pills so that she wouldn't have to take any more.

With her final reasoning, Deborah threw a second pill down her throat, and this time gulped her own saliva, not even bothering to drink water. She looked at herself in the mirror once again and exhaled. She entered her bedroom, walked over to her bed, and kicked off her shoes. She would lie down until the pills took effect. Otherwise, she might end up back at New Day, raising hell.

As she went to pull the covers back, she realized she still had the pill bottle in her hand. She placed it on the nightstand and then crawled into bed. She said a final prayer that when she woke up, she would be back in her right mind. All would be well. She'd be back to her old self again, the one whom Lynox had fallen in love with and married. Anxiety, depression, panic attacks, and all her manic thoughts would be a thing of past . . . if there was a God. Because the Word had told her that God would give her, her heart's desires. Her heart desired to be clean, loving, calm, patient, and whole.

Pulling the covers up to her neck, Deborah said, "Okay, God. Do your thing. I'm going under. Now operate on me while I'm in a deep sleep, the same way you did on others in the Bible. In Jesus's name. Amen."

***

"Deborah! Deborah! Get up! Are you serious right now? You're sleeping?" Lynox was enraged as he paced at the foot of their bed. With each fist balled at his side, he was seeing red. He was about to start seeing black, because if the Holy Ghost didn't hold him back, he was going to black out on his wife. He stopped in his tracks and tried to calm himself down. "Deborah." This time, in his attempt to remain calm, he didn't yell her name, but she did not respond. He looked to see if Deborah was still sound asleep. "Deborah." He said it a little louder this time, trying his best to keep the edge off his tone.

She sighed, as if she was having the best sleep in the world. And if he wasn't mistaken, she had a little smirk on her face.

"Well, I'll be . . . ," he said as he stood there looking at her, shaking his head. He could not believe she was at home, sleeping, without a care in the world. That was it. He couldn't contain himself any longer. "Deborah, get up!" he yelled as loud as he could, snatching the covers off of her.

Deborah began to squirm and wipe her eyes. She let out a couple of grunts and sighs as she desperately tried to pull herself out of her deep sleep. Her mind was telling her no, to stay asleep, that she needed the rest, but her body wanted to get up. It was a struggle that Deborah found herself caught in the middle of.

"Woman, I'm not playing with you!" Lynox snapped.

Deborah managed to pull herself up into a sitting position in bed. "What, Lynox? What's going on?" She was all discombobulated and confused. She patted her hair down.

"The boys! That's what's going on." Lynox began to pace again.

Deborah sat there, confused. "What about the boys?"

Lynox stopped and looked at Deborah as if his look alone could shake some sense into her. "What about the boys?" he repeated. He angrily put his hands on his hips. "Where are they, Deborah? Where are your children?" Lynox waited impatiently for Deborah to reply.

"Well, aren't they . . . they are . . ." Deborah had to think real hard. "With my mother?"

"Is that a question? Because I'm asking you," Lynox said.

"They spent the night with her, didn't they?"

"Yes, where they were safe and sound before you picked them up this morning."

Deborah scrunched her face up. She hadn't picked the boys up from her mother's. As a matter of fact, she had planned on texting Lynox and telling him to go pick them up. "Didn't you get my text? Didn't you pick them up from my mom's?"

"No, I did not!" Lynox said through gritted teeth.

"All right, okay," Deborah said, swinging her legs out of the bed and onto the floor. "Calm down. I'll go get them myself." She looked at Lynox. "What? Did Mom call and fuss about them being there so late?" Deborah stretched and yawned.

Lynox stomped over in front of Deborah. "They are not at your mother's!" He slammed his fist down on the bed next to Deborah, causing her to flinch. "You picked them up already. You took them to church. Don't you remember?" Lynox stood up straight and walked away, slapping his hand across his forehead and wiping away the sweat.

Deborah sat on the bed with her mouth wide open. Had Lynox not just mentioned it, she would have honestly forgotten all about picking up the boys from her mother's and checking them into children's church. That part of the day had been completely lost from her mind.

"Oh, my God! The boys. Church!" Deborah looked over at the clock as she hopped to her feet. It was almost five in the evening. Church usually let out around one o'clock. "I gotta . . . I gotta get back to the church." She went to rush past Lynox.

Lynox grabbed Deborah by the shoulders, stopping her.

"Let go of me!" she yelled, totally flipping out. "I gotta go get the boys."

"Will you stop it?" Lynox said, fussing. "I got them. After failed attempts to get in touch with you, the church called me. Unfortunately, I went to get something to eat after church with Brother Maeyl and his family. I left my cell phone in the car. I checked my messages afterward. It was Pastor Margie. They were worried sick, Deborah." He shook her slightly. "Worried sick. They tried calling your phone, the house phone. They said they even drove by and rang the bell."

"I . . . I . . ." Deborah placed her hand on her forehead. She walked away, trying to put the pieces of the puzzle together. "I must not have heard the phone or the doorbell or . . ." Her words trailed off. She was so embarrassed. So ashamed. "God, my boys. Tyson must have been scared to death. Where are they? I've gotta go see them." Deborah ran toward the bedroom door.

"Wait a minute. They're not—"

"Tyson! Tatum!" Deborah ran out the door and down the hall, calling for her sons.

"They're not here," Lynox called out as he chased her.

Deborah was oblivious to the words her husband had just spoken. "Tyson!" She opened the door to Tyson's room, only to find his race car twin bed with drawers at the bottom empty. "Tyson! Tatum!" She turned to leave the room and head to the nursery. That was when she smacked right into Lynox's chest, almost knocking the wind out of herself. "Ugh," she said.

"They're not here," Lynox told her.

This time the words registered in Deborah's head. "What? But I thought you said—"

"I did get them from church, but then I took them back to your mother's. I was afraid of what I might find when I got back to the house, or of what I wouldn't find. I didn't know if I was going to have to drive around and call hospitals and the police station, looking for you. Because I figured something god-awful had to have happened for you to sign our kids into church and never show back up to get them. So imagine both my surprise and, I suppose, my relief when I came home and found you in bed, sleeping like a baby. Deborah, seriously, what is going on with you? Do you think that maybe you need to—" Lynox halted his words. He wanted to be very careful about what he said. The last time he said something his wife didn't like, he ended up getting slapped across the hand and then the face.

Deborah's eyes began to water. "Do I need to what? Just say it, Lynox."

As Lynox looked into his wife's eyes, his anger started to decrease. And he started to become sympathetic, almost to the point where he felt sorry for her. She seemed lost, overwhelmed, and confused all at the same time. He didn't know what she needed at the moment, but it probably wasn't him making her feel any worse than she already did. All he could do was shake his head.

"What? Say it!" Deborah cried. "Do I need my happy pills again? Is that what you were going to say? Well, just so you know . . ." Deborah stomped off toward their bedroom. "I'll show you." She raced into their bedroom. At first she headed for the bathroom, but then she realized that what she was looking for was on the nightstand by the bed. She headed over to the nightstand and grabbed the bottle of pills. She turned around as Lynox entered the bedroom. "See!" She shook the bottle of pills at him. "I have my happy pills, and for your information, I took them already. I was only trying to do the right thing. I felt so bad about putting my hands on you last night. I wasn't myself. I wasn't in my right mind," Deborah explained.

"I was too proud to apologize last night," she continued. "Then you left for church this morning . . . without me." She swept her hair back with her hand. "I had all these crazy thoughts about you, and then my mom called and asked if I was taking the kids to church. I told her no at first, and then I wanted to go see about you, see if you were okay," Deborah lied. "And so I decided to get them and take them to church too." Deborah was rambling on hysterically. "I tried to find you at church. I couldn't find you at first, but then I saw you. You were sitting next to her, and I . . . I couldn't take it. I had to get out of there before I went postal. I didn't even think about the boys. I needed to get away. I don't even remember how I got home. But when I got here, I needed something. So I decided to take my pills, since they helped me before. I guess I shouldn't have taken two, but—"

"Deborah, you took two?" Lynox said, finally able to get a word in edgewise.

Deborah stood there, nodding like a small child. It was like she'd gone from almost forty years old to four years old.

"Baby, why would you do that?" Lynox said, now completely empathetic toward his wife.

"You could have hurt yourself. What if you hadn't woken up? What would I have told the boys?"

Deborah put her head down in shame. "I'm sorry. I just wanted to be better and happy and to make you happy. I want to be better." Deborah began to weep heavily, her shoulders heaving up and down.

Lynox walked over and embraced his wife. "It's okay. You've been stressed and over- whelmed. I think you need to slow down a little. Take a little time out for yourself." He pressed his wife's face up against him and rubbed her back. "Had you stayed for today's service, it would have been right on time for you. Pastor Margie preached about God blessing you even while you're resting. She talked about how some folks can't even sleep and rest well, because they are already thinking about all the stuff they have to get done the next day."

Boy, oh, boy, if that didn't describe Deborah. She tossed and turned in her sleep at night, thinking about the next day's tasks. Even if it was three o'clock in the morning, she'd some- times get out of bed and do a task, just to get it off her mind.

"Pastor Margie said God wants you to sleep and be renewed and refreshed. Instead of wor- rying about all of the next day's problems, you should sleep soundly, trusting that God has already blessed you in that area," Lynox said, reiterating today's teaching. "She said that when a person is anxious and worried, it's difficult to hear God's voice. But when they stop and rest, they can hear and recognize His voice."

Lynox's words were truly resonating with Deborah. She wished she had stayed at church and received the Word. She'd let the devil run her right out of that church and away from her blessing.

Lynox pulled away a little from Deborah and looked her in the eyes. "God will refresh and restore you even in your sleep, so maybe that's all you really need to get back on track again. Some sleep, some rest, some downtime, or just a relaxing time out with friends." He ran his hands through her hair.

"Well, Klarke did say something about wanting to get together this week," Deborah said.

"I think that would be good for you. I've never known you to have any girlfriends to hang out with and do stuff women do. Having someone to talk to like Klarke might be exactly what the doctor ordered. Even better, that may be why God put her in your life."

Deborah sniffed, then looked up at her husband. "You think so?"

He pushed her hair behind her ears. "Yeah, baby, I do."

"But is she saved? Do you know if their family attends church or anything?"

"Does it matter? I wasn't saved when I met you, and I half attend church now."

Deborah shrugged. "You have a point." Deborah had honestly never looked at things that way. She didn't automatically count folks out because they weren't practicing Christians. It was that she didn't really let them in if they didn't have that in common with her. It was that she tried so hard to be holy. Lynox respected that about her. Deborah wasn't sure that someone who was worldly and didn't know her would, though. She was having enough trouble around saved people, so the thought of trying to get better around the unsaved was daunting.

Lynox kissed Deborah on the forehead. "So just think about hooking up with Klarke. You never know. If she's not already saved, who's to say God doesn't want you to be the one to lead her to the throne?"

That put a smile on Deborah's face. She felt good knowing that even though she'd acted like the devil, Lynox knew her heart well enough to know that she was still usable by God.

"Now, why don't you go get out of your clothes and get showered, and I'll get the boys?" Lynox suggested. "I'll stop and grab pizza or something so you won't have to worry about cooking anything. Okay?"

Deborah nodded. That sounded real good to her. "Okay."

"All right then. I'll be back soon." Lynox kissed Deborah one more time before releasing her. He walked over to the door. Before exiting, he turned around and asked, "Are you gonna be okay?"

Deborah nodded and smiled. "I am now that I've got my husband back."

"Girl, I never left," Lynox said. Lynox returned the smile and then exited, pulling the door closed behind him.

As soon as that door closed, both the husband's and the wife's smile faded. Apparently, neither of them believed that Deborah was going to be okay.

Chapter 7

Deborah had just left the library. She'd met with a prospective client in one of the smaller conference rooms. Deborah didn't like bringing any ole body to her home office, so she quite often reserved one of the public library's conference rooms to hold her meetings.

The meeting had gone well. Deborah was excited about the possibility of beginning work on a project for the aspiring author with whom she'd met. It would involve Deborah doing some editing and adding content to beef up the project. It was a nonfiction work that consisted of several little inspirational stories the author had pulled from her own life. Talking to the woman had inspired Deborah. She had such wisdom and was extremely positive. Deborah was so moved by some of the stories the woman had relayed verbally, she actually would have done the project for free. That was how certain Deborah was that the writer's words would bless her spirit and anyone else who read the book.

Deborah hadn't even realized the meeting had gone over by a full hour until the librarian knocked on the door and told them the parties who had reserved the room next had arrived. Had that librarian not interrupted them, there was no telling how much longer Deborah would have sat there and gotten more than her fill of the woman's sagacity and inspirational nuggets.

That extra hour was a setback timewise for Deborah. Now she sat in her car in the library parking lot, trying to figure out how in the world she was going to be able to prepare the meal she'd originally planned. She definitely needed to have started the meal an hour ago in order for it to be done at a decent time.

She'd served dinner at eight o'clock at night in the past, after not being able to pull herself away from a project. Or perhaps something else had delayed. Like the one time Lynox had needed her to search his computer for a document he couldn't remember the name of and e-mail it to him. That had frustrated her to no end. She had had to search for forty-five minutes and had cracked open dozens of documents before she found the one he wanted. For the millionth time she'd given him a speech about handling his own business, being prepared, and being organized.

As always, though, it had gone in one ear and out the other. The very next day he had called her, wanting her to look all over the house for a piece of paper he'd written a number down on.

Although it wasn't likely, Deborah wondered whether Lynox had taken the liberty of starting dinner once he saw that it was getting late and she hadn't returned home at the time she'd estimated. She pulled out her cell phone and dialed his number.

"Hey, wife," he answered through the cell phone. "What's up?" He sounded all happy and excited, like he'd had a pretty good day.

"Nothing," Deborah replied. "Just getting out of this meeting. It went longer than I had anticipated, which is why I am calling. I was checking to see if maybe you had started dinner."

"No," Lynox said. "You should have told me to, and I would have."

"Well, I figured that when you saw it was getting late, you would take the initiative and do it yourself so that Tyson wouldn't have to eat at midnight." A minute ago Deborah had felt so light and refreshed after speaking to her future client with all that positive energy. The snappishness in her voice showed that a dark cloud was slowly but surely making its way over to the sun.

"My bad," Lynox said, his voice no longer as chipper as it had been when he first answered the phone. Deborah had wasted no time at all figuratively pissing in his Cheerios.

Deborah instantly felt convicted. She'd had a good day; he'd had a good day. Why mess that up? Besides, she didn't want to be accused of stealing her man's joy. She quickly changed her attitude for the better. "It's okay. I'll stop and get something. I'll make tomorrow what I had planned on making tonight."

"Well, Tyson is about to go have pizza, cake, and ice cream next door, anyway. It's CJ's birthday today."

"Oh, yeah. That's right," Deborah said. "Wait a minute. I thought it was tomorrow. Oh, well. Anyway, I wrapped his present and left it out. It's downstairs on my desk. I didn't bring it upstairs, because I didn't want Tyson snooping around and finding it." Deborah kept a mini store in their basement. After Christmas, she would wait until all the stores marked their holiday merchandise at least 70 percent off; then she'd go to town. She'd purchase warm holiday pajama sets, snowflake bath sets, mug sets, and so on. She had bins in their basement that she had labeled WOMEN, MEN, BOYS, and GIRLS. Items that didn't look like they were strictly related to Christmas,

she would place in a separate plastic bin. From
there she would retrieve gifts for birthdays,
anniversaries, baby showers, graduations, and
whatnot, and that was where she had got the
Spider-Man bath set she had all wrapped up and
ready for CJ.

Time didn't always allow Deborah to drop
everything and go out and grab a gift, and if it
did, she'd spend way more money than she liked.
That was what usually happened when a person
didn't have time to compare prices. Even though
she and Lynox were well off financially, there
had been a period of time in Deborah's life when
she hadn't been. She'd been alone and struggling
on her own. She never wanted to revisit that
time, so she made sure she always got the most
for her money and never spent frivolously.

"Don't send CJ over there empty-handed,"
Deborah said. "I don't want them thinking we
sent our child over there to eat up all their food
and didn't even have the decency to get a gift."

Lynox laughed. "They don't care about all
that."

"Well, I do," Deborah said. She'd heard folks
talking in church prior to service starting about
how they'd thrown their child a party at Chuck
E. Cheese's, and so-and-so had shown up with
all their kids and hadn't even brought a gift. No

way was anyone ever going to be able to say that about Deborah. "What's my other boy doing?"

"Keeping me from getting any work done."

Just then Deborah heard the baby coo in the background, as if he knew he was being talked about.

"Now you know what it feels like," Deborah said.

"No, but he's fine. He's tired. I fed his greedy butt and bathed him. He's about to be out like a lightbulb."

"Then it sounds like it's just going to be me and you, huh?"

"I like the sound of that," Lynox said with a hint of seduction.

All of a sudden Deborah pictured a nice romantic dinner of Chinese food with herself and her man, and perhaps catching a game or watching a movie. Maybe she'd even light some candles and incense, like couples in love did in movies. "I was thinking, I have a taste for Chinese, and since Tyson hates Chinese, this would be a perfect time to have it for dinner, when he's not eating with us."

"I'm cool with that," Lynox said.

"Well, I'll stop at that place over in the strip mall where Kroger is. I should be home in about a half hour."

"I'll be waiting."

"All right. I'll see you in a minute. Love you, husband."

Deborah ended the call, and immediately her mind began to play out how her evening with Lynox would go even before it happened. She pictured herself pulling into the driveway. Lynox would come out and help her carry the food inside. The baby would already be asleep, and Tyson would be next door. She would jump in the shower real quick, and Lynox would light candles and incense while she was washing up. When she got out of the shower, she would walk into their bedroom, where the food would be all set up, and the room would be dim, lit only by the candles and the illumination from the television.

That scenario was something both Deborah and Lynox needed. She would finally be taking a moment to chill out, like Lynox had been suggesting she do. And for once Lynox would get some loving that wasn't rushed or that she wasn't too worn out to participate in at all. Yes, she was guilty of sometimes just lying there, hoping Lynox would hurry up and finish so she could roll over and close her eyes.

Besides that, Deborah had been tripping lately, and she knew it. And even though Lynox hadn't said anything more about the whole incident with her taking the pills and leaving the kids at church, he was bothered by it, she was sure. Well, tonight she'd make him forget all about it. Then, once Tyson came home and was put to bed too, they wouldn't hurry up and get anything over with. They'd take it nice and slow.

"Yes!" Deborah said, pulling her thoughts back to reality, but hardly able to wait to make her daydream come true. She pumped her fist after starting the car. "It's on and popping now."

Deborah pulled into the driveway of her home. She didn't bother hitting the button to open the garage door. Since Lynox was home and his car wasn't parked in the driveway, she assumed he'd parked in the garage. Even though they had a two-car garage, only one vehicle could be parked in it at a time since bikes, cases of books, tools, a lawn mower, and whatnot took up all the space on one side.

Looking at all the clutter would sometimes clutter Deborah's brain, so she actually preferred parking in the driveway and bypassing that mess. After putting the car in park and turning it off, Deborah waited for a second. She watched for either the garage door to rise or for the front door to swing open.

Lynox knew she'd stopped to pick up food. He also knew that she'd left the house with her purse and her laptop bag. Therefore, he should have known that her hands would be full upon her return home. But he did not appear. She figured any other husband would have come to help his wife out. "I guess not mine," Deborah huffed. She counted. It worked this time. She was not going to overreact. So this part of her vision wouldn't come to pass. She could live with that. "Pick your battles, D," she told herself.

Deborah got out of the car and walked around to the passenger's side. She struggled to gather the food and all her belongings. She did not want to have to make a second trip back out to the car. Once she got to the front door, she realized she should have thought through her little juggling act a little better. With no free hand to open the door, she risked dropping something if she gave it a try. She pushed the doorbell. She stood there for about ten seconds and then rang it again.

"You've got to be freakin' kidding me," she spat. She tried ringing the bell one more time, but still Lynox didn't answer the door. "Jesus!" Deborah had to set some things down on the porch and then fish her keys out of her purse. This time she used her breathing technique to maintain control.

Once she finally unlocked the door, she
pushed it open and was greeted by the sound
of loud music coming from the upstairs loft. "Is
Lynox playing 'Just Dance'?" Deborah asked
out loud. The song sure did sound like the one
she and Tyson performed whenever she played
the Wii game with him. Well, with that music
playing, there was no way Tatum was asleep.
Deborah didn't let that get to her. Surely, by the
time she got out of the shower, Lynox would
have him settled. Maybe that was what Lynox
was doing; maybe he was upstairs, dancing silly,
trying to entertain Tatum and put him to sleep.

Deborah sat the food down on the table and
one of the two stools in the foyer. She then went
back out onto the porch and grabbed her laptop
bag, which she'd had to set down. She came
back inside and locked the door. She exited the
foyer and entered the living room. Her eyes
immediately found the gift bag on the table, the
one she'd put CJ's birthday present in.

"He forgot to give him the gift, anyway?
Geesh." The next thing Deborah spotted was
a balled-up diaper. A couple of Tatum's baby
toys were on the floor. A bottle was lying on the
couch. Walking into a room that was full of clutter or where things were out of place was as skin
crawling for Deborah as walking into a room full

of roaches. "I can't," Deborah said, not knowing if she was going to be able to keep it together.

She immediately began picking up some of the items. She wouldn't be able to have a nice, romantic, comfortable evening with Lynox if she knew her downstairs wasn't in order. As Deborah was about to pick up the baby bottle, she heard giggling coming from the loft.

"You're beating me!" she heard Lynox shout out.

Deborah wondered who he was talking to. Tyson should have been next door, at CJ's. Deborah called out Lynox's name as she began to climb the steps.

"We're up here," he shot back.

Once Deborah reached the top of the steps, she almost fell down them backward. She was taken aback by the huge catastrophe that she had once called a loft. There were fruit snack wrappers and empty Capri Sun packages strewn about. Tyson had kicked his shoes off in the middle of the floor, and they lay there, instead of under his bed, where she'd taught him to put them once he took them off. The crusts to a grilled cheese sandwich and potato chip crumbs littered a TV tray. Lego pieces were on the floor, instead of on the Lego table she had bought Tyson for Christmas but had let Santa Claus take the credit for.

Lynox and Tyson were having a ball jumping and dancing around to the Wii game. Sitting on the couch in his baby seat, watching it all, just as wide eyed as ever, was Tatum.

No, no, no, Deborah said to herself as she shook her head. This was not happening. "What is going on? The house is a mess, and you two fools are up here jumping around in it. How can you even think straight with all this mess everywhere? And the downstairs is looking just as crazy." There was no turning off the aggravation now. As far as Deborah was concerned, the night couldn't be salvaged, or rather, the night as she'd envisioned it.

"Hey, babe," Lynox said, ignoring the fact that Deborah had come in acting stank.

"Hey, Mommy," Tyson said, not taking his eyes off the television screen while he worked his little butt off, trying not to miss a single dance step.

Deborah didn't respond to either one of them. She immediately began cleaning up the loft in a huff. "Who wants to come home to this mess? Tyson has stuff everywhere. I can't believe you let him tear up this place like this," Deborah ranted. "Looks like a cyclone hit it."

"Oh, he's just a kid. Give him some slack," Lynox said in the boy's defense. He looked over at Tyson. "Say 'Chill out, Mommy.'"

Tyson mimicked Lynox. "Chill out, Mommy."

Lynox and Tyson laughed.

Deborah felt as if they were laughing at her. Not only that, but she felt Lynox was undermining her efforts to teach Tyson to pick up after himself. Maybe Lynox was even trying to pit Tyson against her, make her out to be the bad guy. Deborah was so furious, she absolutely wanted to cry. It was building up inside. She had to unleash her anger.

Deborah got up in Tyson's face and yelled, "Don't you ever get fresh at the mouth with me, you hear me?"

Her sudden outburst stopped the little dancing machine. He looked to see if she was serious or not. Lynox had told him what to say, and when he'd said it, Lynox had laughed, and so he'd laughed too. Didn't that mean it was a joke? But what did he know? He was just a kid.

At the sound of Deborah's harsh, angry voice, Tatum burst out crying.

Lynox shut the game down. "Deborah, are you that upset? Geesh. I'll clean it up."

"Yeah, right. If you were going to clean it up, it would already be clean. No, y'all sitting around waiting for me to do everything, like I don't work all day and take care of the kids too. Not to mention cook and clean." Deborah rambled on as she began picking up the trash in the loft.

Tyson was standing there, looking confused and scared. Poor thing didn't know what to do.

"Tyson, why don't you go in your room?" Lynox put his hand on Tyson's shoulder. He wanted to let him know that everything was going to be all right.

Tyson headed to his room. Tatum still sat in his baby seat, crying. Lynox walked over and picked him up.

"Hey, little guy. It's okay," Lynox told his infant son.

"He's probably ready to go to bed," Deborah declared. "You said he was tired. But how did you expect him to go to sleep with you and Tyson up here making all that racket?" She pointed toward Tyson's bedroom. "And what's he doing home, anyway? Isn't he supposed to be next door?"

"Oh, yeah, you were right. CJ's birthday thing is tomorrow, not today," Lynox said.

"Did they call you and tell you that?"

"No. When I walked Tyson over there with the gift in hand, Benji told me."

Hearing that infuriated Deborah. In her eyes it made them look like bad parents, incompetent. "I told you it was tomorrow," Deborah snapped. "You don't listen. Got my baby looking stupid."

"He didn't look stupid, Deborah. It's not that serious," Lynox told her.

It might not have been that serious to Lynox, but any little mix-up, when it came to her children, stung. She never wanted to look like a mother who wasn't on top of her game. A mother sending her kid to a birthday party the day before the actually party screamed failure in Deborah's book. Couldn't she even keep a calendar?

"Well, what made you think it was today?" Deborah asked.

"Tyson told me that—"

"So you gon' let a kindergartner tell you something, and you run with it?" Deborah tightened her lips and let out a gust of wind that made her cheeks puff out. "Just dumb," she said under her breath.

"Hold up. Did you call me dumb?" Lynox asked.

Deborah stood there with all the trash in her hands. Had she called her husband dumb? No way. There were two things she and Lynox had vowed never to do in their relationship, and calling each other names was one of them, and putting their hands on each other was the other. Well, Deborah had already broken one of those rules, so it would come as no surprise if she had broken the second one as well. Even though she just might have called him dumb, she was not going to admit it.

"I said listening to a kid, instead of to me, was dumb." Deborah cleaned that up as best she could.

"You wanna go get Tatum ready for bed and put him down?" Lynox asked. "I'll finish cleaning up, and then I'll go get Tyson together."

"You can put 'em both to bed," Deborah said. "Heck, I do it all the time by myself. Half the time I feel like a married single mother."

"And what is that supposed to mean?" Lynox asked, offended. No, he didn't do as much around the house or with the kids as Deborah did, but he wasn't some lazy dude who was lying around on the couch, drinking beer and not working, while the woman brought home all the bacon. He was always busy writing to keep up with his publishing house contracts, touring, or engaging his fans on social media. "You make it seem like I don't ever help out."

"Not enough to take some of the slack off of me. But just forget it." Deborah threw all the trash she had collected down on the floor. "I'll take him." She went and snatched the fussy baby out of Lynox's arms.

"Don't be so rough," Lynox said. "Be mad at me all you want, but don't take it out on him."

Deborah looked at Lynox with a twisted face. "I would never hurt my kids, so don't even play like that."

"Deb, I didn't say you would hurt the kids."
Lynox could tell by the defensive mode Deborah
was in that she was not going to let this go if he
pushed the subject. "Just go on and put him
down. He's tired." Lynox kissed his son on the
forehead and picked up the pile of trash Deborah
had thrown down on the floor.

While Deborah got the baby ready for bed,
Lynox got Tyson ready. He then went and
cleaned the downstairs.

Deborah fussed, cussed, and complained
under her breath the entire time she was in the
shower. This night had turned out nothing like
she'd envisioned it. By the time she got out of the
shower, she had a headache from thinking about
how horribly things had turned out. An hour ago
she couldn't wait to get home, but she had had
no idea what she'd be coming home to.

Deborah dried off, put on some lotion, body
spray, and her pajamas, then headed out of the
bathroom. Upon opening the bathroom door,
she froze. She looked into her bedroom to see
candles lit. She could smell the rain forest–
scented incense burning. Lynox had fixed them
each a plate of Chinese food and had warmed
it in the microwave. He stood there with two
glasses in one hand and a bottle of Stella Rosa in
the other.

"I figured this is what you wanted to come home to," he said.

Deborah's heart instantly filled with regret. How could this man stand to put up with her nonsense and flip-flopping behavior? She'd been so mean to him and the kids, yet he'd still made her dream come true. So what if the evening hadn't started off as planned? It was all about how it ended.

"Baby, I'm sorry," Deborah said. She was not going to make the same mistake twice. She was going to apologize to her man when she knew she'd done wrong. "It's just that I had pictured us having this nice, romantic—"

"Say no more," Lynox said. "You think I don't know you by now? Girl, you plan everything out in your head to the tee. The minute one thing gets off course, you act like there's no hope. But you gotta learn to chill out, for real. Things aren't always going to be like some fairy tale. Life has kinks in it. But sometimes those unforeseeable things can turn out to be some of life's best surprises."

Deborah stared at Lynox for a moment. "You are such a writer," she said. "You do have a way with words."

"I do indeed, if I must say so myself, but I wasn't trying to be poetic or anything. That was the truth. Now, let's sit down, relax, and enjoy our meal, now that the house is clean and both boys are asleep."

"The boys," Deborah said. "Let me go peek in on them real quick. I gave off such a mean vibe and negative energy. I need to go give them some Mommy love. I'll be right back." Whenever Deborah felt as though she had been unnecessarily snappy or hadn't shown the boys the attention and love that she should have, it would really bother her. She wasn't going to be able to focus on an evening with Lynox until she went and made it right with them.

She went to Tatum's nursery first. "Hey, little fellow," she said as she softly rubbed his head. He was sound asleep. She kissed him on the forehead. "Mommy loves you so much. She's sorry she came in the house like a hurricane and didn't love on you before you went to bed." Deborah put her hand on the baby's stomach. She closed her eyes and thought good thoughts of how much she loved him. She prayed to God these thoughts would transfer to his little being while he slept.

Next, she visited Tyson's room. He was asleep as well. Deborah sat on his bed and put her hand on his back. Then she leaned down and whispered in his ear, "Hey, Ty."

He moaned and squirmed a little.

"Hey, Mommy's baby. I love you."

Tyson's eyes blinked open a couple of times, then stayed closed. "I love you too."

That made Deborah smile. She was happy that he'd comprehended what she'd said. "I'm sorry for fussing. You forgive me?"

Tyson nodded his head while his eyes remained closed.

Deborah kissed him on the cheek and then returned to the bedroom she and Lynox shared.

When she walked into the room, Lynox was standing there, waiting for her in his birthday suit.

"Well, okay," Deborah said, shocked.

"Dinner is cold, so I figured we'd skip to dessert, which is hot."

Deborah walked toward Lynox, sliding out of her nightgown along the way. "I don't see nothing wrong with a little dessert before dinner, do you?"

Lynox looked his wife up and down while licking his lips. "Sometimes you just wanna get right to the good stuff, and I know for a fact your stuff is good."

Deborah play punched her husband while she blushed.

Lynox held Deborah by her face. All Deborah could see in his eyes was a genuine love for her.

She didn't even feel worthy to be loved. She'd married this man, knowing all the while that there was a chance that even though he brought out the best in her, she could be as bad as the worst. She closed her eyes, no longer able to bear looking at him. She felt like such a fraud.

"I'm going to do better," Deborah said, making a promise to Lynox aloud.

He kissed her on the lips. "I know."

"I'm so sorry," she said in between the kisses he planted on her lips. "I promise I'm going to be good."

He stopped and looked at her. "I hear you, but right now, if you don't mind, I'd like for you to be bad." Lynox passionately kissed his wife as he lifted her up and carried her over to the bed. "I accept your apology," he added, and then they went on to share an evening with no apologies and no regrets.

Chapter 8

"Nevada was nice. I loved the weather, but there's no place like home," Klarke said as she and Deborah sat inside Scrambler Marie's restaurant. It was a nice little café whose specialty was breakfast, which they served breakfast until 3:00 p.m., and then the café closed. "So when Reo suggested we maybe move back to Ohio, I was so ready. Even if it wasn't back to my hometown of Toledo, it was close enough, and it wasn't Sin City."

"Yeah, Lynox and I have talked about relocating to another state," Deborah said, "but whenever he suggests someplace, I find a reason to shoot it down."

"Like where?" Klarke asked, then took a bite from her stack of pancakes. Even though it was one-thirty in the afternoon, Klarke had a taste for breakfast food.

"He mentioned Arizona," said Deborah, who had opted to choose from the lunch menu. "I was all for that at first, until I did my research and learned about those sandstorms." Deborah bit into her burger.

Klarke laughed. "Those don't happen everywhere in Arizona, do they? I thought it was just a certain area."

"I don't know. But I wasn't taking any chances," Deborah said. "Then there was California."

Klarke swallowed her food. "Let me guess. Earthquakes."

"You got it," Deborah said, pointing with her fork before dipping it into her side salad.

"What about some place like Texas?" Klarke asked. "They have nice weather pretty much all year round."

"Nope." Deborah shook her head. "Remember that year they kept having all those tornadoes? And now they be dealing with floods." Deborah shook her head emphatically.

"Oh, girl, then you need to keep your butt right here in Ohio with me," Klarke said, realizing that Deborah would find a reason not to relocate to every place on the map.

"And that's the point I was trying to make."

Point taken," Klarke noted. "You guys can always get a vacation home somewhere. With both your lines of work, you can work anywhere on the map as long as you have Internet. For me, though, now that I have my event-planning business here, I'm pretty much stuck."

"By the way, that was a fantastic job your company did with Reo's party," Deborah said, complimenting Klarke. She then took another bite of her burger.

"Thank you. And it wasn't because it was my husband's event that all the t's were crossed and the i's dotted," Klarke said. "My staff are perfectionists. They see to it that every event is flawless."

"That's great. Good workers are hard to find sometimes," Deborah said. "Lord knows, I've been through my share of assistants. It made me want to go back to the days when I did everything myself, which is exactly what I ended up doing." Deborah's counselor had suggested to her that she get an assistant to help take some of the stress out of her day-to-day life. Finding a dedicated assistant had seemed to cause more stress, so she'd nixed that idea after the third one, who wasn't a charm, but who had stolen her charm bracelet instead. "Where did you find your staff?"

Klarke held up her finger, asking Deborah to hold on while she swallowed the piece of sausage she'd bitten into. "I went through this staffing agency," Klarke answered after swallowing her food. "They are wonderful. You tell them what you want and what you need, and they go through a vigorous interview process with candidates. They narrow them down to only the best, and then you choose from their top choices."

"Oh, wow. I might need to get their information from you."

"No problem," Klarke said. "I have no complaints. All my employees are amazing, even the ones I inherited when I bought the company."

Deborah was surprised to hear that Taylor Made wasn't a company that Klarke had started herself but had purchased. "Oh, you bought the company?"

"Yes. Well, sort of." Klarke picked her napkin up from her lap, wiped her mouth, and then placed it on her plate. Even though she had about a quarter of her meal left, she was full. "I was an event planner for one of the hotels in Vegas," Klarke continued. "It started off as just a part-time gig, something for me to do in Vegas while Reo was touring all the time. Of course, those were the days when author book tours weren't overrated. I wanted to be busy doing something too while Reo was doing his thing. I fell in love with bringing clients' visions to life."

"So how'd you get into the catering piece of your business?" Deborah asked. Even though

Klarke had thrown in the towel, so to speak, and was not going to finish her food, Deborah wasn't going to let that stop her from finishing off her meal. She was going to take her time and eat every last bite. She rarely got to sit down, chew slowly, and simply enjoy a meal. Usually, she was gobbling it down while working on a manuscript, or gobbling it down so that she could hurry and get back to the one she'd pulled herself away from. Sometimes she couldn't even remember what her food had tasted like.

"That happened when we decided to move back here. With almost every event, food is involved. I learned about a catering business that was up for sale. Tamarra already had a thriving business with dedicated customers—"

"Tamarra?" Deborah said, interrupting Klarke. No way was this a coincidence. A former member of New Day named Tamarra had once owned a catering business. She'd sold it once she began having complications due to HIV. She eventually passed away from Pneumocystis carinii pneumonia. "Tamarra Edwards?"

"Yes. Do you know her?" Klarke asked.

A somber look took over Deborah's face. "Yes, she was a wonderful person."

Klarke detected Deborah's change in demeanor. "Was?"

"She's since passed on."

Klarke covered her mouth in despair. "Oh, no. I'm so sorry to hear that. Wow." She shook her head.

"I know. It was sad. She was so young," Deborah said. "Her catering business was her life. We all felt so bad that she had to let it go. But it feels good to know that someone like yourself is successfully carrying on the business."

"Thank you," Klarke said. "We kept her company name for a few months for clientele and name recognition purposes. In doing so, we had to continue serving her menu, per the contract. We did add some new dishes. Once we changed the name to Taylor Made, which is a play on my maiden name, Taylor, we changed it from Tamarra's mainly soul food menu to a more upscale menu. We did keep her macaroni and cheese, though." Klarke winked.

"Oh, the infamous mac and cheese." Deborah smiled while shaking her head. "That was her signature dish, indeed."

"Well, whenever you want any, let me know." Klarke leaned in and whispered, "I had to pay extra for the recipe."

The women shared a laugh.

"But seriously," Klarke continued, "I knew I was going to come back to Ohio and do my own event planning. With Tamarra's business, there was a catering company with a built-in customer base for sale. Most people who need a caterer need it for an event, right?"

"So you said, 'I'm about to take all the money,'" Deborah replied, surmising what had happened.

"Girl, would you leave money on the table? It was a no-brainer." Klarke took a sip of her drink.

"A blessing from God, no doubt."

"A blessing from God for sure." Klarke shook her head. She shook her head as if she was thinking back on all God had done for her. "And He just keeps on blessing me. Even when I found myself sitting in a jail cell, I might not have known it then, but He was even right there with me too."

"Jail?" Deborah asked with a raised octave, pulling Klarke from her daze with her shocked tone. It went without saying that Deborah was indeed curious to hear why Klarke had been in jail, but she recognized that it was probably a sensitive subject, and so she wouldn't push her new friend to talk about anything that she didn't want to. But Deborah made a mental note that if the opportunity presented itself, she'd ask her about it later.

Klarke looked at Deborah, now conscious of the words that had spilled from her mouth and had caused such a reaction from Deborah. "Oh yeah. Well, that's a whole other story for a whole other time." Klarke wiped her mouth and then finished up her drink. "Thank you for agreeing to meet me for brunch. It's been a while since I've had any girlfriend time."

"Same here," Deborah agreed. "I really don't do the girlfriend thing. Not that I didn't want to. I never found anyone like . . ." Deborah's words trailed off as she stared off into space. She then looked at Klarke. "Like you, I guess. Someone who was cool and down to earth." Deborah popped a fry into her mouth. "Can I be honest with you?" She waited for Klarke to reply.

"Of course."

"Well, at first I was even a little skeptical about connecting with you, but then Lynox felt that a friend to hang out with was probably exactly what I needed. I have been so stressed out, moody, and I never take time to just"—Deborah looked down at her plate—"eat." She chuckled, then sipped her drink. "That husband of mine might have been right. I mean, we hit it off like we've been friends forever."

"We do, don't we?" Klarke smiled. "Well, it's not that I don't do the girlfriend thing. I don't have my old crew here to roll with me. I have two best friends. Well, one now." Klarke's face saddened.

"Have a falling-out with one of them?" Deborah asked, guessing that was what had happened.

"No. Jeva lives in Nevada, and Breezy . . ." Klarke took a breath. "She passed away while giving birth." Klarke sniffed and fought to hold back her tears. Breezy had been Klarke's ride-or-die diva. If Klarke had ever decided she wanted to drive off a bridge, Breezy wouldn't have been the friend who tried to talk her out of it. She'd have been the one right there on the passenger side, with her seat belt on.

"I'm so sorry. I didn't mean to bring up memories."

"Oh, no, no." Klarke shooed her hand. "Thinking about Breezy is a good thing." A smile covered Klarke's face. "She was something else." Klarke composed herself, took a napkin, and wiped her nose. "But, hey, let's end this outing on a good note. Hopefully, you'll get to meet Jeva. You never know. God could be stirring up a new threesome."

Deborah nodded and smiled. She liked the idea of finally having some girlfriends to hang out with and doing something other than Bible study, women's conferences, and marriage seminars. Folks thought that because she was a Christian and loved the Lord, everything she did in life had to be church related. There was a thing such as balance, which Deborah was now determined to find in her life. Everything felt so off kilter and unbalanced that this could make all the difference. This little bit of time spent with Klarke had solidified this notion.

"Well, I better get ready to go," Deborah said. She threw her napkin over the last bite of her burger. She really was full to the point where she couldn't eat another bite. "I want to get my little guy from my mom and get home before Tyson gets off the school bus."

"Next time we'll have a girls' night out or something," Klarke said as the waitress slid their check onto the table. "I have someone else I'd like to introduce you to. She's my husband's best friend's wife. She's good peoples too."

"Pay whenever you're ready," the waitress told them, then walked away.

"And remember, the offer is still open for that teenager of mine to keep your boys for you."

"Sounds like a plan," Deborah said, still not 100 percent sure about leaving her children with a teenager, even if the maid, nanny, or whoever was going to help out.

"Don't just be saying that," Klarke said as she went in her purse and pulled out her wallet.

"Really, I'm not," Deborah said. Deborah liked Klarke. She seemed like a really nice woman, someone Deborah wouldn't mind having as a friend. And she'd mentioned God earlier, when she'd talked about being in jail. So even though Deborah was on the fence about the whole babysitting thing, she wasn't on the fence about starting a friendship with Klarke.

"How much is my share?" Deborah asked Klarke as Deborah unzipped her own purse.

"Oh, no." Klarke put her hand up. "I've got this. I invited you out. My treat."

"You sure?"

"Girl, yes." Klarke placed her credit card on top of the bill.

"Well, I sure do appreciate it. Thank you so much," Deborah said.

The waitress walked over to the table. "I'll take this and bring your receipt right back out to you." She picked up the check and the credit card, then walked away.

"So I hear our boys have a playdate planned for next week," Klarke said. "They're supposed to meet at our house and start on their book proposal to present to their publishers."

"Oh, okay." Deborah tried to hide the fact that she was a little upset that Lynox hadn't mentioned this to her. Clearly, Reo had mentioned it to his wife. Deborah pictured Reo and Klarke

that night at his event. They had looked like the
perfect couple. They probably were open with
one another and told each other everything. The
green-eyed monster began to rear its ugly head
in Deborah's heart. Perhaps she was getting
uptight for nothing. Maybe Klarke had assumed
for some reason that the two men were getting
together, or maybe she thought she'd overheard
Reo talking about an upcoming meeting. She
didn't want to believe that she was the only one
left out of the loop. So that she didn't jump on
Lynox for no reason, she wanted to ascertain
how Klarke knew about his plans and she didn't.
"So, Reo told you Lynox is coming over, huh?"

"Oh, no. Lynox told me. I was on the phone
with him the other—"

"Your receipt," the waitress interrupted as
she laid the piece of paper and the credit card
in front of Klarke. She then removed a pen from
her apron and laid it on top of those items.
"Thank you again. We hope you'll come back
and see us."

Thank goodness that waitress had distracted
Klarke. It had prevented her from seeing the
boo-boo face that Deborah was displaying.
There was no way that Deborah had just heard
this woman say she'd been on the phone with
her husband.

"We will definitely come back and visit again," Klarke assured the waitress. She then picked up the pen and signed the receipt. "Snaps! I forgot to add the tip before I wrote the total down. And I don't think I have any cash on me." She began digging around in her purse.

Deborah had cash and could have easily left the tip, but she was oblivious to the situation at hand. Her mind was stuck on hearing that Klarke had learned about Reo and Lynox's meeting through Lynox himself. When had he talked to Klarke? And why? He hardly knew the woman. Why would he be striking up a conversation with her? As calming and nice as her afternoon with Klarke had been, Deborah was starting to feel some kind of way.

"Ah, my hidden stash." Klarke pulled a five-dollar bill out of a compartment of her wallet. She laid it down on the table.

She had to ask Klarke about her conversation with Lynox, otherwise it would bother her to no end. "You said that—" Deborah began, but Klarke's cell phone began ringing, cutting Deborah off.

Klarke held her index finger up to Deborah. "Just one moment." She looked at her phone. "I gotta take this real quick." Klarke answered the call, while Deborah sat there, staring down her throat, anxiously waiting for Klarke to hurry up and end the call. "You've got to be kidding me," Klarke said into the phone, her cheeks turning red. It was clear to Deborah that there was trouble on the line. "Hold on a second." Klarke put the phone against her chest. "I'm sorry, Deborah, but I have an issue with a catering job." She stood and gathered her things while talking to Deborah. "I'll call you, though, so we can plan to meet next week."

"Yes, sure," Deborah said, disappointed that she wouldn't get the information that she so desperately wanted. At least not from Klarke.

Klarke bent down and gave Deborah a hug and said, "Thanks for understanding." She put the phone back to her ear and chattered her way out of the restaurant.

"Humph. But I don't understand," Deborah said to herself, staring down at the table. "I absolutely do not understand why you're talking to *my* husband on the phone."

"Pardon me?"

Deborah was horrified that not only had she said her thoughts out loud, but also that Klarke had heard her. She looked up to see the waitress standing there. Relief consumed Deborah. "Oh, I, uh . . . nothing." Deborah smiled and shook her head, so glad that it wasn't Klarke standing there instead of the waitress.

The waitress picked up the signed receipt and her tip. "Thank you again. Have a great day." She walked away after gathering some of Deborah's and Klarke's dishes.

Deborah gathered her things and exited the restaurant shortly thereafter. She'd have to put on some Yolanda Adams or something to remind her about Christianity, because by the time she got to Lynox, if he wasn't talking right, there wasn't going to be a chance in the world that she'd make it to heaven. Because all hell was going to break loose for sure.

"You got a minute?" Deborah walked up to Lynox, who sat at his desk in their home office, pounding away at the keyboard. He was so focused on the manuscript that he was working on that he hadn't even acknowledged Deborah as she walked down the short flight of steps that led to their basement.

"Oh, hey, yeah," he said, distracted. He looked at the time on the computer. "Man, I didn't realize it was this late. Thank God you do not leave getting Tyson off the bus up to me. I don't know how long the poor kid would be up there, ringing the doorbell, before I even came up for air and realized it was ringing."

Deborah let out a chuckle, just because it was the thing to do. She didn't necessarily find what Lynox had said humorous. As a matter of fact, she'd hardly paid attention to half of what he'd said. Besides, Tyson wouldn't be standing at the door, ringing the bell. He was in kindergarten. They didn't even allow kindergartners off the bus unless an adult was there to greet them.

"You all right? Is something wrong?" Lynox asked. Deborah's mind being a million miles away and that fake chuckle hadn't gone undetected by him. He grabbed her hand as she stood by his desk. "What's going on? Talk to me." He was treating her with kid gloves. After Deborah's erratic behavior in the car a couple of weeks ago, her taking one too many pills after church, and then her clowning in the loft the other day, he was very mindful of the way he interacted with his wife. He had to gauge her and her moods first and then act accordingly.

Deborah didn't appreciate being treated like a fussy baby who needed some cooing to settle her down. "Don't patronize me, Lynox." Deborah pulled her hand out of her husband's.

She could sense he was trying to walk on eggshells around her. She didn't like that one bit. She felt as if he was playing her, trying to butter her up so that whatever lies he tried to tell her would slip on by her. Heck, as far as she knew, he was the one Klarke had been talking to on the phone when she left the restaurant like there was a fire somewhere. Klarke had probably realized herself that she'd slipped up and mentioned that she'd talked to Lynox on the phone. Then, to make matters worse, he'd called her up while she was still having lunch with Deborah. He had probably wanted the scoop on how their brunch went. He'd already told on himself once, anyway, since he'd admitted to having talked to Klarke about Deborah that one time at the Laroques' party, so Deborah wouldn't put it past him to have done it again. Deborah could just hear Lynox asking Klarke, "Do you think she suspects anything?" Well, the answer was yes. She suspected a lot, and now she was expecting some answers.

Lynox was a little taken aback by Deborah's sharp shift in attitude. It wasn't even a gradual shift. She had meowed and then had immediately started barking. *What the heck?* He didn't have to say the words to express how he was feeling about her sudden change in demeanor. His facial expression said it all. *What now?*

"I met with Klarke today," Deborah said, sitting down in the chair next to Lynox's desk.

"Of course, you know that, because you're the one who convinced me that I should hang out with her."

"You say that like it's a bad thing. Why? Did something happen?" Now that Lynox knew that Klarke had something to do with the way Deborah was acting, he felt a little relief. At least she was pissed off at Klarke and not at him.

"I don't know. You tell me." Deborah sat back, with her legs crossed, looking at Lynox knowingly.

Lynox really didn't have time for any guessing games. He was working on a deadline. He started to become a little agitated. Deborah's new attitude, unlike Patti LaBelle's, was not for the better. But like the vows he'd spoken, he was going to hang in there for better or for worse.

"Did she say or do something to upset you?" Lynox questioned, willing to play a couple of rounds of the guessing game to appease her.

"As a matter of fact, she did."

Lynox shot Deborah a look that said, "Okay. Spill it then."

"So you and Reo are supposed to be meeting up, huh?" Deborah began swinging her foot back and forth.

Lynox's eyes followed his wife's foot. As of late, he'd noticed that whenever she started to get anxious, her foot would get to swinging or her knee to bouncing. "Uh, yeah." He couldn't understand why that would have her so upset. "You know that he and I are supposed to be working on a project together."

"Klarke knows too." Deborah sat there, glaring at her husband. She was hoping that he would spit it out without her having to pick.

"Of course she knows. She was standing right there when we were talking about it."

"Yeah, and I was standing right there too when you were talking about it, but I guess neither Reo nor I was present when you were yapping it up with Klarke on the telephone, telling her what day and what time you were coming over." For all Deborah knew, that had been Klarke's way of setting up a secret rendezvous with Lynox. They had made up an excuse for why Lynox would be at her home on a certain day. Reo probably was scheduled to be out of town that day, on a book tour or something. Deborah made a mental note to go online and check his tour schedule.

Ha! If Lynox thought he was slick enough to outslick the slicker, he had another think coming. Her ex and her son's father had been the lowest of the low. He'd cheated on her and done her dirty every way possible. He had tried every trick in the book and had slept with every chick he could, and thanks to him, there was nothing new under the sun to Deborah. He'd prepared her for the next man, who just happened to be Lynox.

Lynox looked puzzled, thought for a moment, and then realized where Deborah was going with this whole thing. "Is that what this is about? Klarke knowing our meeting plans before you? With you being my agent and all, I guess it would have made sense to clue you in."

Deborah had had enough of Lynox's games. She jumped to her feet. "Boy, don't play stupid with me," Deborah snapped. "This ain't got ish to do with me being your wife. You talked to her on the phone, and I'm trying to figure out why. Everyone uses their cell phones for business nowadays, and I'm sure Mr. Laroque is no exception. So I ask, why would you be on the phone with his effing wife? What? Did she just happen to answer his cell phone? Even if she did, you ask to speak to her husband and keep it moving. Why would you want to strike up a conversation with her?" Deborah had a string of other questions that included another string of cusswords, but she figured she'd give Lynox time to weasel out of the ones she'd already presented.

"I can't believe we are having this conversation, but since we are, do you mind if we have it without the foul language?" Lynox had not known his wife to be a cussin' Christian, but almost everything about her attitude these days puzzled him."

"Whatever." Deborah rolled her eyes and sucked her teeth.

"Well, here goes." Lynox exhaled and then proceeded. "I didn't call Reo's cell phone. I called his landline, and Klarke answered."

Deborah honestly hadn't even considered the fact that Lynox had called their home. Who gave out their home phone number nowadays? Most people didn't even have one anymore, unless they had small children, which Klarke and Reo didn't. Their youngest daughter was a teenager. Surely, she had her own cell phone too.

"So when she answered, why didn't you ask to speak to Reo? What made you want to talk to her? You only half want to talk to me."

"That's not true, Deborah." Lynox stood. He recalled getting slugged the other night. He didn't want to be at a disadvantage by sitting, in case Deborah felt like getting her Floyd Mayweather on again. "I love talking to you." He reached down and rubbed Deborah's cheek with his thumb. "Reo had left me a message with a date and a time that he wanted to get together. He also left me the number to return the call. When I called him back to confirm, Klarke answered. Reo wasn't available. She asked if I wanted to leave a message, and I did. I told her to tell him that I was available then and would mark my calendar. She said okay, I said okay, and then that was it. I really don't see why you're so upset about that."

After Lynox had explained himself, Deborah didn't know why she was upset her own self. She had raced home, just knowing she was going to catch him in lie, but everything he'd said made sense. It wasn't some far-fetched story, like the ones her ex used to feed her. Deborah honestly had no basis upon which to argue with or dis-prove what Lynox had told her. That meant it was time to flip the script.

"I feel like we don't communicate anymore. The fact that Klarke knew about you guys meet-ing and I didn't made me feel . . ." Deborah allowed her words to trail off on purpose while she thought of a way out of the unnecessary drama she'd created between herself and her husband.

"I can understand why you would feel that way." Feeling as though it was safe to sit back down, Lynox took his seat. "We are both con-stantly working, and then there are the kids.

We're like two ships passing in the night. Even when we're here, working right across from each other, we don't even speak."

On many nights, after putting the kids to bed, Deborah and Lynox had retreated to their home office to work on their individual projects. They would work for hours yet never say a word to one another, each deeply engaged in his or her work.

"With you and Reo striking up this project, I don't see when we're ever going to be able to, you know, spend some quality time together," Deborah whined. Now she had to make it look like it wasn't about her jealousy or false accusations at all. She'd reacted the way she had all in the name of love. "Even though they are as busy as us, Reo and Klarke seem like they have it all worked out."

"I know, but the book business isn't what it used to be. And we both happen to be in the book business. That's like a husband and wife both being in the real-estate business when housing crises hit," Lynox explained. "I'm a vet author with a very successful brand, so I'm one of the lucky ones. But I still have to work as hard as the new jack to stay relevant. Digital technology is killing the entertainment business all around."

"You are preaching to the choir," Deborah told him.

"We're entrepreneurs. We have to continue to go hard if we want to make sure our family is taken care of."

"Work hard, play later." That had been the commitment the couple had made to one another.

"We have our own thing. It works for us," Lynox said. "Reo and Klarke seem like a really happy couple, but I don't want you to start comparing us to them. What we have works for us. If it ain't broke, don't fix it."

"I hear you." Deborah nodded and took in Lynox's words. She was glad that she'd managed to shift things away from her original suspicions about goings-on between Klarke and Lynox. She would have felt too embarrassed had she outright accused Lynox of having a thing going on with Klarke. He had a perfectly reasonable explanation as to why he'd been on the phone with her. A part of her was definitely pleased, but this meant only that she'd gotten all riled up for nothing. "Well, I better go check on the boys. Tatum is in his swing, and Tyson was playing with his Legos."

"All right. I'll be up later." Lynox turned back to his computer. "Where was I?" he said to himself.

As Deborah turned to head back up the steps, a sudden thought entered her mind, so she stopped in her tracks. Maybe her being upset with her husband wouldn't be in vain, after all. Lynox had managed to explain the Klarke situation away, but there was another situation she hadn't gotten a chance to discuss with him.

"Is there something else?" Lynox asked, noticing Deborah was still standing at the bottom of the steps.

"As a matter of fact, there is." Deborah turned on her heels and faced her husband. She might as well get everything off her chest and clear the air.

"What is it?" Lynox sighed, really hoping he could get back to work.

"It's not what. It's who." Deborah took a step back over toward Lynox.

"Who?" Lynox frowned.

Deborah looked Lynox in the eyes and then said, "Helen."

Lynox looked like he'd seen a ghost. That alone let Deborah know that this conversation probably wasn't going to go as smoothly as the one about Klarke. A baleful grin raised the corners of her mouth. She couldn't wait to see if Lynox was able to weasel his way out of this one.

Chapter 9

Because of the whole episode with Deborah taking more happy pills than prescribed and leaving the kids at church, she wouldn't have dared drill Lynox about sitting next to Helen on the very day it happened. It had been too soon. Well, now it was later. She'd already gotten to the bottom of the whole Klarke issue, so since she was already at the bottom, she might as well stay there and continue digging at the surface.

"In church, you were sitting by her. There were tons of other vacant seats you could have sat down in, and yet you sat down and decided to praise the Lord with her," Deborah said.

"You're kidding me, right? First Klarke and now Helen." Lynox picked up a pen on his desk and threw it across the room. "Darn it, Deborah!" She had totally put the brakes on his creative juices. There was no way he was going to be able to get his mind right and dive back into his work.

Lynox's abrupt action startled Deborah. She jumped.

"Are you bored? Is that what it is?" Lynox asked.

"Don't try to get sarcastic with me. Just answer my question." Startled by Lynox throwing an object across the room or not, Deborah wanted answers. He could throw however many pens he wanted. She wasn't letting him be until she found out everything she wanted to know.

Lynox stared at Deborah momentarily. "I don't even know why I continue entertaining you, but since we're already at the circus . . ." His wife was wearing him out. "For your information, I was already sitting down when the usher led Helen and her son to my row. What was I supposed to do? Get up and leave?"

"If an usher sat someone who is crazy"— Deborah used her fingers to make quotation marks when saying the word *crazy*—"and who I despised next to me, you dang right I would have gotten my black butt up and gone and sat somewhere else."

"Well, I didn't. I thought that would have been rude. Besides, I was there to keep my eyes on Jesus, not her."

"So when Pastor Margie did what she always does at the end of service and told you to hug three people before you left, did you hug her?"

Lynox stared at Deborah. So far he'd made it through her questioning without having to lie, but in this case he knew the truth might push Deborah over the edge. Even so, Lynox was a straight-up kind of dude. He didn't believe in telling a lie to prevent the hurt the truth might cause. Everything always came to light, and when the truth behind a lie finally did, its uncovering would hurt even more than the truth itself.

"Did you hug Helen?" Deborah demanded.

"Yes, I . . . I think so. Her and her son," Lynox stammered.

Deborah cringed at the thought of Lynox's arms wrapped around that heifer. "Keeping your eyes on Jesus, huh? You are such a joke. A clown. You are indeed a clown at the circus you just referenced, and now you're trying to clown me. Here you were a few nights ago, ranting and raving about how Helen was crazy and you don't do crazy. I guess it's okay to hug crazy, though. The way you were talking, if the usher had sat her next to me, I would have gotten up and gone and sat somewhere as far away from that woman as I could. Guess you were just talking." Deborah used both her hands to make a talking gesture.

"You're the one who is just talking, and you're talking crazy."

Deborah snapped her head back and put her hands on her hips. "Oh, now I'm crazy again?"

"I'm not going to do this with you, Deborah. I love you, but, baby, we got to figure out what's going on with you, or else—"

"Mommy, the baby is crying."

Both Lynox and Deborah looked at the top of the steps to see Tyson standing there.

Lynox turned back to his computer. Even though Deborah had surely stifled his creativity, he was still going to try to get some work done, even if it was only replying to fan mail.

"Or else what?" Deborah said in a loud tone as she walked up on Lynox.

"Go get the baby," Lynox said in a warning manner. In other words, he was telling his wife that it would be better for them both if she got out of his face and went to tend to the baby.

"No. Not until you tell me what you were about to say. Or else what, Lynox? What you gon' do? Say it." Deborah's voice got louder and louder as she stepped to her husband.

"Deborah, you need to go get the baby," Lynox said in a "You better go somewhere" tone.

"You get him."

"Fine. I will." Lynox stood up and headed for the steps.

"Oh, no you don't." Deborah charged behind Lynox, huffing and puffing. "You will not try to walk away and get out of this. You son of a b—"

Lynox stopped and turned, causing Deborah to run smack into his chest. He was not about to let her call him out of his name yet again. She'd already called him dumb. No way was he going to allow her to insult his mother in an expletive directed toward him.

"Ugh!" Deborah shouted after slamming into Lynox's chest. She then covered her mouth with her hand. Her eyes watered from the throbbing pain in her mouth.

"Let me see." Lynox pulled Deborah's hand away from her mouth.

"Get away from me." She snatched her hand away and put it back over her mouth, but not before Lynox could see that her lip was bleeding from her tooth having cut it.

The sound of crying coming from the top of the steps reminded both Lynox and Deborah that Tyson was still standing there . . . and had watched everything that had just transpired.

"Mommy!" Tyson cried out. He then looked at Lynox with an angry face. "You hurt Mommy."

Deborah brushed past Lynox and climbed the steps. "Mommy's okay, baby," she said, her voice muffled from her hand still covering her mouth. When she reached Tyson, she placed her free hand on his back and escorted him up the steps that would take them to the next level of their home. "Mommy's okay. It was just an accident."

Lynox could hear Deborah consoling their son. In disbelief about what had just taken place, Lynox sat down on the steps and ran his hands down his face. His and Deborah's life together had been no picnic. There had been Helen, who had first tried to break up their relationship, and then there'd been Tyson's father, who had actually broken up their relationship. Even when they got back together, they hadn't simply picked up where they'd left off. After a game of cat and mouse, or perhaps dog and cat in their case, they had finally been on good enough terms where they could share a meal together. Lynox had been first in catching Deborah up on his life during the time they were apart. He'd shared with her that he'd dated a couple of women who potentially would have been great life partners, but that his deal breaker was a woman with kids. He did not want to have to deal with baby daddy drama and "You're not my daddy" drama. Lynox had dropped this bomb before Deborah had the chance to tell him that during their time apart, she'd actually given birth to a son, Tyson.

Poor Deborah had given herself a nervous breakdown by trying to jump through hoops to keep Lynox from finding out that she had a child. In the end, though, Lynox had learned to love Tyson as if he were his own son. With Tyson's father having passed away in an earthquake over in Chile, where he had been playing professional basketball, there had been no baby daddy drama for Lynox to contend with. And there had been no "You're not my daddy" from Tyson, either, given that Lynox was the only daddy he'd ever known. And even though Lynox hadn't gone through the court system with Deborah to legally adopt Tyson, Tyson still called Lynox "Daddy." That was something he had started doing on his own, even before Lynox and Deborah got married. And only a few months ago, when Deborah had sat Tyson down and explained to him that Lynox wasn't his biological father, the boy had still refused to call him any other name but Daddy.

As Lynox sat in the basement, thinking about Deborah's actions recently, he wondered if he should start legal proceedings to officially adopt Tyson. That would make it a lot easier for him to get custody, or at least visitation rights, if he ended up having to file divorce papers on Deborah. Lynox loved Deborah. God knew that much. But in the past couple of weeks he had been pushed pretty hard and had come close to putting his hands on her. He'd always promised himself something: before he hit his wife or cheated on her, he'd leave her. Deborah already thought he was cheating on her. He'd been inches away from retaliating physically. Deborah was slowly but surely pushing him close to the edge. . . . And a promise was a promise.

"My man, Mr. National Bestselling Author himself." Reo greeted Lynox, then stepped back into the foyer to allow Lynox into his home.

"And my man, Mr. *International* Bestselling Author," Lynox said as he walked into the house. He looked around. "What a huge difference from when I was here a couple of weeks ago," Lynox said. "Your wife had it looking like a hotel ballroom or something. Now it looks like a real home. I can feel the love." Lynox started bouncing his shoulders, acting silly.

"Aw, you know I try, man." Reo rubbed his chin with pride. "Naw, but I can't take the credit. The wife makes it her business to make this place feel like home. My baby and I might have gone through hell and back to be together, but now life is like heaven."

Lynox looked down and nodded. He wished he could say the same about himself and Deborah. Yes, they'd been through hell and back to be together, but it still felt like hell. Well, for about a year it had felt like heaven. They had been newly married, both of them had been striving in their careers, Deborah had found out she was pregnant, and then she had had a healthy, bouncing baby boy. Even after the baby was born, things had been lovely, but it had been very short lived. Perhaps the extra responsibility brought on by the baby had been a little too much for Deborah. Maybe Lynox could have helped out more. But how would he have known to help if she never asked? He wasn't exactly sure who or what was to blame for the state of his and Deborah's marriage, but he was sure fault lay with him somewhere.

"Hey, you all right?" Reo asked with his always happy-go-lucky self.

Lynox didn't respond. His mind was too far away as he thought about his and Deborah's issues.

"Hello. Earth to Lynox."

Upon hearing his name, Lynox snapped out of his daze and looked up. Reo stood there, looking as if he was waiting on Lynox to respond to something. "Huh? What?" He gave Reo a "Did I miss something?" look.

"You cool? You were, like, a million miles away a second ago."

"Uh, yeah, yeah. I'm good," Lynox lied, and it was clear to Reo that he was, in fact, lying.

"Come on. Let's go out to the patio for a minute, before we get to working on our proposal," Reo suggested.

Lynox shrugged, conveying that he was cool with that.

"It's this way." Reo led him through the foyer to a space off the kitchen and then out the sliding doors and onto the patio.

"Wow. It's as beautiful out here as it is inside." Lynox stood on the brick-laid patio. Over to the right was a round patio couch. Across from that was a brick wall for sitting, and in the middle was a fire pit. To the left was a patio table with an umbrella and chairs. Straight ahead was a bar, a grill, and a cooking area. Looked like someone could live right outside.

"Deborah and I are definitely going to have to step our decorating game up. Heck, both inside and outside the house," Lynox said. "It's just that we're both so busy, we don't have time to settle down and focus on stuff like that."

"Make time, my friend," Reo said to Lynox as he walked straight over to the bar. Behind the bar was a refrigerator with double glass doors. One could see everything stacked neatly inside without even having to open the door. Reo pulled it open. "Brewski or wine?" he asked Lynox.

"I'll take a beer."

Reo looked back over his shoulder and gave Lynox the side eye. "I got some Cîroc back here if you want that." He nodded at the bar. "By the way you were looking inside the house, you may need something a little stronger."

Lynox held both his hands up and made a sour face. "Oh, no. I'm good."

"You sure, bro? Going once, going twice . . ."

"Beer will suffice," Lynox assured his pal. "You mind?" he asked Reo as he went to sit over on the couch by the fire pit. Lynox's father had taught him that a man always asked permission to sit in someone else's home.

"Oh, not at all. Make yourself comfortable," Reo said as he grabbed a bottle of beer for both himself and Lynox. Reo walked over and handed Lynox a beer, then went and sat down on the brick wall seating area, taking a swig from his bottle. He allowed Lynox to take a drink from his own bottle before he dove right in. "I'm really excited to be working with you on this project. I want to create a proposal and an outline that are solid."

"Same here," Lynox agreed.

"When we walk into my writing cave, that's the only thing I want to be on our minds."

Lynox nodded. He could tell where Reo was about to go with this.

"You know the saying 'Don't take your work home?' Well, since you're a writer, I'm sure I don't have to tell you that we can't take what's going on at home to work. Something's weighing you down. I'm a perfectionist when it comes to my craft. With this project in particular, I know that it's not only my name on the line, so I'm going to make sure that I'm focused, that I have no distractions and nothing blocking my creativity." He took another swig of beer. "Something tells me that at the moment, you can't say the same."

Lynox looked down at the beer he was cradling in his hands. He took a swig, then sat the bottle on the edge of the unlit fire pit. He thought for a moment, exhaled, and then spoke. "It's me and Deborah," Lynox began, then thought better of it. He stood. "You know, maybe this isn't a good time in my life. As much as I'd give my left arm to actually be able to work with a legend in this game, my idol, I'd give my right to make things good with my wife."

"Is it something you want to talk about? I mean, I know you and I aren't homies that go way back or anything like that, but I'm here. Your words are safe with me. Promise I won't write a story about you."

Reo's last comment brought out a chuckle in Lynox. Writers were good at writing about what they knew first and foremost, even if it was what they knew about somebody else.

Lynox thought for a moment. Perhaps hanging out with one of the fellas wasn't a bad idea. Here he'd been telling Deborah that maybe she needed to make some friends, hang out, and have some other women to talk to. Maybe he should have been listening to his own advice and been spending some time in the company of men. Who knew? God could have brought Reo into his life for such a time as this. It was possible that they were supposed to be something more than writing partners. A confidant outside of his home didn't sound so bad.

Since reconnecting, both Lynox and Deborah had made life about themselves . . . their family. There had been no couples' night, no girls' night out for her, and no night out with the boys for him. Having someone to talk to besides each other might be a good thing. With that thought, Lynox sat back down.

"Things are crazy between us," Lynox said, picking his beer back up. "We're arguing and fighting about every little thing. Even things that aren't there. She picks, picks, and picks."

"My grandmother used to tell me that it takes two people to argue," Reo said. "So surely, you've got a part in there somewhere, right?"

Lynox shrugged. "I mean, yeah, I guess. But I have to respond to what she's throwing at me. I can't just stand there and take the hits."

"No, but you can stand there and listen. If what she has to say calls for a response, then reply in a non-argumentative manner. It's called giving thoughts to your ways. You can't act or react to things based on emotions and circumstance. Don't let other people determine how you're going to act. Always remember that you have the right to remain silent." Reo let out a chuckle as he thought back to something. "I did that for about three months with Klarke—I remained silent—before she got tired of hearing herself."

"Nah. This is different." Lynox shook his head. "You don't understand. Deborah has . . ." Lynox paused. He was rethinking whether or not he wanted to talk about his wife to Reo.

Reo had been right in saying that he and Lynox weren't homies. They had corresponded through social media more than anything. Reo's book release was the first time Lynox had ever been to his home. Reo had never been to his. Sharing this beer was the first nonwork-related thing the two men had ever done together.

Some men didn't seem to confide in other men about any and everything as freely as other men did, and as women generally did, and Lynox was one of them. But there was something about Reo that came off as genuine, and Lynox couldn't imagine Reo betraying his trust by putting his business out there, verbally or in a book. Lynox felt a sense of peace come over him, so he went ahead and continued with the discussion at hand.

"Deborah has had some issues in the past where she had to be prescribed some medication to deal with life situations. I understood all that going into our marriage. She's a full-time mother, a wife, and she edits, she agents, she goes to church, and she takes care of the home. That's a lot, and before me, she was doing it all on her own." Lynox stared down into his beer bottle. "I hate to say it, but even with me around, she's still doing pretty much all of it on her own. I'm putting out two books a year, so my life consists of writing, marketing and promoting, touring, and then writing again."

"You know, I understand all that," Reo said. "But you guys have little ones. At least Klarke and I have only one teenager at home to deal with. We have one kid off to college, and Vaughn and HJ are grown." Vaughn and HJ were the two stepchildren Reo had inherited when he married Klarke.

Reo and Lynox had quite a lot in common. Lynox, too, had inherited a stepchild. Lynox and Deborah had had a breakup, only to make up again, and so had Reo and Klarke. In between those breakups, babies had been conceived. The difference with Reo and Klarke, though, was that they had weathered the storm for years and seemed to have come out of it pretty well. Lynox was pulling out his umbrella, trying not to get too wet.

"Deborah's emotions have been on level ten lately," Lynox said.

"Maybe her doctor should consider changing her medication dosage or her prescription, period," Reo suggested. "It's not unheard of that a medicine can stop doing what it's supposed to do. She could need something stronger."

Lynox shook his head. "She doesn't even really take her old prescription anymore. When she found out that she was pregnant with our second child, she stopped taking the pills. That was a year ago. She was good up until a little while after having the baby. I suppose things have been going downhill since, I never paid as much attention to this as I am now. Then, not too long ago, she tried to self-medicate by taking some of her old pills. She took too many.

It was a mess." Lynox shook his head. "I don't know what to do. It's like she's happy there for a second, then depressed one minute and anxious another. Up, down. Up, down. Like a horse on a carousel."

"Sounds crazy." Reo realized what he'd said and put his hands up in his defense. "She's not crazy. I mean the *situation* sounds crazy."

"Relax. I know what you mean," Lynox said. Thank God Deborah wasn't in the vicinity and hadn't heard Reo *almost* call her crazy. She would have flipped the script!

"So how are you dealing with it?" Reo asked. "Have you guys tried counseling?"

"You mean marriage counseling? Or like a counselor, therapist, or something?"

"Heck, both, if need be."

"Once upon a time Deborah was seeing a counselor. It was very helpful. She was in a good place."

"I can understand her not wanting to take any meds while pregnant, but why not continue to see her counselor?"

Lynox shrugged, then took a swallow of his beer. "Like I said, things were going well. We got busy. We got pregnant. I think she felt like she was okay. She had everything in life keeping her mind right and keeping her happy. Guess I ain't doing the trick anymore." Lynox guzzled the remainder of his beer.

"Oh, no, partner. I'm not even going to sit here and let you blame yourself. You are not responsible for somebody else being happy or unhappy. You can't control other people's emotions. Folks have got to get to the point in life where instead of chasing happiness, they create it."

"I hear what you're saying, brother, but happy wife, happy life. She's not happy, and as a man, I can't help but blame myself. Plus, kids pick up on their parents' emotions. Our oldest son witnessed us getting into it the other day. It wasn't pretty. I never want that kid to think I'm this big, bad wolf who is mean to his mommy, but, man, she be taking me there."

"Maybe Klarke can talk to her."

"Oh, no." Lynox shook his head repeatedly. "If she thinks I'm telling another woman her business . . . no, thank you."

"It won't even be like that. I'm serious," Reo said. "Trust me when I say Klarke knows a little something about this. She used to have her ups and downs emotionally, but she managed to get it all under control, in a way that I really never expected her to." He let out a chuckle. "Kind of unorthodox, to say the least."

"Now, your wife ain't 'bout to introduce my wife into no mess where there are secret meetings and they have to wear masquerade masks, is she?"

Reo burst out laughing, spitting some of his beer out. "No, no, no. Nothing like that.

"Well, I had to ask."

"Right, right," Reo said, finishing up his beer. "How 'bout we enjoy another brewski and just shoot the breeze? We can reschedule working on the proposal for another time. Sound like a plan?"

Lynox exhaled. "The best plan I've heard in a long time." He put his hand behind his head and leaned back. "You know, I feel good after having talked to you."

"Can't keep everything bottled up inside," Reo said, scooping up Lynox's empty bottle and heading back over to the bar area. "We have to be able to talk and express ourselves too."

"Yeah, and you were cheaper than a therapist." Lynox laughed.

"Oh, but you haven't seen my bill yet. I'm taking this session out of your royalties on our book."

Both men laughed.

"And I appreciate you agreeing to talk to Klarke," Lynox added. "Just make sure she doesn't let on to Deborah that I said anything."

"I got you, bro. Trust me." Reo walked back over and handed Lynox a second beer.

"I trust you." Lynox smiled. The two clinked their bottles and drank. He trusted Reo just fine. It was Deborah he wouldn't trust if she caught wind of the fact that he'd mentioned their issues to Reo. He said a silent prayer that that wouldn't happen.

Chapter 10

"Are you sure two little ones aren't going to be too much for them to handle?" Deborah said as she and Klarke got in Klarke's Range Rover. Deborah had driven her car over to Klarke's house to drop the kids off before she and Klarke went out. Klarke had decided she would drive to their destination.

"I told you, my daughter is great with kids," Klarke said. "You see how they warmed right up to her. And Elsie is the best when it comes to kids. I've watched her with her grandchildren. She's brought them to work a couple of times. Besides"—Klarke reached over and patted Deborah on the shoulder to comfort her—"they have our numbers, and we have theirs. Your boys will be fine." Klarke put the key in the ignition and then started the car up.

"I don't mean anything against your daughter. It's just that my mother's house and my children's church are the only places the kids have been without me and Lynox being present.

I mean, Tyson has gone over to his best friend's next door, but that's about it."

"I understand. I know what it's like to be apart from your kids when they're young." Klarke looked regretful as she backed out of the driveway.

"I take it you're referencing the time you were away in jail," Deborah said, sensing that an opportunity to delve a little deeper into Klarke's incarceration was presenting itself.

Klarke nodded. She looked to make sure no cars were coming as she pulled out of the driveway and onto the road. "It was awful."

"I can only imagine," Deborah said. "It's a mother's worst nightmare to be separated from her children, knowing she can't go to them whenever she wants."

"It was a nightmare," Klarke said as she drove. "As a matter of fact, the nightmares haunted me for quite some time. I saw a lot while I was locked up, things I wish I could forget. My kids went through a lot while I was gone. I used to wake up out of my sleep in a cold sweat, crying and hyperventilating. I truly thought I was going to lose my mind."

Deborah let out a harrumph. "I know the feeling." She turned her head and looked out the window. Thinking about her own issues pulled her away from wanting to find out about Klarke's.

"What do you mean?" Klarke asked, fishing. Reo had already had a conversation with Klarke in which he shared some of the things Lynox had told him. Klarke hoped Deborah would open up to her on her own. She really wanted to be there for her and help her, simply because she knew firsthand what Deborah was experiencing. If she could help her new acquaintance, she wouldn't hesitate.

Deborah turned to look at Klarke. Her words had popped into her head and had shot out of her mouth before she had had a chance to think about their impact. She hadn't meant to admit out loud that she felt as though she was losing her mind. And now Klarke was questioning her about this statement. She hesitated. She'd already stormed out of Reo's book event, probably leaving Klarke to believe she was a little off her rocker. That hadn't deterred Klarke from inviting Deborah to brunch. Had Klarke not had to take that emergency phone call and run out of the restaurant, Deborah probably would have come off as a crazy and deranged wife, because she'd had every intention of drilling Klarke about her phone conversation with Lynox.

Once Deborah talked to Lynox and was able to cool off and think things through, she'd realized that believing something was going on between Lynox and his mentor's wife was foolish. So now she really wanted to make an honest attempt at forming a friendship with Klarke. In doing so, the last thing she wanted to do was scare Klarke off by telling her about her issues. But by the same token, if she really planned on starting a real friendship with this woman, she didn't want it to be built on lies, secrets, and half-truths.

Deborah exhaled. "A while back I got counseling. My life was so overwhelming."

Klarke nodded, letting Deborah know that she was listening.

When Deborah noticed that Klarke wasn't acting funny about what she'd revealed, she continued on. "I was snapping at my child, my mother, church members. Heck, even my pastor."

"What about Lynox?"

Deborah thought for a moment. "No. I did a good job of hiding the ugly side of me from him. I mean, he knew I was a little fresh at the mouth and could hold my own. But he never saw me when I was completely turned up, if you know what I mean. By that time my therapist had prescribed me meds to help me, you know, keep calm." Deborah shook her head. "I cringe when I think of some of the things I did." Her eyes watered. "I was so mean to my son. I didn't beat him or anything, not with my fists. But I bruised his poor spirit up real good with the words that came out of my mouth. Every little thing used to make me pop off. He had no idea what was going on or why I acted the way that I did. He just loved his mommy."

Klarke opened up her console and grabbed a napkin. She handed it to Deborah.

Deborah took the napkin and wiped the tears that were now sliding down her cheeks. She sniffed and continued speaking. "All my mom did when I was growing up was yell, scream, fuss, holler, and call me out of my name. It was the way she communicated with me. It used to hurt, and it was embarrassing, because she would humiliate me out in public. And I'm not saying it's a race thing, but I rarely see as many white folks cussing their kids out in public as I do black folks. As black people, we've been broken down enough. Why break each other down, let alone our own children?"

"I hear you," Klarke said. "It was my daddy who had the tongue on him and who was like a raging bull. My mother was the opposite. Quiet and meek. She'd give me treats after he would go off on me. I think it was her way of apologizing for not being able to protect me from his wrath. But I understood. How could she protect me when she couldn't even protect herself?"

"Did your dad used to hit your mom?"

"No," Klarke answered, "but like you said with your son, sometimes the verbal beat down was worse. You know?"

"Yes, I do," Deborah said, wishing she didn't. "Between my counseling sessions and my meds, I got back on track. Lynox and I were doing well. He proposed, we married, and then shortly thereafter, I got pregnant. My life was bliss, bliss, and more bliss. I was consumed by happiness. And I had Lynox to talk to, so not only did I stop taking the meds—because I was pregnant, of course—but my visits with the therapist and the counselor became far and few between. As far as I could see, I had no problems and issues that I needed to talk about. My career was going well too. Then, after I had the baby, everything changed. Well, not everything. Me," Deborah said, pointing at her chest.

"Baby blues?" Klarke asked.

"Like you wouldn't believe. I was sad, depressed, tired, and I felt like a bad mother and a bad wife. I wasn't excited about any of my clients' projects. I was going through the motions of doing them."

"What did your doctor say about that?"

"I didn't really tell my doctor. The whole postpartum depression thing sounded like white people's stuff."

"Girl, please," Klarke said. "And weaves and extensions used to be thought of as black people's stuff. People better stop putting a color on issues if they want to get right."

"I know. I know." Deborah sighed.

"Did you at least start going back to see your counselor?" Klarke asked as she continued to drive.

"No. Well, yes. Kind of," Deborah stammered.

"Girl, did you or didn't you?" Klarke asked.

"A few weeks ago I found myself in Dr. Vanderdale's office." Deborah frowned. "But it felt so useless. I don't need a doctor and happy pills to function. I know I can do this on my own, with the help of Jesus, of course. I have to get focused."

"And how's that working out for you?" Klarke asked sarcastically.

Deborah looked over at her and chuckled. "Funny." She rolled her eyes. "But seriously, I pray about it, asking God to heal me."

"And I truly believe that He will," Klarke said. "He's going to heal you with His power and His anointing, but more importantly, with

His resources, and sometimes, honey, I'm sure those resources come in the form of a pill."

Deborah pulled her head back and looked at Klarke. "Okay, and just what makes you the expert on all this?"

"Like I said, I've been through some mess, child. Jail was no joke. Dealing with Reo's ex, my children. I, too, was on cloud nine for a minute, until reality set in and kicked my butt right off the cloud, and I had to come tumbling back down to reality. After all the drama of jail, Reo and I got back together. Everything was good. But once the dust settled, my idle mind started really messing with me. I'd have nightmares about everything that had taken place in my life. No matter what good was going on in my life, all the—"

"All the bad thoughts consumed you," Deborah said, jumping in.

"Yes, exactly," Klarke confirmed.

Deborah exhaled. "You get it! Oh, my God, to meet someone who finally freaking gets it," Deborah shouted, excited and relieved. She was not alone.

"I would get all snappy, then depressed, and when anxiety kicked in, child, watch out," Klarke said, shooing her hand. "My mind moved faster than my body did, so it was always working a day ahead of me and what I could physically keep up with."

Deborah buried her face in her hands and began weeping. To know that Klarke really could comprehend and relate to what Deborah was going through was such a relief. Not only that, but Klarke spoke as though she had gotten through it personally and wasn't just talking in order to be talking. That meant there was hope for Deborah too.

Klarke gave her new confidante a moment to take it all in. Klarke understood the pain of being a prisoner in one's own mind and thinking that no one else could relate. Sure, the counselors, doctors, and therapists could scientifically explain the issue, but they didn't know what it felt like. They couldn't fathom the actual torment.

"It's okay," Klarke told Deborah, reaching over to pat her on the back.

"Thank you, Jesus," Deborah mumbled into her hands. "God, thank you." After a few more seconds, Deborah lifted her face and wiped it with the napkin Klarke had given to her earlier. "I can't explain to you what it means to know someone who has experienced firsthand what I'm going through."

"You don't have to explain it to me. Oh, I get it. As a matter of fact, the women we'll be hanging out with tonight, they *all* get it."

Deborah looked over at Klarke. She now felt a little iffy about revealing all this. "What do you mean?"

Klarke sighed and thought for a minute. When sharing the information that Lynox had relayed to him, Reo had been clear about the fact that Klarke couldn't reveal her source to Deborah. So how in the world was she going to let Deborah know that she had long been privy to her situation without telling her that Lynox had spilled the beans?

"Can I be honest with you?" Klarke asked, knowing she was going to be only partially honest.

"Absolutely," Deborah said. She'd been completely honest with Klarke, so she expected the same in return.

"The first night I met you, I saw how your mood suddenly shifted out of nowhere. Then I noticed it again at our brunch. You seemed to get a little antsy, or anxious maybe, there toward the end. It takes someone like me to notice those kinds of things. Me and Michel'le."

"Oh, my God!" Deborah said, once again excited to be with a like-minded person. "You watched that *R&B Divas: Los Angeles* show too. You saw what Michel'le was going through when she had that anxiety episode and her therapist was there to help her?"

Klarke nodded. "I saw it, and I cried, because I sympathized with her. I had worn those same exact shoes many times." Klarke got a little choked up. "I know reality television gets a bad rap. But there is nothing new under the sun that goes on, on those shows. And I strongly believe that everything doesn't have to have a Christian label or some other religious tag on it to minister to and reach people."

Deborah's eyes filled with tears. "I agree. I watched that show with Lynox sitting right there in the room. It took everything in me to keep my tears at bay and stop myself from shouting out, 'That's me. I get it. Michel'le, girl, I know how you feel.'"

Klarke laughed. "And, see, it was the opposite with me. Reo was sitting there, watching it with me, and he turned and said to me, 'Baby, so is that how you used to feel?' And he touched my hand and smiled at me."

Deborah was a little taken aback. "So you explained to Reo what was going on in your head?"

"Sure did."

"And he didn't leave you and think you were crazy?"

Klarke laughed. "Oh, he thought I was crazy. It was he who urged me to put my pride aside and go get some help. He even went with me to my first couple of sessions. Sitting there and listening to him tell my therapist how my actions were destroying our relationship, it hurt. And I knew it was tearing us apart, yet I insisted on trying to work my way through it alone, thinking that as long as I focused on being happy, it would all be good. I had every reason in the world to be happy, yet I couldn't climb in the pocket and stay there."

"You're like this jack-in-the-box. Up, down, up, down," Deborah said as she raised and lowered her hand.

"Exactly, and God forbid, someone try to interrupt your routine. Talk about heads rolling."

"Girl, you are preaching to the choir," Deborah said. "I couldn't seem to keep it under control. I mean, yes, the pills helped. But I didn't want to have to function the rest of my life based on what was in my medicine cabinet. I'm a control freak. The pills took away my control, it seemed. Like a kid with ADD who doesn't know how to act unless they're on some Ritalin." Deborah rolled her eyes and shook her head.

"I'm definitely not trying to diagnose you, but it sounds like you really might have experienced a case of postpartum depression. It could have taken you back to that dark place, and you haven't been able to pull yourself up out of the pit."

Klarke was speaking the truth. The truth was hurting Deborah. She liked to think that she was strong enough to get through this on her own, and if not on her own, then with the strength of Jesus. But she was failing miserably.

Deborah looked at Klarke. "You keep saying you *used to*, as in the past tense. How did you get over it? Do you take meds? Do you see a shrink or something?"

"I still see my therapist a couple of times a month. Like you said, sometimes you just need to talk to someone who is on the outside, looking in. Someone who isn't family or a friend. With friends and family members, you might leave little details out because you are afraid they will judge you. People like us really need to get everything off our minds and chests. God knows what will happen when it builds up and builds up and builds up."

"What about drugs? Do you take anything prescribed by your doctor?"

"Well, yes and no."

Deborah didn't understand. "What do you mean?"

Klarke had finally reached their destination, and she pulled up in front of a two-story stucco home. She put the car in park. "Well, you know I used to live in Nevada, right? And California was only a drive away."

"Yes." Deborah couldn't wait to see where Klarke was going with this.

"Well, I would drive over to one of my doctors in California, and he was, let's say, environmentally connected, you know, with nature. God's natural herbs."

Deborah sat there, looking as confused as ever. She wasn't getting it.

Klarke let out a sigh. "Well, even though no doctor here in Ohio has prescribed for me what my green doctor prescribed for me, I still take it, and it still seems to do the job."

Deborah sat there, still looking as clueless as ever. As if her mind didn't do backflips all on its own, Klarke talking in circles had Deborah's mind spinning.

Klarke saw that she wasn't getting anywhere with Deborah. "Forget it. I think I can show you better than I can tell you. Let's go." Klarke turned off her vehicle, and her car door automatically unlocked. She pushed a button to unlock Deborah's door, and the two of them got out of the car.

As they walked up the walkway to the front door, Deborah noticed the yard. Even though the sun was going down, she couldn't help but be drawn to the beautiful landscaping. Flowers lined the walkway. About three feet out from the house, on each side of the porch, was a flower bed. The variety of flowers really popped in the deep, rich soil they were planted in. On each side of the house was another bed of soil with evenly trimmed bushes. Once they stepped onto the porch, she saw a wrought-iron plant stand with different planters resting on it. All the plants appeared nice and healthy.

It reminded Deborah of her neighbor's house across the street. The older woman paid a crew to tend her lawn, her plants, and her flowers all spring and summer long. She had even had a sprinkler system installed. Some days the woman would go outside and tend her yard herself, showing her horticultural creations some love.

Almost every car that drove by would slow down to look at her neighbor's yard and some of the other yards on the street as well. Not everyone had professionals come out and take care of their landscaping. Some did it themselves. Deborah often wished she had the kind of time it took to create such a beautiful scene.

She'd promised herself the past two seasons that she would get out there in her yard and get her hands dirty, but she never had. But that didn't keep her from appreciating nature's beauty.

"Your friend's flowers and plants and everything are just lovely," Deborah said to Klarke as Klarke rang the doorbell. "She must have a green thumb."

Klarke looked over her shoulder and said, "If you only knew." She then turned back around to face the door, while repeating under her breath, "If you only knew." As the front door opened, Klarke braced herself, knowing that it was now only a matter of time before Deborah actually did know.

idea what the woman was talking about. When Klarke remained silent, Deborah said, "Get what party started?"

"Uh, no. I, uh . . ." Klarke thought for a moment and then stuffed a strawberry in her mouth. With her mouth full, she began to talk to Persia. "I didn't get a chance to eat today, is all." She stuffed a pineapple chunk in her mouth. "So, uh, Persia . . ." Klarke picked up a napkin and wiped some pineapple juice that was dripping from the corner of her mouth. "On the way here, I was telling Deborah about my situation, everything I went through mentally, you know, back when I went to jail and all."

Persia nodded. "Uh-huh." She confirmed that she knew all about it. "It took a mental toll on you, for sure. We all go through things in life, not necessarily incarceration, but things that can just make us feel . . ." Persia searched for the right word.

Then, at the same time, all three women said, "Crazy." They each laughed.

"Exactly," Persia said. "And even though one might not deem one person's issues as serious as detrimental as another's, what we all have concluded is that a molehill to one person can be a mountain to another."

Chapter 11

Deborah looked around the Victorian-style house, wondering why it seemed that every home she walked into felt like what she wanted her own home to feel like. Like a home. Deborah wanted a life and a home that she didn't feel like she had to take a vacation from, but that felt like a vacation instead.

Klarke, who was walking behind Deborah as they followed their host into the kitchen, noticed Deborah eyeballing the home. "Persia did all the interior decorating in her home," Klarke said to Deborah. "Isn't she the stuff?"

The introductions had been made between the home owner, Persia, and Deborah when Persia greeted them at the door. Persia was Reo's best friend's wife. Every month Klarke made it her business to connect with Persia. Her hope was that Deborah would ultimately find it beneficial to meet with them monthly as well.

"Yes, indeed," Deborah agreed as they entered the kitchen. "Persia, your lawn is magnificent as well. You definitely know your stuff when it comes to the green stuff."

Klarke had a little coughing spell and just about choked.

"That's what they tell me," Persia replied in a singsongy voice. "Thank you so much for the compliment, Deborah." Persia escorted her guests over to the kitchen's center island, which held various appetizers and snacks. "If you need any decorating ideas for your own home, I'm your girl," Persia said. She popped a grape in her mouth from the fruit platter that was sitting on the island. "You ladies, help yourselves." She pointed to a stack of small red plates.

"I don't mind if I do," Deborah said, grabbing a plate and placing a couple of pieces of fruit on it, some salami, a few crackers, some cheese, and veggies.

"The punch is over there on the counter," Persia pointed out. She looked at Klarke. "A special ginger ale blend with a hint of sherbet, something I learned from one of the best caterers in the business." She winked at Klarke.

"Shhh, girl," Klarke said, putting her index finger on her lips. "I'll have to kill you if you be telling folks my punch recipe."

Persia shooed her hand. "I didn't tell h everything."

"You told enough," Klarke said seriousl

"Girl, I'm just playing." She laughed and the followed behind Deborah, placing snacks o her own plate. "So where's the other girls Downstairs?" Klarke asked.

"Yep." Persia gave Klarke a questioning look behind Deborah's back. Deborah was too busy helping herself to a cup of punch to notice.

Klarke mouthed the words, "Wait a minute," to Persia as she continued to load up her plate.

"Dang, did you two get the party started without us before you got here? Look at that plate." Persia pointed to Klarke's loaded plate. "Or do you just not want to have to make another trip back up here once those side effects kic Persia laughed.

Klarke's eyes bucked out as she tighte lips and gave Persia an evil look. "I sai minute," Klarke mouthed harshly.

Persia shrugged her shoulders, n standing why Klarke was mean mu "*What*?" she mouthed at Klarke ri Deborah turned around with both h her cup in hand.

Deborah looked at Klarke, waiti answer Persia's questions, becau

"And vice versa," Klarke added. "The straw that broke this camel's back felt like a big ole oak tree landing on me and breaking me in two."

"I know exactly what you guys are talking about," Deborah said, taking a sip of her punch. "I think that's why I keep most of what I'm dealing with or feeling to myself. You turn on the television and see real crises, and then you feel stupid and selfish for thinking you're actually going through something."

"When, in all actuality," Persia said, "your mind is suffering a crisis."

Deborah looked from Persia to Klarke, then back to Persia again. "You two look so well put together, like nothing in the world could bring you down." Whether Deborah realized it or not, she looked well put together too. She was doing as good a job hiding behind a mask as the next woman. "It's hard to believe that you've been through what I'm going through mentally."

"And sometimes I still go through it," Persia said.

Klarke nodded her support of Persia's statement. "Which is why we meet here every month." She popped a piece of cheese in her mouth. She then gave Persia a look, letting her know that now was the time to begin clueing Deborah in on things.

Deborah looked down at her plate. She was starting to feel a tad uneasy. Klarke had mentioned that they met every month. Deborah assumed that included the other women who were downstairs. "I don't know. You two really seem cool. Talking to you is like talking to someone who has known me all my life and gets me. But I can't even religiously talk to and tell my story to a counselor, let alone a group of strangers." Deborah looked at Persia. "I mean, I think it's a great idea that you open up your home and hold monthly group counseling sessions, but I don't think that's the way I want to deal with things right now."

Persia looked at Deborah strangely. "Me either. This isn't a Psychos Anonymous meeting." She laughed, looking at Klarke. She turned her attention back to Deborah. "This is where we meet for the cure, not to discuss the ailment."

This entire evening had too many weird bits and pieces for Deborah to put together. She felt as if both Klarke and Persia were speaking in riddles. "Let me tell you this. If a sista didn't think she was crazy before tonight," Deborah said, referring to herself in the third person, "she sure does now. What's really going on here?"

Klarke and Persia looked at one another.

"I really don't think words can explain it," Persia said to Deborah.

"Me either," Klarke said. "Because, trust me, I tried." She had an exasperated expression on her face.

"How about we just show you?" Persia suggested.

"Please do," Deborah said, just as exasperated as Klarke.

Klarke had already told Deborah she could show her better than she could tell her. Well, it went without saying that Deborah was ready to *see* for herself.

"Then let's go, ladies," Persia said, opening the door off the kitchen that led down to the basement. After walking down a couple of steps, Persia stopped in her tracks and turned back around to address the women behind her. She looked at Klarke. "I trust your judgment, Klarke, but are you sure your friend is going to be okay with this?"

Klarke looked back at Deborah before turning to Persia and replying, "I guess we'll find out soon enough, now won't we?"

"What in the world?" Deborah took the plate she was carrying and sat it on top of her cup as she walked down the last step in Persia's basement. She used the index finger and thumb of her free hand to pinch her nose closed. "Did someone hit a skunk on their way over here or something? I'm not trying to be funny, but I hit one last week on my way home and lit my living room up when I walked into my home." Her face twisted up, Deborah closed her eyes and shook her head.

Klarke chuckled as they followed Persia down a hallway and into an open area.

Ahead Deborah could see a cloudy-looking room. "A smoke bomb?" she said to Klarke. Persia had such a beautiful home, and Deborah couldn't imagine why she would allow someone to set off a smoke bomb in it. Maybe this woman was crazy . . . in every sense of the word and according to every legal definition.

"There's smoke, and it's the bomb." Persia laughed as she disappeared into the smoke-filled room.

When Deborah entered the room, she saw about five other women conversing with one another. A couple of them were sipping on drinks, and one was nibbling on her own plate of food. It was what the other two were doing that gave Deborah pause. She froze right in the entrance to the room.

"Everybody, this is Deborah," Persia announced as she walked over to the two women Deborah's eyes were frozen on. "Deborah, this is . . ." Persia's words stopped when she turned to find Deborah standing there, on the verge of shock.

The other women waited for Persia to finish the introductions.

"Deborah, are you okay?" Persia asked.

Deborah's head nodded yes, but her appearance screamed no.

Persia looked at Klarke and gave her a "Handle your girl" look, then went and handled her own business with the two women. Seeing that Persia had no intention of finishing the introductions, the women all went back to their business and the conversation at hand.

"We got two going," one of the women said as she passed Persia the skinny white little thing she'd been puffing on.

"Thank you," Persia said as she accepted it and then took a puff. She exhaled smoke, and it shot from her nose like from the nostrils of a dragon.

Klarke walked over to Deborah and stood next to her. "You good?" she asked softly.

"I . . . I . . ." Deborah was truly at a loss for words. She continued looking around the room for a moment. She watched as the two joints made their way around the room, the women puffing and puffing and then passing them along.

She finally looked at Klarke. "You do that too . . . what they're doing?"

Deborah's question was laced with so much disgust that Klarke almost felt too bad to answer. "Yes," Klarke said, shaking her head no. Realizing that she was saying one thing and doing another, she added, "No," all the while nodding yes. Klarke threw her hands up. "Clearly, I do. I can't seem to get my brain to coordinate my mouth and my gestures."

"So is that what they mean when they say, 'This is your brain on drugs'?" Deborah asked.

"No, honey, this is my brain off of drugs. I need a hit." Klarke set down the plate she had in her hand and went over and took a hit from one of the joints. She closed her eyes and tilted her head back as she blew out the smoke. "Yesss," she said, as if that was exactly what she needed. She gathered herself and then walked back over to Deborah. "Okay, and you were saying?"

Deborah looked at her strangely. "You just took a puff of that joint, Klarke." Deborah hadn't gotten rid of her tone. Only now Klarke thought she heard a hint of judgment behind the disgust.

This time Klarke wasn't confused about her reply. "Yes, yes, I did," she said matter-of-factly.

Deborah scrunched up her face. "And they did too." She looked over at the women, her face still scrunched up.

"Yes, they did too," Klarke said.

"Disgusting. With everyone's mouth on that one little thing, aren't you afraid you might catch herpes simplex one or something? Or catch a cold? Ew." Deborah shook her head in repulsion.

Klarke stared at Deborah for a moment. She had to make sure Deborah's only concern was germs. "Are you serious right now? You entered a room that looks like Snoop Dogg was the interior designer, and all you're worried about is catching cooties?" Klarke asked, then waited on an answer with a straight face.

"Well . . ." Deborah thought for a second. "Yeah, and I can't believe it's not a concern for you. I mean, how do you go home and kiss your husband after repeatedly putting your mouth on something a hundred other people had their mouth on?" Deborah put her plate down too, as well as her cup of punch. "I just lost my appetite."

Klarke watched Deborah make a boo-boo face for a moment longer before she burst out laughing. Klarke laughed so hard, tears welled up in her eyes.

Persia walked over with a joint in hand. "What's so funny?" she asked Klarke. "Don't tell me you got the giggles. Acting like a rookie."

Klarke put her hand on Persia's shoulder while she laughed. She tried to gather herself, but she couldn't stop laughing. She bent over and put her other hand on her stomach. Eventually, Persia started chuckling. Her chuckle turned into a laugh, and then before she knew it, she was having a laughing fit also. Eventually, the other women came over to see what was so funny. The next thing Deborah knew, every last one of the women was laughing, all except her.

They looked so silly, happy, and carefree. A smile covered Deborah's face first; then she allowed a little chuckle to slip out. A little laughter eventually escaped her mouth. Granted, she wasn't laughing nearly as hard as the others, but she was laughing. Laughing was good.

"Okay, okay," Deborah said. "It wasn't that funny. Cut it out."

"What wasn't that funny?" Persia managed to ask Deborah through her laughing. "I'm laughing at this crazy fool." She pointed at Klarke.

Deborah thought for a moment, and her laughter disappeared once she realized she had no idea why Klarke thought what she had said was so funny. Was Klarke laughing *at* her?

Finally, Klarke was able to gain her composure and speak. "Whew-wee. That was funny."

"What?" Persia insisted on knowing. "What was so dang funny?"

Klarke pointed at Deborah. "I was afraid she would trip off the fact that we, you know, smoke weed"—Klarke held the joint up—"since I wasn't certain if she'd ever smoked before or knew anyone who smoked."

"I don't," Deborah was quick to confirm.

"You don't what?" Persia asked. "Smoke or know anyone who smokes?"

"Both," Deborah told her.

"Come on now," one of the other women said. "E'erybody know somebody who gets high."

"The highest myself, my friends, and my family have ever been is thirty thousand feet up in the sky when traveling via airplane, thank you very much." Deborah crossed her arms across her chest and rolled her eyes.

Now that the conversation was turning serious, everyone's laughter died down.

Klarke cleared her throat. "I could see the look on your face when you first walked down here and saw that we were weed smokers. Well, for someone not accustomed to the art of weed smoking, I found it hard to believe that all you had to say about it was that we could pass germs. That was funny to me. No offense, but it was."

Deborah shrugged. "To each his own. I'm sure I have done and still do plenty of things that other folks wouldn't, so who am I to judge what you do?"

"I know that's right," one of the women said. "Judge not, lest ye be judged."

"Amen," Deborah said. "Wait a minute. Are we speaking the Word and praising it over a joint?"

All the women eyeballed each other and then, once again, burst out laughing.

"Oprah said God is nature," Klarke said, looking down at the joint. "Well, this is as natural as it gets." She took a hit and then passed the joint to Persia.

Persia took a hit, exhaled, then said, "Let the church say amen."

Chapter 12

All the women now sat around the coffee table in Persia's basement. The two joints that Deborah had witnessed being passed around had been smoked down to the roach and now rested in an ashtray.

Deborah recalled asking whether or not Klarke was saved when Lynox had first encouraged her to befriend the woman. Now she couldn't help but address this subject. "So all y'all are members of a church?" Deborah asked the women. She would be in utter disbelief if she were to learn that for the past fifteen minutes she'd been in a room with some weed-smoking Christians who claimed to love the Lord. She didn't care what those women said about marijuana being natural, like an herb grown in the ground. It was a drug, and the last time she'd checked, in the state of Ohio possession of illegal drugs could lead to an arrest, which could result in imprisonment. And although she had no intention of condemning and judging the women for choosing to smoke the substance, it just wasn't something she wanted to do herself. Even if they did legalize it in Ohio, she couldn't get past the idea of putting her mouth on something that everyone in the room had put their mouth on. *Yuck!*

"I am," Persia and another woman, who had been introduced to Deborah as Cinnamon, said simultaneously.

"No. I'm not," Klarke said. "Not on the regular. But Persia has invited me to her church, and I've gone."

"I've invited you to mine too," Cinnamon said, jumping in, "but you've never taken me up on my offer." She didn't hide her attitude about this.

"Next Sunday. I promise," Klarke told Cinnamon. "No. Wait a minute. The Sunday after that one. I forgot, I have a gig this Sunday."

Cinnamon twisted her lips up, as if she didn't believe a word Klarke was saying.

"For real, I'll be there," Klarke promised. "Just text me the info."

"And don't think I won't," Cinnamon said.

Klarke looked at Deborah. "I might not belong to a church, but I believe in God. Reo doesn't belong to a church, either, but he can pray his butt off. We owe that to our oldest daughter. She is one praying lady. Even when she was young, she always had a relationship with God. She did that on her own, because I can count on one hand how many times I ever took my children to church."

Persia asked Klarke about her daughter. "Isn't Vaughn a co-minister or something like that at a church in Nevada?"

"Yep. That's one of the reasons why I couldn't convince her to move back to Ohio," Klarke said.

"I'm not a member of a church," one of the other women said, "but I've been attending the same one for about a year now."

"Then why don't you just join?" Deborah asked.

"Because sometimes I like to attend other churches too," the woman replied. "My focus is being committed to God—and He's every-where—not to a church, which is in just one place. I have to have a gym membership and belong to my home owners' association. Is the church the same way? If I don't have a church membership, I can't belong to the Kingdom?" She rolled her eyes. "Let a sista worship and fellowship."

"I hear you," Persia said. "I'm committed to God, but as with having any other type of membership, I like the security that comes along with being a member of something. It's not only about me being committed to something, but about something being committed to me as well. It feels good to be able to call on a group of my fellow church members to pray for me in my time of need. Being called on by them is equally rewarding."

Deborah feared the conviction within of being called on spiritually by someone after having had a glass of wine, let alone after smoking a blunt. She didn't voice that to Persia, though.

"But wouldn't God's children pray for and be there for a complete stranger off the streets?" the woman countered. "Would you not bury a dead person who was not a—quote, unquote—member of the church and pray for his or her soul?"

"Okay, okay." Deborah put her hands up. "Forget I asked." She had had no idea that posing that simple question was going to lead to a near argument. "I was asking only because it seems weird that churchgoing Christian women get high."

"It's not about getting high," another woman snapped. "It's about keeping our sanity. You try raising four kids, only for your husband to leave you for the babysitter, who is barely legal. You struggling to take care of the kids that he don't even wanna get on his every other weekend court-ordered visitation, and yet he's taking care of the new wife and their new baby and threw me and my kids away." The woman's bottom lip began to tremble, and her hand balled into a fist. "Oh, Lord, somebody light another one up."

Cinnamon, who was sitting next to the woman, laughed and patted her on the shoulder. "Calm down, Deidra."

Klarke looked at Deborah, who was trying to take in everything Deidra had shared. "That was a very rough time for her. She was hospitalized and everything," Klarke informed Deborah.

"Mind you that I was handcuffed while I was hospitalized," Deidra added.

"Handcuffed?" Deborah said.

"Yeah," Klarke said, answering for Deidra. "She was already struggling to deal with the situation of losing her husband to another woman. Hadn't slept or eaten in weeks."

"And I finally get her out to a restaurant to eat something," Cinnamon said, "and her ex and his new, pregnant wife are at the same restaurant." She shook her head. "Now, you know that wasn't nothing but the devil."

"I didn't know she was pregnant at the time," Deidra said. "I just know that I had not only paid her to watch my kids, but apparently, I had also been paying her to suck my husband's—"

"Dee, come on now," Persia said. "Bring it back. Reel it in."

"I'm sorry," Deidra said, apologizing. "I know you don't cuss. I'm not trying to disrespect your house."

"It's okay," Persia said.

Deborah sat there thinking, *Really? She can't cuss in your house, because you find that disrespectful, but she can smoke weed in it?* This was more than Deborah could even begin to comprehend.

On the ride over here she really had started to feel like her connection with Klarke was becoming stronger. When she met Persia, that same connection had existed. Klarke had told Deborah that the people she would be surrounded by tonight all knew where the others were coming from and had a way of dealing with life's issues. Deborah had been hopeful that she'd find the answer to her situation here tonight. God had been the provider of all her resources. But it would take some major convincing for Deborah to believe that marijuana was, in fact, one of those resources. Maybe it wasn't a good idea, after all, to try to be friends with someone who wasn't saved.

"Klarke," Deborah said, "I don't want to ruin your evening, but I think I'm ready to head out.

If you're not ready to go, I can call my husband or a taxi or something."

"Oh, no. Don't leave yet," Klarke said, truly disappointed that Deborah was ready to dip out on them.

"I don't want to be Debbie Downer." Deborah looked at the women. "No pun intended, but this whole group smoke therapy thing isn't for me." Deborah went to stand.

"Well, how do you know if you haven't tried it?" Klarke said.

"And never in my life have I had a desire to try it," Deborah said.

"Well, neither had I, but then I actually gave it a chance," Klarke retorted.

Deborah stared curiously at Klarke for a moment. "And what exactly made you try it?" She looked at the other women. "What made any of you sit there one day and say, 'I feel like I'm losing my mind. Let me smoke a joint and see if that will help'?"

"Research," Persia interjected. "I researched it. After hearing so much about medical marijuana and the various things it was being used for treatment-wise, I wanted to know more."

"Yeah," Cinnamon said. "I was receiving court-ordered therapy. I remember seeing a special on CNN about marijuana. It was, like, in the middle of the night. I'd had a bad day that day. Terrible depression and anxiety had been plaguing me all that week. I'd been praying and getting hands laid on me, you name it. I continuously cried out to Jesus for help. But on that particular night, when I was minutes away from taking my own life, what pops on television?"

"I saw that special too," another woman said. "They said that when there is an imbalance in the brain, there are too many receptors associated with intense emotions."

These women definitely had Deborah's attention now. Her being on overload with intense emotions felt like an understatement. But it was a statement, nonetheless, that connected with something in Deborah, causing her to focus fully on what was being said about marijuana.

"The emotions can be fear, anxiety, and stress," Cinnamon said. "And there's not enough of a chemical that binds to those anxiety receptors to keep them calm and in check."

"Girl, you are quoting that show verbatim," the other woman said.

"Honey, I rewound it so many times, took notes, you name it," Cinnamon declared. "I swear, it was like God was speaking to me through that TV show. Call it blasphemy if you want to, but then I'll rebuke you," Cinnamon said, wholeheartedly convinced about her findings.

"Please continue," Deborah practically begged, hoping those anxiety receptors could remain at bay while she waited in anticipation for Cinnamon to proceed.

"Anyway," Cinnamon said, "science has proven that marijuana is filled with a chemical that can bind to these receptors and help restore balance in the brain."

Klarke jumped in. "With me, as I'm sure it is with Cinnamon, my flashbacks, depression, and anxiety are similar to those of people suffering from PTSD. People suffering from PTSD need a substance that can quiet those receptors that are associated with anxiety, but not completely shut down other parts of the body. Marijuana has some of those properties."

Cinnamon nodded in agreement. She was in accord with everything Klarke had said. "Marijuana farms are popping up all over the world. And God has the whole world in His hands," she said matter-of-factly.

Deborah took in everything the women had to share. The more they talked, the more Deborah started to think that maybe marijuana wasn't just a natural resource, but a scientific one as well.

"I didn't bring you here tonight to take you back to the high school days of peer pressure," Klarke said to Deborah. "I felt like the least I could do was inform you about something that I know for a fact works for me. For most of our lives, have we known it to be an illegal drug? Yes," she said. "But you think about it. How many people smoke a dime bag, jump in their car, enter the freeway via an exit ramp, and take out a family of five? Not many. Yet some people who drink alcohol, which is legal across the map, do it daily."

Deborah nodded. The way she saw it, Klarke really did have a valid point.

"Again, I don't want to pressure you," Klarke said. "I felt compelled to share with you, that's all." she exhaled. "So if you're ready to call it a night, I brought you here, so of course I'll take you home." She stood.

The women began telling Deborah how nice it was to have met her. Klarke started to walk away but then realized that Deborah was still sitting on the couch, staring off into space.

"Deborah, you ready?" Klarke asked.

Deborah looked up at Klarke, then responded, "Not quite."

***

"Oh, my God!" Deborah roared in laughter as she passed Klarke the joint she'd just taken a puff from. It was actually the second joint she'd partaken of since deciding to stay at Persia's house and give the nonprescription medical marijuana a try. "You actually did that to that poor woman?" Deborah asked Klarke. For the past several minutes, she'd been sitting with Klarke and listening to her tell stories about how she'd met Reo and how they'd broken up and then made up, and about all her experiences with his ex-wife in between.

The other women were sitting in clusters throughout the room, except for Cinnamon, who had left for the evening. But she hadn't left without first confirming Klarke's attendance at her church and then inviting Deborah to come visit as well. Both Klarke and Deborah had promised her they'd be there.

"Poor woman, my foot. Meka was the devil," Klarke said. Meka was Reo's ex-wife, the mother of Reo's teenage daughter, who lived with them. "I'm just getting started on her foul self. Believe me when I say you ain't heard nothing yet when it comes to her." Klarke took a puff from the joint. "Heck, she's the main reason why I need this here." Klarke held up the joint. She took another puff and then passed it to Deborah.

Deborah took the joint. "I thought I put Lynox through some shenanigans in order to catch his heart, but you playing secret pen pal to get Reo to take interest in you was as much of a roller-coaster ride for you too."

Reo was actually Klarke's second husband; she'd been married to her son and daughter's father prior to that. But when she found out that his cousin's daughter was actually his love child, she'd flipped the script on her first husband. She'd beat everybody down. That divorce had been so painful for her physically, mentally, and financially. Trying to raise two children while depressed and not wanting to see another day of life had been hard. Klarke had wanted the easy way out. While most women had been trying to snag NBA players, she'd figured a semi-world-renowned author would suffice, so she'd schemed her way into Reo's life via sexy little pen pal e-mails. Her intentions weren't to find love. She was done with love. Her goal was to find a man who could provide for her children. This was back when authors' publishers paid them obscene advances and kept them on the road, touring. She figured she wouldn't even have to be bothered with the man; she could just cash his checks. She had no idea she would actually fall in love with Reo. But like a Prince Charming in a fairy tale, he swept her off her feet.

Unfortunately, Meka, who was then his ex-girlfriend, was not having it. If she couldn't have Reo, nobody could. Meka put Klarke through the ringer as she tried to get her man back, and her conniving actions landed Klarke in jail.

"It was a roller coaster," Klarke confirmed. "And a haunted house and every other crazy attraction at the amusement park." She took the joint back from Deborah and took another hit and exhaled.

"Uh, you know I hadn't taken a puff yet, right?" Deborah chuckled. "I'm no pro, but I thought it was puff, puff, pass. You took three puffs."

"Oh, my bad. Girl, got to keep my receptors in check." Klarke laughed and extended the joint to Deborah.

Deborah put her hand up. "No, that's okay. I was kidding. I think I better slow my roll, anyway."

"It's only two joints." Klarke took another puff. "Well, one and half for you."

"Yeah, but I'm a newbie, and I don't want to overdo it, especially when I'm not sure of the effect it might have on me."

Klarke was not going to argue with Deborah. She definitely didn't want to come off as having coerced Deborah into this whole weed-smoking venture. She was coming from a good place.

On top of that, she most definitely didn't mind finishing off the joint on her own.

Deborah leaned back against the couch and closed her eyes.

"You all right?" Klarke asked her.

Deborah sat there for a minute and then opened her eyes. "I'm better than before I came, I know that."

"See, girl? I told you God was all up in this here," Klarke said. "Just like at church."

Deborah furrowed her eyebrows. "Come again." She sat up, waiting to hear Klarke's response.

"You know how church is supposed to be for sick people and how you're not supposed to leave the same way you came? Well, there you go." She held up the joint and took another puff.

Deborah leaned back against the couch and closed her eyes again as she laughed. "Whew-wee. You are something else."

"Actually, I'm hungry." Klarke dropped the doobie in an ashtray.

Once again Deborah opened her eyes. "Girl, me too, and I ate that whole plate of food I fixed when I first got here."

"I'll go grab us something else."

"No. Everybody might think I'm a pig."

Klarke looked around the room. "Child, ain't nobody stuttin' you. Besides, it's just one of the side effects of weed. Everybody who smokes it gets it. It's called the munchies." Klarke stood up and went and got herself and Deborah some more snacks. When she returned, she sat down, and the two of them began to devour the food.

"I know you've mentioned it a couple of times already," Deborah said, biting into a cracker with cheese on it, "and I hope you don't think I'm being nosy." She paused.

"About what?" Klarke asked, tossing back a cherry tomato dipped in ranch dressing and chewing it.

"The whole jail thing," Deborah said.

Klarke shrugged her shoulders in a nonchalant manner. "What about it?"

"I didn't really want to ask. I was waiting on you to tell me, but you never did." Deborah ate a piece of salami. She chewed it, swallowed, and then asked, "But what exactly were you in jail for, if you don't mind me asking?" She continued stuffing items from the plate of food into her mouth.

"Girl, you could have Googled that," Klarke said. "I was all over the paper when that all happened."

"I'm not a Googling type of chick, unless I'm fact-checking a book or something," Deborah said. "If I want to know something about someone, I simply ask that person."

"Okay. Well, then, you should have just asked, because I don't mind telling you at all."

Just then Persia walked over and handed Klarke a lit joint. Klarke took a puff, then exhaled. Staring at the joint between her fingers, she said, "Murder."

Deborah didn't even have any smoke in her lungs, but she began coughing. She was choking either on the words stuck in her throat or the words Klarke had said.

One of the other women walked over and asked Deborah, "You okay?"

Deborah was too busy choking to reply. Persia, in all her concern, began patting Deborah on the back, while Klarke, just as cool, calm, and collected as ever, took a hit from the joint.

"She'll be all right," Klarke said, exhaling. She looked over at Deborah, who had a horrified look on her face. "I know you said you were done for the night, but something tells me you're going to need another hit."

Without hesitating, Deborah took the joint from Klarke and puffed her little heart out.

Hopefully, the chemicals in the marijuana would not only help her depression, anxiety, and stress but, with any luck, would make her so high that come morning she'd forget all about the fact that she'd spent the night doing drugs with a murderer, an ex-felon, and a woman who had very good taste in home decor.

Jesus, take the wheel!

Chapter 13

"You go ahead and sign them into children's church," Deborah said to Lynox as they headed toward the church building with their two boys in tow. She released Tyson's hand. "Go on with Daddy." Lynox was already holding the baby in his carrier.

"Why? What's wrong?" Lynox asked Deborah with concern in his voice.

"Nothing. It's just that I left my Bible bag in the car. Can't go to church without my sword," she said. "I'll meet you inside soon, okay?" She smiled.

"Well, all right," Lynox said. "Or I can run back and grab it for you."

"No, no, no. I got this," Deborah assured him as she started to backpedal to the car. "You go on in there. I don't want to make you any later."

Lynox hesitated but then gave in. "Okay. I'll try to get us the closest seats to the front as I can."

By now Deborah's back was to Lynox and her heels were clicking as she made her way back toward their car. "Thanks, honey," she yelled over her shoulder.

She remembered those times she had either prayed for or thanked God for the days when Lynox would enter the church doors with her. To her, there was nothing more intimate than a husband and wife being in the house of the Lord together. There was quite a number of married women at church, but one rarely ever saw their husbands join them. Deborah felt truly blessed for the days when her husband joined her and her sons and they all worshipped together. If the man was going to be the head of the family, then he needed to lead the way into the sanctuary. With one son who was old enough to look to his father to set and be an example, this was a day Deborah should have held dear. Instead, she was opting to allow the males in her life to enter the church without her.

Lynox had driven them to church in his vehicle. Deborah carried a key to his car on her key ring, so she used it to let herself back in on the passenger side. Once inside the car, she grabbed the Bible bag, which she'd deliberately left behind. She'd needed an excuse to come back to the car. This morning had been like a zoo in their home. To the ordinary mom preparing her family for church, it might have been a regular Sunday morning, but to someone with anxiety issues like Deborah, it was enough to make her want to crawl up under her bed and hide until everyone else left the house.

The baby had woken up whining an hour before he usually did. Deborah had actually stayed up later than usual to meet an editing deadline, and so she was exhausted this morning, and the sound of the baby crying was like nails down a chalkboard. She had turned to see Lynox sleeping like a baby himself, totally unaffected by the screaming coming through the baby monitor. Oh, how Deborah had wanted to wake him and ask him to go see about the baby, but last night he'd still been up when she'd gone to bed. He and Reo had spent the past three months putting together a proposal that included an outline and the first few chapters of their joint book, which both Deborah and Reo's agent had presented to their respective publishing house editors. Reo's imprint had ended up being the one that would publish the book. After negotiations the book deal had been finalized. Most authors felt the days of lucrative book deals were over, but this deal involved the two African American authors with the most name recognition, and so it was like the nostalgic days of 2005 advances.

Knowing she had a couple more hours of sleep on Lynox, she decided to let him rest and to go take care of their baby herself. No sooner had she gone into Tatum's nursery than Tyson came in, asking for cereal. She took both boys downstairs and prepared to feed them. She placed the baby in his seater and had Tyson sit at the table. While she warmed the baby's bottle the old-fashioned way, in a pan of water, she prepared some cereal for Tyson. After serving Tyson, she sat down at the table and said grace with him. As she went to get up, Tyson began telling her about a kid in school who had hit him. In getting to the bottom of it, Deborah forgot about the baby's bottle and the water in the pan almost boiled away, which meant the milk was scalding, way too hot for the baby to drink.

Deborah had to run the bottle under cold water. The impatient baby fussed. In the meantime Tyson flipped his cereal bowl and its contents ended up all over him. She sent Tyson upstairs to take off his sticky, wet clothes while she finished cooling off the bottle. Finally, the milk was at a temperature the baby could tolerate. She put the baby in her arms and fed him as she went upstairs to check on Tyson. In an attempt to be a big boy, Tyson had dressed himself in the clothes Deborah had ironed and laid out for him the night before, only he hadn't cleaned himself up first, and so the milk and the fruity cereal had stained his shirt. Not only did she have to help him shower quickly, but she had to pick out and iron a new outfit for him to wear.

In getting Tyson together, she forgot to burp the baby. Consequently, he spit up all over himself, so a sponge bath was in order for him. Once she got the baby clean, she laid him on his changing table to dress him. Before she could get his diaper on him, he started whizzing. Some of it hit Deborah, and before she could cover his wee-wee up with a towel, he'd already gotten his outfit, which was lying on the edge of his changing table, wet. So she had to sponge him clean again, plus pick out a new outfit for him to wear.

After getting the baby dressed, she secured him in his little bouncy chair and went to make sure Tyson had gotten his clothes on okay. He had gotten dressed okay and had brushed his teeth on his own as well. She was about to praise him for brushing his teeth without her help when he turned around, and she saw blue toothpaste plastered on his shirt. She wanted to cuss. She couldn't remember if she cussed out loud or in her head, but a cussword or two definitely came to mind. She changed Tyson's shirt, then sat him down on his bed and ordered him not to move a muscle until she came back for him.

When she raced back into her bedroom, Lynox was coming out of their bathroom, looking all cool, calm, and collected. She wanted to slap the smile right off his face and kick him in the chin when he said, "Good morning, honey." It had been anything but a good morning.

Deborah went into the bathroom to take a quick shower herself. She'd handled Tyson, with all his sticky milk and cereal, along with the baby and his throw up and pee. No way would a washup in the sink suffice. She felt so cruddy. She went and turned on the water in the shower, and it shot straight out of the showerhead and onto her. That meant that Lynox had simply turned the water off without first turning off the showerhead. She'd told him about this on numerous occasions. No, he didn't leave the toilet seat up after he used the bathroom, but to Deborah, not taking an extra moment to turn the showerhead off before turning the water off was just as disturbing.

She quickly fumbled around to turn the water off, but not before the water had dampened her hair. Typically, Deborah wouldn't be too upset about this. She'd be irritated, but not upset.

Today wasn't a typical day, though. Today she wasn't wearing her hair in the natural two-strand twist she would set it in at night. No, yesterday she had gone to Synergi Salon and had had it flat ironed. Getting a natural two-strand twist wet and getting natural hair that had been flat ironed wet were two completely different animals. It was only a matter of minutes before her roots would turn into a puffy Afro.

That was it for Deborah. That was the straw that broke the camel's back, and she broke down in tears.

Lynox knocked on the door, apparently after hearing her sniffling. "You okay in there?" he asked.

"Yeah. Runny nose. I think I might be coming down with something," she lied.

Lynox had been tiptoeing around her and handling her like a fragile piece of china. She didn't feel like dealing with his wannabe Dr. Phil self. So she put on her big girl panties, pulled her puffy, wet hair into a puff on the top of her head, and pressed forward.

Surprisingly enough, they made it to church only a few minutes behind schedule. At one point, while Deborah was doing that quick washup in the shower, she hadn't wanted to go at all. The morning had already been too much.

Her mind hadn't been in a place where she could focus on church. She had refused to give the devil the victory, though. That was probably exactly why he'd had his foot all up in her behind, kicking her around, that morning, trying to get her to give up on church first and then give up on God. Deborah had refused to give in. She and her family had piled into Lynox's car, and they had headed on to church. All was well until Lynox realized he was practically on empty and they needed to stop and get gas before driving the rest of the way to church.

"We could have taken my car if you knew you didn't have any gas," Deborah said, fussing.

"I forgot, babe. It's okay. We'll be fine, as long as we get there."

"It's not only about getting to church. It's about getting to church on time. When we have meetings and appointments, we show up on time. We should give God the same respect."

"I hear you. I hear you," Lynox said while pulling into a gas station. "But God knows our heart. He sees us trying."

Deborah simply rolled her eyes, while Lynox got out to pump gas. In her head she was cussing him out, calling him every kind of idiot in the book, then, in the next breath, repenting and asking God to help her control her emotions. By the time they pulled up at church, there were no parking spots left in the main lot. Deborah was completely done at this point. They had to park in the overflow lot. There was no way she was going to be able to sit, relax, and focus during service unless she did a little self-help. Her self-help came in the form of a Baggie with green stuff in it.

"Yes," Deborah said to herself as she undid the Baggie, closed her eyes, and inhaled the aroma. Time was of the essence, so thank God, Deborah was prepared. She had two joints pre-rolled in the Baggie. She didn't plan on smoking them both right now; just a couple of hits off one, she figured, would do the trick.

Deborah pulled one of the joints out of the Baggie and dug a pack of matches out of her purse. Before striking one of the matches, she thought for a minute. The vehicle was a small, enclosed space. Deborah worried that if she smoked in the car, the odor would not be cleared out by the time church was over. She feared that a couple of hours might not be enough. She usually smoked in her own car, after telling Lynox she had to run to the store or something, any excuse to get out of the house. And, of course, she'd gone to Persia's a couple of times since her indoctrination into their green club. One time she had smoked at home, in the upstairs hallway bathroom. No one ever used that one, except for Tyson, and it was where she bathed the baby.

"Bathroom," Deborah said when a sudden idea entered her mind. She could probably go into the church bathroom and smoke. Not the women's or the men's bathroom, but the single family bathroom, which lay between the men's and the women's bathrooms. It was the one most mothers would take their sons to if they were around the age of seven or eight, not wanting to send their boys into the men's bathroom alone. Daddies with daughters around that same age did the same. All the kids around that age were more than likely in children's church right now, so no one would be using the single family bathroom for quite some time. Her chances of getting caught were pretty slim.

On second thought, though, this wasn't like being back in high school and sneaking cigarettes in the girls' bathroom. This was the house of the Lord, and even though Deborah had done her research and discovered that marijuana was grown in the earth, like green beans and collard greens—the earth that God had created—no way could she go inside the church and disrespect God's house like that.

Not when she was one of the members who
had brought to Pastor Margie's attention that
parishioners taking cigarette breaks right outside the church was tacky and disrespectful.
Wouldn't that be the pot cooking on the stove
calling the kettle right next to it smoky? So with
that final thought, Deborah decided to go ahead
and smoke in the car.

She placed her smoking items in her lap and
then put the key in the ignition and started the
car. She leaned over to the driver's side and
rolled down each of the electric windows about
two to three inches. She then turned the car off
and put the keys back in her purse. She looked
around the parking lot. There were a couple
of latecomers straggling in, but none of them
paid any attention to her, as they were too busy
scurrying about, trying to get inside the church
as quickly as they could since they were already
late.

Deborah lit the joint, took a hit, then leaned
back while she exhaled. She took another hit,
inhaling the herb that gave her an instant sense
of relaxation. "Mmm," she moaned as she
exhaled. She took a couple more hits before
she put the joint out. She then placed all her
paraphernalia back into her purse. She stayed in
the car, with her head leaning back against the

seat and her eyes closed. She wanted to marinate right there for a minute while the drug traveled through her veins and to her brain. What had started off as the most hectic day ever was now calmed.

A smile rested on her face. "Dang, I see why Snoop rapped so smooth and laid back," Deborah said aloud, conjuring up an image of the famous rapper Snoop Doggy Dogg, who was known for constantly smoking weed. The weed seemed to have put her on cloud nine. But it wouldn't take but a few raps on the driver's side window to kick her right off that cloud and back down to earth.

Deborah nearly jumped out of her skin when she heard the sound of knuckles tapping on glass. Her body jerked against the seat. She looked over to see Brother Willard, church security, leaning down and looking in the driver's side window.

"You okay in there?" he asked through the crack in the window.

"Huh? What? Oh yeah," Deborah said, jittery. "I was just . . . praying." Instantly, her spirit was convicted. Could that be considered using the Lord's name in vain? Even if it wasn't, it was still a lie, which meant it was still a sin.

"All right. Well, I wanted to make sure," Brother Willard said. "Sorry for interrupting."

He tilted his security hat, then stood erect and moseyed on, going about his business.

Deborah watched him to see if he looked back or gave any other sign that he was suspicious. He continued to troll both parking lots. Over the past few months some churches in the area had suffered automobile break-ins during church service. New Day had upped security to deter would-be thieves and prevent this from happening to its members.

Deborah looked around the car and started fanning the smoke, which was now barely visible. Even if security hadn't smelled anything, there was still the possibility that he'd noticed smoke in the car.

"Jesus, help me," Deborah said as she continued to fan. Once she got a nice-size cramp in her wrist, she stopped fanning. She looked down at herself and brushed away any ashes or marijuana remnants that might have fallen on her. She reached into the glove box and pulled out a bottle of air spray. Not only did she spray the car, but she sprayed herself as well, making a mental note to carry a bottle of body spray in her purse from now on.

After putting the air spray back in the glove box, she opened the door and got out of the car.

She stood with the car door open and brushed herself off yet one more time. She grabbed her purse and the Bible bag, then scanned the car's interior to make sure she hadn't left anything behind that would expose her. After doing so, she clicked a button to lock the car doors, closed the door, and then headed back toward the church.

Brother Willard had already made his way to the main church parking lot. He acknowledged Deborah from two cars away with a smile and a nod.

Deborah returned the gestures. Then once he looked elsewhere, she rolled her eyes and stomped off into the church, fussing, "Shoot. I went through all that, and that fool messed up my high."

"You smell that?" Lynox said once he was settled in the car and was about to put the key in the ignition and turn the car on. He began looking around the car as he sniffed.

"Smell what?" Deborah asked, shrugging her shoulders. Her heart began to beat a hundred miles per hour. She honestly thought her heart was going to plain old stop and she'd die right there, without a buzz. Any little bit of buzz she'd had left after her encounter with Brother Willard had been danced off when she caught the Holy Ghost in church. Yes, she had blazed in the church parking lot before service and then gone in and praised the Lord.

Lynox looked at Deborah with squinted eyes. "Are you kidding me? You gon' sit there and try to tell me that you really don't smell that?"

Deborah tucked her lips in and cast her eyes downward. She was cold busted. She could have kicked herself for thinking that the smell of the weed would be completely gone by now. Now she had no choice but to tell her husband how she'd been self-medicating, controlling her jumping-bean emotions with narcotics that could land her straight jail time if a real officer of the law was ever to bust her, and not Brother Willard's mall cop self.

Deborah looked back at her children, who were secure in the backseat. Even though she knew this conversation had to go down, she didn't want it to be in front of her children. She took in a deep breath and turned to Lynox. She opened her mouth to tell him that of course, she smelled it, but that she'd discuss it with him once they got home. Before she could get a word out, though, Lynox spoke.

"Uh-huh. I knew you smelled it," Lynox said. "It's that little stinker right there." He looked at the baby in the car seat, cooing. "What you be putting in that milk you be feeding that boy?" Lynox fanned his hand in front of his nose. He then looked back over at Deborah. "And you tried to play it off like you didn't smell it, just so you wouldn't have to change him. Nuh-uh." Lynox shook his head. He put the key in the ignition and started the car. "You're the one taking him back inside to change, while I sit here and air out the car."

Deborah took note of the windows. They were still open a crack. *Jesus*, she said to herself. She'd forgotten all about rolling them back up. Now Lynox was probably going to ask her why she rolled the windows down, and she'd end up having to tell him the truth, anyway. She couldn't win for losing today. But to her relief, Lynox hit the buttons to roll the windows all the way down without even noticing they were already open a bit.

On the bright side, at least it hadn't started raining while they were in church or anything. Because God knows, when it rained, it poured, or at least that was how it seemed to be in Deborah's life.

"Go on. Get funky man on out of here," Lynox told her.

"The baby let a stink." Tyson laughed, then pinched his nose closed with his index finger and thumb.

Deborah had no qualms at all about taking the baby back inside the church and changing him. She needed to get out of that car before she hyperventilated, anyway. There had been way too many close calls today.

A few minutes later, Deborah found herself changing her son's diaper in the exact same bathroom she'd considered smoking in earlier. All she'd wanted to do was smoke a little bud to calm her nerves after a rough morning so that she could relax during church service. It would have been too much like right for that to have gone down smoothly. Deborah was now more on edge than she'd been before she blazed up. It didn't seem worth it. Anything God was in had a peace about it. Well, trying to smoke weed had been anything but a peaceful experience.

"You know what, little guy?" Deborah said to her son as she changed his dirty, stinky diaper. "The grass may be greener . . . literally, but it's still the same ole—"

Before she could utter the expletive that was about to come out of her mouth, the baby let out the last poop.

"Yep. That's exactly what I was about to say," Deborah said.

Deborah got the baby changed and then went back out to the car. She placed Tatum back in his car seat and climbed in, and Lynox drove them home. As soon as Deborah got home, she asked Lynox to get the boys out of their church clothes and into some lounging clothes. Meanwhile, she went into her bedroom. She took the Baggie out of her purse and then walked into her closet. She stood on a stool and reached up and pulled down her Coach duffel bag. She opened it and pulled out two big bags of weed. She got down off the stool, then peeked her head out of the closet. Seeing that the coast was clear, she ran into the bathroom and closed the door behind her. One by one, she emptied the bags of weed into the toilet and then tossed in the one and a half rolled joints she had in the Baggie.

She had honestly thought that marijuana was the answer to her prayers. She had to admit that it did mellow her out. If she hadn't had to be so secretive about it, and if it were more accepted by society as a medical drug, then she probably would have continued using it. And who knew? It might have been beneficial for her. That wasn't the case, though. She felt so hopeless as she watched the weed swirl around in the toilet bowl. She closed the lid before she could see it go all the way down. That had to be about two hun-

dred dollars' worth of the stuff. She couldn't bear
to witness flushing what was essentially money
down the toilet. Sure, she probably could have
given it or sold it to Klarke, Persia, or somebody
else, but she knew the longer she held on to it,
the more she was apt to keep using it, simply for
recreational purposes.

"Oh, well," Deborah said, throwing her arms
up in the air and letting them fall to her sides
as she stood looking at herself in the bathroom
mirror. "I tried a therapist. I tried pills and
weed." She shrugged her shoulders, feeling like
it was time to give up and just live with the fact
that her brain functioned at a level that made it
hard sometimes for her to keep up with it.

Before exiting the bathroom, she gave the
toilet one last flush for good measure. She
then drew an invisible cross on her chest with
her index finger. "So long, Mary Jane. You was
my homegirl there for a minute. May you rest
in peace."

Chapter 14

"The girls told me to tell you hey," Klarke said as she and Deborah drove toward Marcus Theatre to catch a movie. "They really miss you."

"I miss them too," Deborah said.

"You know, just because you don't want to, you know"—Klarke used her hands to mime smoking a joint—"doesn't mean you can't come hang out with us sometime."

"Okay. Well, maybe I'll take you up on that offer," Deborah said, knowing she had no intention at all of doing so. That would be like being on a fast and meeting them at a buffet.

"When you first stopped accepting my invitation to hang out, I thought that maybe it was, you know, the whole thing about me going to jail."

"Oh, heavens, no," Deborah said.

"I mean, finding out that I'd been incarcerated for murder was one thing, but being incarcerated for murdering a child was a whole other thing."

"But you explained to me what happened," Deborah said. "It wasn't you who killed Reo and Meka's first baby. It was that evil baby mama of his, Meka herself." Deborah shook her head. "I can't believe she let you go to jail for it."

"While she ran off with the love of my life and got pregnant with another kid." Klarke fell silent for a moment. "I know we shouldn't question God, but I don't get it. There are women who would give their sight to know what it feels like to give birth, to hold and smell a child of their own. This woman kills her baby and then, just like that"—Klarke snapped her fingers—"she gets another one."

"I know what you're saying," Deborah said.

"And you know what really pisses me off whenever I think about it?" Klarke said. She didn't wait for Deborah to answer. "Not only did that witch let me go to jail for a crime I didn't commit, but she let my baby girl go to jail too."

"What?" Deborah said, totally surprised. "I guess I *am* going to have to Google you," she joked, "because this is all news to me."

"Save yourself the time and just read the book," Klarke said.

"Wait a minute." She held her hand up. "A book has been written about this?"

Klarke nodded. "Uh-huh. Reo wrote it."

"But I've read all of Reo's books, and I've never read a book about you guys' life story."

Klarke bit her bottom lip, as if she was debating whether or not to continue. This was a secret that no one knew outside of the Laroques and Reo's publisher.

"What?" Deborah said. "Girl, don't stop now. Don't leave me hanging. You know how anxious I get. You gon' have me smoking again."

Klarke laughed. "Okay, okay," she said. "Reo did write a book about our lives, but he wrote it under a pseudonym. It's called *The Root of All Evil*. He wrote it under the name Joylynn M. Jossel."

Deborah thought for a minute. Her eyes then lit up. "Wait a minute. You talking about that book that famous producer turned into a movie?" she asked excitedly.

Klarke had a mischievous grin on her face. "That's the one."

"Oh, my God!" Deborah put her hand on her chest. "That movie was so frickin' good. I went right out and bought the book. It was even better than the movie. I tried to research the author. All I could find was the Web site and a Facebook fan page, with more posts from fans than from the actual author. I couldn't find author tour dates or anything."

Klarke turned to Deborah and winked, then put her eyes back on the road.

"Oh, wow," Deborah said. "Guess that explains it."

Klarke smiled and nodded.

"Can you imagine how many more copies of that book would sell if readers knew that the author was none other than Reo Laroque?"

"I know. I know," Klarke agreed. "That's the same thing his publisher told him, especially when J. K. Rowling did the same thing with that book she put out under another name."

"I remember that. When the book first dropped, nobody was really buying it," Deborah said. "Her publisher had given her a nice-size advance and had put marketing dollars behind it, which they weren't making back. They didn't see themselves recouping unless they revealed the author's true identity."

"And when they did," Klarke said, picking up the story," that book shot to number one on Amazon within minutes."

"And that's exactly what would happen for you guys," Deborah mused.

"The movie pushed up the sale of the book very well. And, of course, it recently came out on DVD. It can be ordered on pay movie channels, and a deal with Netflix was just negotiated.

Plus, whenever they run an advertisement for the movie, book sales go up again. When Reo initially wrote the book, he said it wasn't all about money, but about getting our story out."

"But it was written like it is fiction," Deborah said.

"Reo figured the public would be more apt to purchase it if they thought it was fiction, versus a book based on the life of someone who wasn't like a movie star or something. Granted, in the book world my hubby is a pretty popular guy."

"Tell me about it," Deborah agreed. "He's won more NAACP awards for best fiction than I can count."

"But a popular author doesn't compare to a famous music artist or actor."

"Yeah, I know," Deborah said with a sigh. "In my make-believe world, books have as big of an influence on society as music does." Deborah shifted the conversation back to their initial subject matter. "There's a part in the book I was wondering about."

Klarke nodded, a signal for Deborah to go ahead.

"If I'm not mistaken, didn't I hear you mention a few months back that Jeva is still one of your good friends?" Deborah asked Klarke.

"Uh-huh," Klarke confirmed.

"But in the story it says that her daughter's father was a man she'd had a one-night stand with in a strip club when she used to strip. Later it was learned that the man was, in fact, your husband at the time, Harris, who is now your ex-husband."

Klarke nodded.

"Was that part true or something you guys added for drama, to beef up the story line?"

"No, it's true," Klarke said without hesitation.

"And you're still friends with her to this day?" Deborah said with a strained tone.

"Yep." Klarke nodded again.

"If you can forgive ole girl for all that, then I guess my beef with Helen is plain stupid," Deborah said.

"Helen?" Klarke questioned. "Who is Helen?"

"Girl, never mind," Deborah said, shooing her hand. "I'd have to write a book about that one for you to read."

Klarke laughed.

Deborah stared at her for a minute.

"What?" Klarke asked, feeling Deborah's eyes staring at her.

"You have to be one of the strongest women I've ever met," Deborah said.

Klarke smiled humbly. "It was all Him." She pointed upward. "We can do all things through

That was true. Lynox recorded every reality television show that aired. He'd watch them all, then figure out a way to incorporate the story lines into his books, putting his own signature twist on them, of course.

Being a connoisseur of the written word herself, Deborah knew that if an author had a great idea, then there were thousands of other writers across the map with that very same idea. It was a matter of how each author told the story. No idea was new. There was nothing new under the sun taking place in books, songs, and movies. The artist just had to craft it in such a way that the consumer didn't feel as though it was the same old story, different writer.

Deborah thought those reality TV shows were scripted or just ignorant. Lynox insisted that with everyone addicted to one reality show or another, right down to Christians and their preacher shows, preacher's daughters shows, gospel artist shows, and what have you, there was something in them that resonated with people in society, and he wanted to capture it in his books. With everything he penned hitting the *New York Times* best sellers' list, he was doing something right.

"All right. We can watch it." Deborah gave in.

Christ Jesus, who strengthens us. That's what Vaughn tells me all the time. Hey, I might not have been raised in the church or had a praying grandmother, but I have a praying daughter."

"I know that's right," Deborah said. "As long as somebody is praying for you, you can't go wrong."

"Amen," Klarke said. "Prayer has surely helped me."

"There are times when I've felt that nothing could be worse than what I'm dealing with, and then I hear your testimony. Umph, umph, umph."

"I hear you, girl. Somebody talks about us, steps on our toe, and we ready to lose our mind. Cussing people out, throwing wineglasses at folks. Then you look at all Jesus went through, and that man never said a mumbling word."

"Don't even remind me," Deborah said. "The smallest things set me off, and I lose my mind. I have even put my hands on a person or two."

"You preaching to the choir," Klarke said. "When I found out my ex-husband had fathered a baby with another woman, I went to that broad's house and mopped the floor with her. Now that's when a sista should have gone to jail. I wasn't even in my right mind when that happened. Talk about snapping. That was not a good time in my life at all."

"I know he's the father of your children, but that Harris was a low-down cheating dog all the way around, wasn't he?"

"Girl, sleeping with folks right up under my nose and having babies with them. These men are something else."

Something Klarke had just said triggered a thought in Deborah's mind. "Not all men, though, right?" She let out a nervous chuckle. All men would include her own man, and Klarke's too, for that matter. "Reo's a good guy. You haven't had to deal with any type of cheating in your marriage, have you?"

Klarke paused. "I'm not one to ever put my husband's and my business out there, but I can say that our marriage has been tested with infidelity."

Deborah was truly shocked to hear that. "Oh, my goodness. I can't see Reo as the cheating kind."

Klarke stopped at a red light, turned to Deborah, and asked, "Who said anything about Reo being the cheat?" With that, Klarke turned back, waited for the light to turn green, then pulled off.

For the past couple of days, ever since Klarke had alluded to having stepped out on Reo,

Deborah's mind had been blown a[...] were so many questions she had wa[...] Klarke, but clearly, if Klarke had wante[...] orate on something, she would have. [...] she had pulled into the movie theater [...] lot, and they had enjoyed the movie.

Afterward, Deborah hadn't broache[...] subject again. She didn't want to be the [...] of friend who pried and asked questions. [...] she had to admit that her opinion of Klar[...] had changed greatly. This was why she really[...] needed the facts about the situation. Had Klarke cheated on Reo years ago, early on in their marriage? Had Klarke cheated on him as payback perhaps for not believing in her before she went to jail and for getting back with Meka? Not that Deborah ever condoned cheating, but an explanation might give her a different opinion about the situation.

"Ready to watch some *Love & Hip Hop*[...] Lynox asked as he exited their bathroom a[...] walked over to the bed, upon which Deborah [...] already lying, racking her brain about Klark[...]

"Do we really have to tonight?" Del[...] whined. She had her own reality show g[...] in her head.

"Come on. You know I get some of [...] stuff for my books from ratchet te'[...] Lynox climbed in bed and grabbed th[...]

Lynox already had the television on and was viewing the list of recorded shows before Deborah even replied.

Not even three minutes into the show, Deborah was shaking her head. "I don't understand how he managed to have two women and neither one of them knew about the other."

"Oh, they knew. Women don't care. They turn a blind eye just to say they have a man or was bad enough to steal somebody else's man." Lynox laughed.

Deborah turned toward him, irritated that he thought women being played for fools was funny. She instantly got an attitude. "Well, I hope you don't ever think I'll let you get away with that kind of crap."

"Oh, girl, stop." Lynox laughed again. "You wouldn't do nothing, just like these women ain't doing nothing." He pointed to the television. "You know you love me, girl."

"I do, but I love myself enough not to be sharing no man when I know there is one out there who will want only me. One I'll be enough for."

"You are more than enough woman for any man," Lynox said, "but it's not about that. Men don't cheat because their woman isn't enough. They sometimes cheat because she's too much."

"And just what does that mean?"

Lynox was trying to have a conversation with his wife at the same time that he watched television. "It's just that, you know, today's woman is so independent. It's not her fault. Men have failed women to the point that roles get reversed. If the woman isn't paying half the mortgage and the bills, she's paying the majority of them. Some men sell women a dream, but then they break the promise and leave them alone . . . with two or three kids to take care of. They have no choice but to be the head of the family and the head of the home. So when a good man who knows his role comes along, there are two things going on," Lynox said.

By now he had paused the television, realizing he'd opened a can of worms that Deborah wasn't going to let him worm his way out of.

"Go on," Deborah urged, as if waiting for him to scratch his throat with his toenail, now that he had ended up with his foot in his mouth.

"That woman is going to be so used to taking care of everything that it's not going to matter when a man comes along and isn't the provider he's supposed to be. Another thing that can happen is that that woman does have a man who is helping out, and she's so happy to have him that she'll take more crap than a little bit. That woman who feels that she doesn't need a man

can't make a man feel needed. Then someone
else comes along who makes him feel needed.
It's not about what she looks like, but what she
makes him feel like." He raised his hand up to
the paused television. "And there you have it.
That's life." He hit the PLAY button.

"That's BS," Deborah said, then turned her
attention to the television.

For the next ten minutes Deborah and Lynox
watched as one of the male reality stars got the
two women he was seeing at the same time to
meet up and talk.

"He is the man," Lynox said, as if he was
cheering the guy on.

Deborah turned and looked at Lynox, who was
grinning from ear to ear. She couldn't believe
her husband was cheering on this man for his
shenanigans. In her eyes, that meant that he was
condoning his behavior. Or maybe even Lynox
was living vicariously through this man, wishing
this was something he himself could engage in.

"That's what they get. They ain't nothing but
some gold diggers, anyway," Lynox said, talking
to the television.

Even though she knew it was only a show and
even though it was labeled reality, there was a
lot of acting going on in front of that camera.
Deborah couldn't believe some of the beliefs

Lynox was expressing. Did he really think it was ever okay for a man to treat women the way the man on the television was treating women? The more Lynox laughed and chuckled, the more the water in her mental pot began to boil.

"I can't even believe you condone that type of behavior from a man," Deborah finally said. "If you feel what he's doing is okay, then who is to say you won't turn around and treat me like that?"

"I'm not condoning it," Lynox said. "But you heard the guy. He's in love with two different women. It happens."

"It happens?" Deborah was in shock now. "You can't be in love with two women. When you love someone, you don't do something that you know will hurt them. Him starting up a relationship with another woman while he's already in a relationship with one is not love. You are defending this jerk, which makes me wonder."

"Wonder what?" Lynox asked.

"For one, I wonder why you know so much about why a man cheats, and for two, I wonder how you can be okay with something like that." Deborah was fit to be tied.

"I'm not saying that I would ever do it. I'm just saying I can understand why some men do."

Lynox was speaking his mind, but he did not realize that he was about to make Deborah lose hers.

"I honestly had no idea this is what you thought about infidelity. Talk about unequally yoked." Deborah rolled her eyes and turned her attention back to the television.

Lynox paused it once again and then placed the remote on the bed, between himself and Deborah. "This is stupid. We are the ones arguing, and this doesn't even have anything to do with us."

"It has everything to do with us when you are rooting for him and cheering him on, blaming the women and calling them gold diggers. I'm an independent woman in the sense that I do my own thing. I don't clock in for anybody. I started my own business, and I'm my own boss. Is that too much for you? Does that intimidate you? Make you feel less needed?"

"I don't even want to watch it if it's going to cause us to argue." Lynox went for the remote, but Deborah quickly grabbed it so that he couldn't turn the television off. "Then you can watch it by yourself. I'm not doing this." Lynox pulled the covers over himself as he simultaneously turned away from Deborah.

Before he knew it, Deborah threw the remote at the sixty-inch flat-screen television, which was mounted to the wall, cracking it.

"What the . . . ?" Lynox said, quickly sitting up in bed. His eyes traveled in the direction of the cracked television. "What the heck is wrong with you, woman? I know you have lost your mind now. Look what you've done to our television." Lynox wasn't furious as much as he was shocked.

Deborah looked at the television, shocked herself that she'd snapped that quickly. She hadn't taken the consequences of her actions into consideration before acting.

Lynox snatched the covers off of himself and walked over to the television to take a closer look. Realizing that there was nothing that could be done with the now fizzled-out screen, which emitted only sound, he looked to Deborah. "You really wanted to throw that at me, didn't you?"

Deborah put her head down.

He walked over to Deborah's side of the bed as he spoke. "I'm not going to put up with this, Deborah. All of this because I didn't want to finish talking about that nonsense of a show? Something that ridiculous set you off? That scares me."

"Well, you had plenty to say at first, when you were talking about that cheating bastard. I was watching you watch television as if you wished you were that man. That's what scares me."

"Well, do you want to hear something really scary?" Lynox said, not waiting for Deborah to reply before continuing. "If things get to the point where I feel like the next time it's my head and not that television, I'm not sticking around. And just know one thing. If I go, my boys go with me."

Hearing that—hearing Lynox say that he would take her boys away—hit a nerve with Deborah. She jumped up out of that bed like a cat and landed square on her feet in front of Lynox. "Nigga, I wish you would!" Deborah snapped.

Lynox was appalled. He did not care for the use of the *N* word in any shape, form, or fashion. *Nigga, nigger*, and *Negro* were all ugly words in his book, even though he usually let her slide with the word *Negro*. He would never use those words around his sons or ever allow them to use them. And he dang sure wasn't going to stand there and allow his wife to call him one.

"What did you call me?" Lynox had heard his wife very clearly. He wanted to give her a moment to think about what she'd just said and take it back, right before she vowed never to use that degrading word in their home again.

"You heard what I said, *nigga*," Deborah said, not backing down one bit. He'd expressed to her many times that he didn't care for that word, no matter the color of the person who was saying it. This time Deborah put so much stank on the word, it was like she'd taken her nails and scratched them down Lynox's bare chest as hard and as deep as she could.

"Wow. And you call yourself a Christian."

"Oh, honey, if I wasn't, you best believe I'd be calling you something far worse than the *N* word, what with you talking crazy, saying some you gon' take my boys from me." Deborah rolled her eyes.

"Oh, I guess you've watched so much ratchet reality television that you're acting like these women." He flung his hand back toward the broken television. "I guess next you gon' start clapping your hands to each and every syllable that you pronounce. You already calling me out of my name, so I guess next you'll be calling our sons out of their names too."

"I'm warning you, Lynox. You better stop bringing my boys into this."

"*Our* boys," Lynox retorted, correcting her. "And whenever it comes to the safety, well-being, and peace of mind of my boys, I will not bite my tongue."

"You know darn well I'm a good mother, so don't even go there. I wish you would try to take them from me. No judge in his right mind would give you custody. You're always somewhere writing or away touring. At least when you were always writing, you'd be here at home. Now you're not even home, for the most part, when you're writing." Deborah was referring to the fact that Lynox had been spending a great deal of time working with Reo. "I'm the one at the PTO meetings, the parent-teacher conferences, the doctor's appointments. I'm the one doing homework and everything else."

Lynox typically didn't engage in all this tit for tat with Deborah. Actually, for the better part of their relationship, they had never really argued. But in the past few months, that was all Deborah seemed to want to do. Now it was to the point where she was forcing Lynox to act out of character and respond to her.

"Yeah, but I'm the one who makes enough money so that you can stay home and do all those things," Lynox retorted.

"Stay home and do all those things?" Deborah repeated, the very words leaving a bad taste in her mouth. "I don't just stay home. I work too. Yeah, you might pay for the mortgage and all the bills, but you would be doing that whether I was here or not. But as far as you taking care of me and paying my personal bills . . ." Deborah shook her head. "I don't think so. I pay my own car note. I get my own hair done, nails—"

"As you should," Lynox snapped back. "It's your car, it's your hair, and they're your nails. Why do black women think a man has to do all that for them?"

"Oh, so let me guess. Now I'm a gold digger, like the women on television? All black women just gold diggers with attitudes. Well, need I remind you that you are married to a black woman? But I guess you want you a white woman, then. Or one of them light-skin girls, like Klarke." Deborah thought for a minute. "I bet she's why you like being up over at Reo's so much. Writing this book with him is an excuse."

"Now you're really talking crazy," Lynox said, letting a chuckle come out under his breath. "Why would I be over in that man's face, trying to get at his wife?"

"As far as I know, they might be into that type of thing," Deborah said. "Wasn't one of his little freaky-deaky books about a couple who did that type of thing?"

"That was just a book."

"Yeah, but Mr. Reo has a thing about hiding his and his wife's life behind the written word."

Deborah thought for a minute. "You know what they say. Writers always write about what they know. Wouldn't surprise me if the three of you were over there getting it on." Deborah didn't actually feel that way. Yes, Klarke had alluded to the fact that she might have cheated on her husband, but Deborah didn't honestly believe they were all over there making out.

"You disgust me right now," Lynox said through his teeth. "I swear to God on everything, I really do just want to go get my sons and get out of here. Give you time to get your head together, because I'm really starting to believe that you are a nut job."

"Threaten me about taking my kids one more time." Deborah was enraged, partly because her husband had called her a nut job, but anything about her children superseded that.

"It's not a threat. If you don't get it together, you are going to wake up one morning and find me and my sons gone."

"Ha. Tyson ain't even your son, so I'd call the police and charge you with kidnapping so quickly . . ."

Lynox had stopped hearing Deborah after she professed that Tyson was not his son. She had said some cruel things tonight, had even called him out of his name, but that right there had taken the cake. She might as well have snatched his heart out of his chest, thrown it on the ground, and stomped all over it. He was frozen, with hurt etched all over his face.

The look that showed on her husband's face was one Deborah had never seen before. A pain streaked throughout her being. If only she could reach out and take her words back. But they were long gone, embedded in Lynox's heart, his mind, forever.

Lynox gritted his teeth together and began shaking his head. His look of hurt and pain quickly resolved into one of anger. "Tyson's not my son, huh? Well, I guess if I told the judge about how children's services got called on you before and how you denied even having a son for the sake of getting a man, perhaps he might end up not being your son, either. And that reminded me of something. I was at the peak of my career when we got back together. The fact that you went as far as even denying having a child, because you knew that was a deal breaker for me, just might make you a gold digger."

At that point, not only was Deborah glad she'd struck Lynox in the heart with her previous comment, but she also wished she had more daggers to throw at him. Since she didn't, she resorted to throwing her fist. Like a windmill, she began swinging on Lynox. "Muthasucka, don't you eva, you son of a witch." She cussed at him and hit him. Cussed at him and hit him. "I wish the eff you would, you witch-butt nigga!"

Lynox tried his best to grab her arms, but she had the strength of a madman at this point. She'd clocked him so hard on the ear that he liked to think his eardrum had busted. She was definitely getting the best of him, but that was only because his mother had raised him better, had told him never to put his hands on a woman. Like he'd told himself before, before he put his hands on his wife, he'd leave her first, and that was what he was going to do if he could get her to stop hitting him and scratching him up.

But her fists were continuously coming at his face, and she was landing some pretty good blows. After so many blows and so much name-calling, Lynox couldn't take it anymore. He turned his head and pushed her, hoping she'd land on the bed, but when he heard a thump and the cussing stopped, so did his heartbeat. Without even looking, in that split second, he knew something was wrong. He turned to see Deborah lying near one of the night tables, her head leaning up against it.

"Deborah, Deb, honey," he said, racing over to where she lay. Deborah was nonresponsive.

"Deb?" Lynox lifted her head, and that was when he felt the moisture on his hand. He pulled his hand from behind her head and noticed it was covered in blood. He then looked at the edge of the night table and saw a streak of blood on the front corner, which was where her head had slid down. "Jesus." It was a low call to his Lord and Savior at first, and then it was a loud cry. "Jesus! Deborah, what have you done? Look what you made me—"

"Mommy, Daddy." There was knock on the door, and Tyson's voice could be heard calling out on the other side. "Mommy, Daddy. I'm scared." Terror was in the little fella's voice.

As badly as Lynox wanted to comfort him, he couldn't let the child bear witness to the scene in the bedroom.

"Tyson, son, go back to bed. Wait there until Daddy comes and gets you. It's okay."

"But I heard Mommy. She screamed. I'm scared. I want Mommy. Did you hurt her again?" Tyson began to cry.

Lynox tucked his lips in and thought. "Tyson, please. Everything is okay. Go back to your room, and Daddy will be in to talk to you in a minute."

"I want my mommy. I want to see Mommy." He began to cry even harder.

"Tyson, son, okay. Just wait a minute. Go to your room and wait."

"But I want—"

"Tyson!" Lynox's voice was so thunderous, it echoed off the walls.

This only made Tyson cry even louder. Then the baby's cries filled the room through the baby monitor.

"God, help us," Lynox said, his eyes filling with tears as well. His family was hurting right now, and he felt so helpless. He didn't know what to do. But there was one thing he had to do, and that was to call for help for Deborah.

Lynox went and grabbed his cell phone from off the dresser. He dialed 911. Once the operator answered, he spoke into the phone. "Yes, we need an ambulance. My wife was hitting me. I pushed her and . . . she's bleeding. Please help." Lynox gave the operator their address, since he'd called from his cell phone and the address hadn't automatically popped up in the system. After that, the operator asked him a series of questions while she dispatched help to their house.

"Is your wife breathing?" the operator asked Lynox.

He walked back over to Deborah and put his hand on her chest. He could feel her heart beating. "Her heart is beating."

"Check her pulse."

Following instructions, Lynox took Deborah's flimsy wrist and held it between his index finger and his thumb as he took her pulse. "Yes, I feel it."

"Now put your ear to her nose."

Lynox did so. A tiny wind hit his ear. "Yes, yes. Thank you, Jesus. She's breathing. She's breathing."

By now Tyson had stopped wailing so loudly, but Lynox still could hear his tiny whimpers through the door. The baby must have cried himself back to sleep, because his wails were no longer blaring through the monitor.

"Good. That's good," the operator said.

The operator kept Lynox on the phone, instructing him not to move Deborah, in case she had some type of spinal injury. Since Deborah seemed to be as stable as possible for the moment, the operator decided to throw in some questions for Lynox.

"What happened to your wife again?" the operator asked. "You said you pushed her?"

"Yes. We were fighting. Well, she was fighting me," Lynox said. "I pushed her. I didn't mean to hurt her." As strong as Lynox had tried to be thus far in speaking with the operator, he now broke down in tears.

"Sir, the medics are at your door," the operator told him.

Lynox heard the doorbell ring. "I hear them. They're here."

"Okay. We can end the call, and they will take care of your wife."

"Thank you. Thank you so much." Lynox was more than grateful to the operator for helping to make sure Deborah was stabilized and for sending help. He ended the call and walked over to the bedroom door. He turned and looked at Deborah. "I'll be right back, baby. You're going to be okay." Lynox opened their bedroom door and darted right down the steps, not even paying attention to small Tyson, who was sitting against the wall next to the door.

Lynox was going down the steps so fast, he missed one and fell. He managed to grab on to the handrail to stop his fall, but not until he'd slid down about four steps. He pulled himself up and then ran to the front door.

"She's upstairs," he said immediately upon opening the door to the medics. He turned and ran up the steps he'd just fallen down. Halfway up the steps, he heard a piercing screech. "Tyson!" The blood drained from his body as he imagined the fear Tyson must be feeling from seeing his mother lying on the floor in a pool of blood. The last thing Lynox had wanted for him was to see his mother like that.

"Mommy, my mommy," Tyson cried out when Lynox entered the room, followed by the two medics.

By this time, two officers in separate patrol cars had arrived on the scene. One of them rapped on the door while simultaneously entering the house. Upon hearing the commotion going on upstairs, and especially Tyson's screaming, they drew their guns and scaled the steps. They couldn't take any chances with a domestic violence call. When they entered the master bedroom, Lynox was trying to pry Tyson off of his mother.

"Mommy." Tyson had blood on his hands and a death grip on his mother.

"Come on, Tyson. Help is here to take care of Mommy," Lynox said. "She's going to be okay."

"No. Get off of me," Tyson cried. "You hurt my mommy again. You hurt my mommy."

"Sir, step away from the boy," one of the officers said upon hearing Tyson's words. He tucked his gun back in his holster, but the other officer kept his drawn.

"I need to take care of my son!" Lynox exclaimed.

"Sir, move now," ordered the officer with his gun drawn.

Lynox looked over and noticed the gun for the first time. The man in him—the husband and the father—just wanted to protect his son, his wife, his family. But that black man in him knew better than to do anything but what the officers had requested. There wasn't anybody videotaping this event, which might provide a modicum of safety, but then Lynox considered the fact that even when there was proof positive of police misconduct in incidents involving a black man and law enforcement, the officers still got away with unjustifiable shootings and/ or injuries. With that thought, Lynox did what he would teach both his African American sons to do, and that was to obey the police regardless. Human survival was based on human behavior. Not only did Lynox want to survive this ordeal, but he wanted Deborah to survive it too. And he could see that his little situation with the officers was distracting the medics, so he released Tyson, put his hands up, and then backed up.

The officer who had put his gun away immediately snatched up Lynox and put him in handcuffs. This only made poor Tyson even more hysterical.

"Come on, son. Let us help your mommy," the female EMT said to Tyson. "You want us to help your mommy wake up, right?" She spoke in as tender a voice as she could muster.

Tyson nodded and wiped his tears as his shoulders heaved and he tried to catch his breath.

"Okay, then I'm going to need you to go with the nice officer while we help your mommy." She nodded at the second officer.

Tyson's eyes followed the direction of her head nod. "Nooo," he said. "I saw on TV the police shoot black boys like me. He's going to shoot me." Tyson cried harder.

"No, baby." The EMT shook her head. "That was the police officer on TV. This isn't that police officer. See? Look at him." She once again nodded at the officer.

Once again Tyson's eyes went back to the officer. He examined the police officer. Just as some white people might think all black people looked alike, for little Tyson, all police looked alike, and he wasn't having it. He adamantly shook his head.

"Hello? Is everyone fine in here?"

A voice could be heard calling out from downstairs.

"That's Mr. Charles," Tyson said. "My best friend's daddy number one."

The second officer looked at Lynox for confirmation.

"Sounds like our neighbor," Lynox confirmed.

"I'll go talk to him," the second officer said, while the first officer had Lynox off to the side in handcuffs.

The male EMT had managed to work on Deborah this entire time, while the female EMT had engaged Tyson in a conversation that had distracted him from his mother.

"Ugh." The sound of Deborah moaning caught the attention of everybody in the room.

"Deborah!" Lynox shouted out.

"Mommy!" Tyson cried.

"See, baby? I told you your mommy was going to be all right," the female EMT said to Tyson.

The second officer came back up the steps and into the room. Charles was with him.

"Sir, is this your neighbor?" the second officer asked Lynox.

Lynox looked over at Charles, who had a look of shock on his face as he examined the scene before him. Deborah was on the floor, in a pool of blood; Tyson was crying over her, with blood on his hands; and Lynox was in handcuffs. So many scenarios ran through his mind, but right now, Charles's concern was for the young boy, who shouldn't have been witnessing any of this.

Lynox confirmed that Charles was, in fact, his neighbor.

"Tyson, son, come with me," Charles said. "I'll clean him up and then take him next door."

"Whoa. Hold up," the first officer said, raising his hand to stop Charles from moving toward Tyson.

"It's okay. Let him go with him," Lynox said. "I don't want my boy seeing this."

"Is this gentleman family?" the first officer asked.

"No, but—" Lynox began before the officer cut him off.

"We can't turn him over to anyone who isn't family. We'll have to call children's services."

"What? Are you kidding?" Lynox snapped. "Can my sons at least go with our neighbor until we call a family member to come pick them up?"

"There's more children in the house?" the first offi-cer asked.

"They have an infant son," Charles interjected. "Tyson comes to our house all the time and plays with my son. It's okay. They know us and trust us." He looked at Lynox for confirmation.

"Yes. That's right," Lynox confirmed.

"Sorry. We can only release them to family." The first officer was adamant about following regulations.

Lynox felt the officer was being a prick. But he was not about to jump bad with the officer, considering this officer might be the one in charge of driving him to the precinct if he were

to be arrested. No way did he want this officer to Freddie Gray him, God rest that young
black man's soul. So Lynox was going to be as
cooperative as possible.

"Can we at least call my mother-in-law to
come pick them up?" Lynox asked.

"She better get here soon," the officer said. He
nodded at Deborah. "Looks like she's going to
the hospital and you're going to jail."

The thought of going to jail horrified Lynox.
He wanted to defend himself and explain why
he should not go to jail. But right now making
sure his boys were safe and sound was his main
priority. Making sure his wife was okay would be
his next.

"Charles, can you please call Deborah's
mother?" Lynox asked.

Charles whipped his phone out of his pocket.
Lynox rattled off her phone number as his
neighbor dialed.

"Tell her to get here as soon as she can," Lynox
ordered. "Tell her you'll explain everything when
she gets here."

Charles stood there with the phone to his ear.
After the second ring, Deborah's mother picked
up. "Hello? Yes, this is Charles, your daughter's
neighbor." He stepped out into the hall to finish
the conversation out of Tyson's earshot. The boy
had already heard and witnessed too much.

"How is she? How is my wife?" Now Lynox could concern himself with Deborah's well-being.

"She's been able to tell us her name, the date, and everything," the female EMT replied.

"Deborah's mother is on her way," Charles said, reentering the room and tucking his phone away.

Just then the baby could be heard crying through the monitor.

"Can I at least take Tyson with me to go check on the baby?" Charles asked the officer who seemed to be running the show. "We won't leave the house." Charles, too, wanted to be as cooperative with the officers as he could. Even though he wasn't black and his chances of suffering police brutality were slimmer, he knew that a white man could get it too. Not too long ago he'd watched a video on the news of a white officer body slamming a white male he had in custody. The white male had died as a result.

"Yes," the first officer replied, then nodded at the door.

"Come on, Tyson. Let's go check on your brother," Charles said, opening his arms for Tyson to come with him.

"But my mommy," Tyson whined, grabbing hold of Deborah's hand and looking at her.

"It's okay, Ty," Deborah groaned. "Mommy needs you to help her take care of your baby brother right now. Can you please go with Mr. Charles?"

Tyson thought about his mother's request, then nodded his head while he wiped his eyes.

"Good boy." Deborah smiled and gave Tyson's hand a squeeze.

Tyson stood up and walked over to his best friend's dad. He took Mr. Charles's hand and was escorted out of the room, but not before he gave Lynox a glare.

Lynox's eyes filled with tears. He hated that Tyson thought he'd hurt his mother intentionally. How would he ever get the boy to understand otherwise?

The second officer bent over Deborah and asked, "What's your full name?"

"Deborah Chase," she replied, still somewhat groggy.

"Who is this man to you?" The officer pointed at Lynox.

"My husband," she replied.

"Mrs. Chase, can you tell us what happened? How did you get hurt?"

"My head," Deborah said, reaching for her head.

The male medic pulled her hand back down as the female medic was cleaning and examining her head.

"I hit my head on the nightstand," Deborah added.

"Did you fall?" the second officer asked. "Were you pushed?"

Deborah looked over at Lynox. Lynox couldn't tell what the look Deborah was giving him meant. She still seemed a little out of it to him.

The first officer, the one who had Lynox in cuffs, spoke. "Ma'am, did this man push you into the night table?" The tone in which the officer spoke conveyed that he was hoping, wishing, and praying that Deborah would answer in the affirmative.

Lynox felt that the officer wanted Deborah to give him a reason to manhandle Lynox and throw him in the back of a police vehicle.

Deborah stared at Lynox for a few more seconds before she cast her eyes downward and replied, "Yes," while simultaneously nodding her head. "He pushed me."

Chapter 15

Lynox didn't know what to think as he sat in the back of the police car. The first officer had cared nothing about what Deborah said after accusing him of pushing her and hurting her. Immediately after her statement, Deborah had begun yelling that it was all an accident, but he hadn't tried to hear her one bit.

"Can't you hear what she's telling you?" Lynox had asked the officer as he pushed him down the steps. "She's trying to tell you that it was an accident, which it was. I did not hurt my wife, not on purpose, anyway. This is all a big mistake."

The officer had said nothing. He had heard that same old song and dance a thousand times. He had simply escorted Lynox to his squad car and thrown him in the back.

Lynox now sat there feeling as though he was in a nightmare. His only encounter with the law had been the time he was in a car accident. Even then it hadn't been a moving violation. As a matter of fact, it hadn't been his fault at all.

It was his car that had been hit. And like the last time he had any involvement with the law, Deborah had been involved. She was the one who had actually backed her car out of a parking space and into his vehicle. Now here the two of them were again, dealing with the police. Only this time it was no fender bender.

"Sir, can you please go back inside and get my wife's story?" Lynox asked the cop through the partition that separated them. "Just really listen to what she's saying, and not to what you want to hear."

The police officer completely ignored Lynox as he talked on his CB. From the few details Lynox could hear, it sounded as if the officer was running Lynox's name. Lynox wasn't worried about them finding anything on him. The only law he'd ever broken was not feeding a parking meter in a timely matter, and that had got him a parking ticket.

As Lynox sat in the police car, which was parked in his driveway, behind the ambulance, he noticed the headlights of a car pulling up in front of their house. He turned as much as he could and saw that it was his mother-in-law. "Oh, great," he said under his breath. The last thing he wanted was for her to see him hand-cuffed like some common criminal in the back of a police car.

Once Lynox saw her getting out of her vehicle, he turned and faced forward. At first, she stepped on past the police car, but then she decided to look over her shoulder and back at the car. That was when a look of shock covered her face and she grabbed her chest.

She came back and spoke to him through the rolled-up window. "Dear Lord, Lynox, what in the world is going on here?"

All Lynox could do at first was shake his head. He knew he had to answer her, though. By the time Lynox went to speak, the officer had gotten out of the vehicle and was on his way around it to address Ms. Lucas.

"Ma'am, are you the boys' grandmother?" the officer asked her.

"Well, yes, I am," she said, her eyes shifting back and forth from the officer to Lynox. "What's going on? Why do you have my son-in-law in the back of your car?" She looked at the ambulance. The next expression on her face was one of pure horror. "Deborah! Where's my baby?" She no longer gave a care about Lynox. All she wanted to know was where her daughter was. "The boys? Are they okay?" And her grandchildren.

"Ma'am, there's been an accident," the officer told her. "But the boys are fine. They're inside the house with the neighbor." The officer went to escort Ms. Lucas to the boys. As they were going inside the house, the second officer was coming out.

The second officer whispered something in his partner's ear. His partner turned and looked toward Lynox. He then passed Ms. Lucas off to the second officer, to be escorted to where the boys were. Lynox watched as the officer who had placed him in the vehicle came back in his direction.

"Can you step out of the vehicle?" the officer asked upon opening Lynox's door.

Lynox scooted over and struggled to get out of the car. When it seemed like he was unable to lift himself off the seat, the officer finally assisted him.

Without saying a word, the officer took out his flashlight and began examining Lynox's face, head, and arms. He made a mental note of the bruising that was forming on his face. Lynox had scratches on him as well. "How did you get all these bruises and scratches?" he asked Lynox. "Did your wife do this during your fight?"

Finally, Lynox thought. This jerk was actually going to give him an opportunity to tell him exactly what had happened. "Yes!" he exclaimed with a sigh. "She was hitting me, and all I was trying to do was get her off of me. I pushed her.

I didn't mean for her to fall and hit her head against the table. I was trying to defend myself from the blows. I swear to God, that's what happened. I would never intentionally hurt my wife."

The front screen door opened, and the medics walked Deborah out of the house. Her head was bandaged. Ms. Lucas came out next, with the baby in her arms, wrapped in a blanket. The neighbor followed, holding Tyson's hand. The second officer was behind him. That officer made his way around them all and over to his partner.

"Does his story match hers?" the second officer asked his partner.

His partner nodded his reply.

"My wife, how is she?" Lynox asked. "Where are they taking her?"

The officers looked at one another.

The officer who had detained Lynox spun him around and began uncuffing him. "Well, regretfully, your story checks out," he said. "It matches what your wife told my partner, that she was hitting you, and you were simply defending yourself."

"That's what I've been explaining," Lynox said. He rubbed his wrists where the cuffs once were. "Now where is my wife going?"

"Well, first, she's going to get a few stitches in her head," the first officer said to Lynox. "Then she's going to jail." He walked over to Deborah as the medics were about to put her in the back of the ambulance. "Ma'am, you are under arrest for domestic violence."

"What?" Ms. Lucas yelled out, frightening the baby. He began crying.

"Oh, my God," Deborah said under her breath, in disbelief.

The officer began reading Deborah her rights while she stood there in what was truly a surreal moment. "You have the right to remain silent—"

"Wait a minute," Lynox yelled. "I'm not pressing charges."

"You pressing charges?" Ms. Lucas shot back at Lynox. "My daughter is the one whose head is busted open." She looked at the arresting officer. "You had it right the first time. He's the one you need to be handcuffing and taking to jail."

The officer ignored both Ms. Lucas and Lynox and continued reading Deborah her rights. By now what was about to take place was clearly registering in Deborah's head: she was about to be arrested and taken to jail for putting her hands on her husband. Tears began to stream down her face.

"Do something!" Ms. Lucas shot at Lynox. "You're her husband. Protect her from these fools."

Lynox might have been between a rock and a hard place, but Ms. Lucas was like a boulder rolling down a hill and tumbling on his head. The way she was looking at him, if she didn't have that baby in her arms, there would probably be two people catching a case.

"Officer, I don't want to file charges against my wife." This time Lynox spoke to the second officer, who didn't seem to have anything against him.

"Sir, you don't have to. The state will," the second officer responded. "In the state of Ohio, when it comes to domestic violence, the victim doesn't have to press charges. The state is the plaintiff, and the victim is the state's witness," he explained. "Your wife broke the law. What your wife did to you is unacceptable. She has no more right to put her hands on you than you do on her."

Lynox knew that what the officer was saying was right, but to him it was different. Deborah, even though she had gotten the best of him upstairs in their bedroom, could never win a physical altercation with him. He'd suffered some bruises and scratches, but she could never do the physical damage to him that he could do to her. With one blow, he could have knocked her out cold. That would have kept her from windmilling him. He wasn't the type to hit a woman, not even in self-defense.

"He's a big ole man," Ms. Lucas said in her daughter's defense. "And he's still standing. She didn't hurt him, not to the point where she needs to be hauled off to jail."

"What if the next time she uses a weapon or something? Cracks him over the head with a bat? Maybe even doesn't see her son behind her when she's swinging it back and cracks his skull?" the officer said.

He did have a point, one that both Lynox and Ms. Lucas couldn't deny. But that hadn't been the case in this situation, and Ms. Lucas voiced this. Her words fell on deaf ears, though, as the officer turned his attention to Deborah.

The first officer began speaking to Deborah. "Ma'am, they are going to take you to the hospital to be treated, but then you will be taken to jail."

Deborah couldn't speak or even nod her understanding, like she had done when the officer had asked her if she understood her rights. She understood her rights, but what she didn't understand was how her life had been turned upside down because she couldn't control herself. She felt so weak right now, physically and mentally. It tore her apart even more that her children were here to witness this.

The medics put Deborah in the back of the ambulance.

"Don't you worry, baby. Mommy is right behind you," Ms. Lucas called out.

Charles, who had stood there, remaining silent, trying not to interfere in the family's domestic situation, finally spoke up. "Do you want Tyson to spend the night with us, so you can handle things?" he asked Lynox.

Lynox looked down at a very sleepy, worn-out Tyson. Too tired and drained, and all cried out. He stood there, holding his neighbor's hand, letting the grown folks take care of things.

"If you don't mind," Lynox said to Charles. Lynox looked down at Tyson. "Buddy, why don't you go help Mr. Charles pack you an overnight bag? And don't forget your book bag for school tomorrow."

"I'll make sure he and CJ get on the bus all right," Charles said. Both Tyson and his son went to the same school and rode the same bus.

"Okay, Daddy," Tyson said, rubbing his eyes. "But is Mommy going to be okay?"

"Yes, she is," Lynox answered. "I promise."

With Tyson seeming to be convinced, Charles escorted him into the house to do what Lynox had asked.

"This is crazy," Lynox said, smacking himself on the forehead. He looked at the second officer. "You have to admit that this looks crazy." He pointed to the ambulance in which Deborah had been placed. "She's no match for me. Besides, this is the first time any of our fights have ever gotten physical."

"So you two have fights on a regular basis?" The officer raised an eyebrow.

"Yes. I mean no. Well, lately things have been . . ." Lynox could hardly answer the officer because he was watching one medic get out of the back of the ambulance and close the door while the other tended to Deborah. "What hospital are you taking her to?" Lynox asked the medic, who was about to hop into the driver's seat.

"Mount Carmel East," he replied, then got into the vehicle.

"I need to move this vehicle to let them out." The first officer nodded to the ambulance, which he had parked behind. "Rob, can you finish taking his statement? Get some photos of his injuries. I'll go to the hospital and finish speaking with her."

Officer Rob agreed, and his partner got into his vehicle, backed out, then followed the ambulance.

"I'm going to see about my baby," Ms. Lucas said. "Where's Tatum's car seat?"

Lynox helped his mother-in-law get the car seat out of his car. He put it in her vehicle while she went inside and packed up the baby's diaper bag. After she drove off with the baby in tow, Lynox and Officer Rob took things inside, to the living room.

"I know this isn't easy for you," Officer Rob said as he stood in the living room, taking note of what Lynox had to say. "I know you love your wife, but abuse is never okay."

"My wife doesn't abuse me," Lynox said as he sat on the couch, wiping his hands down his face. "And I won't be taking any pictures of any injuries either. I'm fine."

The officer could see that Lynox was not going to accept the fact that even though he was bigger and stronger than his wife, that didn't mean it was okay for her to get physical with him. If they knew a man wouldn't hit them, some women felt it was safe to come at him. But what about the woman who was wrong in thinking that, and whose mate totally lost it and retaliated against her, causing her great harm or even death?

Women had to understand, just like men, that it was never okay to take an argument from the verbal realm to the physical one.

For the next fifteen minutes the officer questioned Lynox and had him write down a statement as to what had taken place that evening.

"What's going to happen to my wife?" Lynox asked the officer after he had taken Lynox's statement.

"Well, she may end up spending the night in jail. They may let her out. Depends on her criminal record."

"She doesn't have one," Lynox said.

"Well, she might get let out on her own recognizance. Depends on the judge. They all take domestic violence pretty seriously."

The words *domestic violence* made Lynox want to cringe. The fact that the world would think his wife had beat him up was embarrassing. But hadn't she?

"You can probably call downtown, or you can wait for her to call you." The officer pulled a card out of his shirt pocket. "Feel free to give me a call if you have any questions regarding the case."

"Thank you," Lynox said, taking the card.

Lynox showed the officer out. He closed the front door and then went over and sat on the couch. He had to take a minute to get his mind straight. He had no idea what lay ahead, but he knew that it wouldn't be easy and that he couldn't do it alone. So before he began inquiring into Deborah's arrest, he did what he knew he had to do in order to get through everything. He got on his knees and called on Jesus.

Chapter 16

Lynox didn't know how to feel about the fact that Deborah's one phone call hadn't gone to him, but to her mother instead. He'd always been the first person she called on if she was in need. She had never called her mother first when she got a flat tire, and that time she took a client out to lunch, realized she'd left her wallet in her other purse, and needed someone to bring her money to cover the bill, she hadn't called her mother. She'd called him. But now, at the most crucial time in her life, when she had been arrested, she hadn't called him.

Receiving a phone call from his mother-in-law the morning after the incident and getting updates on his wife from her had not been what he expected, or what he felt he deserved. From the tone of Ms. Lucas's voice when she called, he'd deduced that she felt that he didn't even deserve her phone call. Lynox wasn't sure exactly what Deborah had told her mother, but he could

tell by her sharp, short, and sassy tone that she
blamed him for the predicament her only child
was in.

"I'm sorry about all of this," Lynox had said,
trying to apologize, but Ms. Lucas had already
hung up in his ear.

He hadn't even gotten a chance to ask his
mother-in-law if Deborah had asked about him.
Was she angry at him? He had no idea where
her mind was at. All he knew was that she had
received seven stitches in her head, had been
taken to jail, and was waiting for bail to be set.
Getting out on her own recognizance had not
been an option.

Lynox paced the floor, not knowing what to do
at this point. He looked over at the baby's empty
swing. He hadn't even thought to ask Ms. Lucas
how Tatum was doing. The doorbell ringing
snapped him out of his thoughts. He raced over
to the door, not knowing if it was Deborah coming home or what. She hadn't taken her purse
with her when the ambulance took her away, so
she didn't have her house keys to get in.

"Coming!" Lynox called out, practically tripping over his own feet as he raced over to the
door. Without even looking out the peephole,
he flung the door open. A huge wave of disappointment covered his face when he saw that the
person standing on his doorstep wasn't his wife.

"Well, dang, I'm glad to see you too, partner," Reo said. He would have had to be blind not to see the look on his writing partner's face.

"I'm sorry, man. I thought you were Deborah," Lynox said when he opened the screen door to let Reo in. He'd forgotten all about the fact that the two of them were supposed to spend time today working on their manuscript.

"Something wrong with Deborah?" Reo asked. Lynox had already walked away, so Reo closed the door behind them.

Lynox, still in the same clothes from last night and not having had a wink of sleep, flopped down on the couch and exhaled, as if he'd been holding his breath for hours.

"This looks serious," Reo said. "What's going on? How can I help?" Reo was very sincere in his query, and he stood there, waiting for Lynox to reply.

Lynox stared up at the ceiling for a minute, deciding whether or not he wanted to share with Reo all the details of last night. The last thing he wanted was for some type of stigma to be attached to his wife. He didn't want people looking at her funny for having been arrested for domestic violence. But Reo's wife had been arrested for murder. Reo would be the last person to judge Deborah. And he would know, more than anybody else, how Lynox was feeling right about now.

"From the looks of things," Reo said, "it seems like what you need more than anything is prayer. And I don't need to know what's going on with you to pray for you." Reo bowed his head and began praying. "Dear God, I come to you as humbly as I know how. I ask that whatever is going on with my brother, you be in the midst of it all. Please order his steps, touch his mind, and give him peace. Surround his family with a supernatural barrier of protection. Lord, anything that looks bad right now, we ask that you turn it around and add your favor to it."

"Yes, Lord," Lynox mumbled, truly moved by his friend's words.

"Lord, send down your power, grace, mercy, glory, and anointing. Shower down, Lord. Shower down. In Jesus's name, I pray. Amen."

"Amen," Lynox said. He then looked over at Reo. "Thanks, man. Whew. I really needed that."

"Anytime," Reo said. He stood there. "Well, you're clearly in no mood to write. So why don't we take a rain check?"

"That sounds like a good idea, because with Deborah being in jail, I can hardly put a sentence together, let alone a paragraph."

"Jail?" Reo said, shocked at the news his ears had just heard.

"Yeah, man. Deborah was arrested last night."

"For what?" Reo really didn't mean to pry. It was just that Lynox had spilled the beans, so he couldn't wait for them to spread all over the place.

Lynox hesitated. "Domestic violence."

"Against you?" Reo looked Lynox up and down, questioning with his eyes whether Deborah had really whopped on his big self. The minor bruises and scratches really weren't as visible as they'd been under the flashlight last night.

Lynox nodded. He didn't even want to say it.

"Wow," was all Reo could say.

"They arrested her and took her to jail. Well, not straight to jail. They at least allowed her to go get stitches put in her head first." Lynox said it as if Reo had been present last night and knew all that had gone on.

"Stitches? Wait. You're losing me." Reo shook his head. "Deborah got charged with domestic violence, but she's the one who's hurt?"

"Yeah, she busted her head when I pushed her against the night table."

Reo raised both hands as he stood there. "Whoa. Hold up, man. You my dawg and all, and I'll definitely continue to pray for you, but I can't condone men hitting on women."

"No, no." Lynox began to shake his head. "I didn't hit her. She was clobbering me, man. And since I would never hit her, I tried to push her away. When I did this, she fell backward and hit her head. She corroborated my story. That's why the police didn't arrest me."

Reo put his hands down.

Lynox was lightweight offended that Reo had even thought he was that type of guy. "Man, you know that's not who I am," Lynox said. "I would never put my hands on a woman."

"My bad. I didn't know what to think. I mean, you hitting me with the one-two right now."

"I know. I feel you," Lynox said. He looked at Reo. "You was really gon' cut me off just like that?" he asked.

"Yeah," Reo said without hesitating. "I can't even look at a man who puts his hands on a woman, let alone hang with one. Even more, write a book with him. All I can do is pray for a brother like that and hope he gets delivered, so we can kick it again. But as long as a cat is abusing a woman, I ain't got no holler."

"That's what's up," Lynox agreed. "But so you know, I've never put my hands on my wife or any other woman." He paused for a minute. "Can't say in these past couple of months I haven't wanted to, though."

Reo chuckled. "You preaching to the choir on that one. Like Chris Rock said, a brother may not hit a woman, but, man, there are times when he wants to shake her butt."

Lynox let out a harrumph and shook his head. "You ain't never lied."

Reo finally sat down. He took the chair opposite Lynox. "So I take it things haven't gotten any better as far as the way Deborah has been acting." Klarke had shared with Reo how Deborah had tried marijuana but hadn't stuck with it long term. Reo wasn't sure if Lynox knew about her little experiment, so he didn't mention it.

Lynox stared off into space, thinking about how bad things had actually gotten. "I really do wish I understood how her mind is working. She's changed. She's not the woman I married. And if something doesn't give, between you and me, I don't know if she's the woman I want to stay married to."

"Yo, hold up with all that," Reo said. "You in your feelings right now. Don't let emotions that are on ten right now make decisions that your heart will regret. First thing's first. You two need to get through this whole jail and court situation, and then go from there."

"Yeah. You're right," Lynox said. "This is so crazy. It's like a nightmare."

"I hear you," Reo said. "Do you have any idea when they're going to let her out?"

Lynox shook his head. "No. She hasn't called me or anything. She's been communicating with her mother. My mother-in-law in turn gives me an update."

"The heck with all that," Reo said. "That's your wife. Get yourself together and come on." Reo walked over to the front door.

"For what?" Where are we going?"

"Where do you think we're going?" Reo asked. "We're going to go see about your wife."

Reo was right; Lynox needed to go see about his wife. Not call the jail or the courts on the phone and possibly get the runaround, and definitely not get the information secondhand from Ms. Lucas. He needed to go downtown personally and get some answers.

With his friend's final words, Lynox went upstairs, washed up in the sink, brushed his teeth, and changed into a jogging suit really quick. He'd put off going downtown to see about Deborah. It had seemed like a waste of time if they weren't going to let her out. On top of that, Ms. Lucas had been giving him updates. But knowing his mother-in-law and her attitude toward him, he wasn't so sure that if Deborah was to get out, she'd even call him and let him know.

"All right, man. I'm all set," Lynox said after taking the steps two at a time back down to the living room. "Let's go."

Reo was still standing by the front door. "Make sure you have your ID, your wallet, credit cards, cash, or whatever, just in case you have to bail her out or something."

"Got all that," Lynox assured him, tapping his front pants pocket. He snatched his keys off the table next to the door and then went and opened the door. But he froze solid when he saw what was waiting for him on his doorstep.

Chapter 17

"Deborah, honey, I was on my way to come see about you," Lynox said. He wanted to throw his arms around his wife and pull her in for a hug, but he wasn't quite sure what type of head space she was in. He restrained himself and stared at her with a glowing look on his face. The look was comparable to love at first sight. No matter what they'd been through the night before, he was glad to lay eyes on his wife.

Deborah looked like death warmed over. Her hair was a mess, as the doctors had had to mess with it in order to put the stitches in. She didn't even have on light make-up. She hadn't washed her face or brushed her teeth. She hadn't had the strength to do it. As far as she was concerned, they might as well have had her locked up in a crazy house, because that was where it felt like she'd been.

She'd shared a cell with some career criminals, the kind she'd only read about in books

or seen on television. Now she had put herself
in a position to be labeled as one of them. And
she wouldn't be telling the truth if she didn't
admit that a part of her felt that Lynox was at
least partly to blame. It probably was best that
he didn't try to hug her. She'd probably catch
another case.

Standing there, in the married couple's pool
of silence, Reo decided to excuse himself. "Well,
I guess I better go." He patted Lynox on the back.

That quickly Lynox had forgotten Reo was
standing there. "Oh, yeah, man. Thanks, anyway, partner." Lynox gave Reo some dap.

Reo walked out the door. He nodded and
acknowledged Deborah by saying her name as
he passed by her and walked off the porch.

"How'd you get here?" Lynox asked Deborah,
but just then he saw Ms. Lucas coming up the
walkway with the baby.

"I'm tired," Deborah said. "I need to take a
shower."

"A bath," Ms. Lucas said as she walked up
behind her. "Remember the doctor said no
showers for a spell and not to wash your hair."
Ms. Lucas looked at Lynox standing in the
doorway and at Deborah on the porch. "Well,
go inside," she told her daughter. "You can go
inside, can't you?" She then glared at Lynox.

"Or did he file a restraining order against you too?" She brushed by Lynox and went right into their home like it was hers.

"We already have a lot to deal with," Lynox said to his mother-in-law. "Please don't add to it. You weren't here. You don't know what all went on last night."

Ms. Lucas spun around, as if she wasn't carrying the baby in his seat. "I know my child went to the emergency room last night to get stitches in her head through no fault of her own."

Deborah stepped inside the house while her husband and her mother argued.

"Again, Ms. Lucas," Lynox said, "you don't know everything that happened to be able to speak on it."

She sat the baby's seat down. "Then why don't you tell me what happened?"

Lynox looked at Deborah. She was his main concern right now. All he wanted to do was get things right with her. Getting things right with his mother-in-law would have to play second fiddle, and it was time he let her know. "Look, I appreciate everything you've done to help us out," Lynox began.

"To help my daughter and my grandbabies out," Ms. Lucas said, correcting him.

Lynox continued without addressing her last comment. "But right now Deborah and I need to take care of some things on our own. Preferably, before Tyson gets out of school. So if you don't mind . . ."

"If I don't mind what?" Ms. Lucas asked. "I know you're not suggesting I leave, are you? What for? So I can drive right back over here and take her to get more stitches, if she's even so lucky the next time?"

Lynox could see that things were really about to get ugly between him and his mother-in-law, a person with whom he'd had a wonderful relationship prior to last night. He looked at Deborah, begging her with his eyes to intercede.

It took a second or two, but Deborah finally spoke up. "Mom, I'm going to be fine. I just want to get cleaned up." She looked herself up and down. She then looked over at the sleeping baby. "If you could get him situated in his crib while I do that, I'd appreciate it. Then you can go. I'll be fine."

"But don't you want me to make you something to eat?" Ms. Lucas asked, almost begging.

Deborah had pretty much told her mother exactly what she'd told the police, that she had been the one out of order and that Lynox had merely been trying to protect himself when he pushed her down, causing her to bust her head open on the night table. For all Ms. Lucas knew, though, Deborah could have been saying all that out of fear of her husband. Ms. Lucas hadn't truly discerned the full truth yet and therefore wasn't taking any chances.

"Mom, I'm fine," Deborah said. "There are a lot of things I have to work out with my husband. I have a court date coming up, and we need to make sure our stories are straight."

Perhaps Deborah should have worded that differently, because she raised a red flag with Ms. Lucas.

"You have to get your stories straight only when you plan on telling a lie," Ms. Lucas said, poking her lips out and crossing her arms. "The truth is as straight as it gets. It's a lie that's all crooked and twisted."

"That's not what I meant." Deborah grabbed her head. She was in no mood to debate with her mother.

"Well, what exactly—"

Deborah put her hand up, cutting off her mother's words. She rested her forehead in her hand while shaking her head. "Mom, please." Her voice almost cracked, and she fought back the tears threatening to escape her lids.

The baby began whimpering a little bit while he slept. Deciding to go ahead and tend to her grandson, Ms. Lucas didn't put up a fight. She turned her attention to Tatum and left the other two grown folks in the room to do what they had to do. "Come on, Ganny Ban Banny's baby."

Deborah sighed and then made her way toward the steps.

"I'll come help you. I'll get your bathwater together while you—" Lynox began, but Deborah cut him off.

"I'm going to take a shower," she said, in spite of her mother's orders. She was grown enough to take a shower without getting her head wet.

"Well, okay," Lynox said after a quick pause. "I'll, uh, go start the water for you. You know how long it takes for the water to get hot in the master bath."

Deborah started walking up the steps.

Lynox came up behind her. He put his hand on the small of her back. "Let me help you up the—"

Deborah turned sharply to face Lynox. "I don't need you," she snapped.

Lynox was caught off guard. Hearing his wife say those words stung him.

Looking at her husband and seeing the hurt in his eyes, Deborah added, "I don't need your help. I don't need you to help me up the steps."

Although it was Deborah's intention to be apologetic, Lynox still held on to her first words. He heard all sorts of things between the lines of that initial comment. His wife didn't need him anymore. She didn't want him anymore. He heard that and so much more. He slowly put his hand back down at his side. "I was trying to help."

"You've done enough."

Those words were uttered by Ms. Lucas, who had witnessed the exchange while she held the baby in her arms.

Deborah didn't say a word about her mother speaking on her behalf. Instead, she continued up the steps. Lynox waited until she was at the top of the stairs before he followed her up. When he got to their bedroom, Deborah was over at her dresser, pulling out underclothing to put on. Lynox went and sat on the bed.

"I'm sorry about last night. It was an accident," Lynox said.

Deborah closed the dresser drawer after retrieving a bra and underwear. She turned to face Lynox. "You say that like you're trying to convince me. No need to. I was there. I know that it was my own actions that led to me ending up with stitches and a night in jail. I don't blame you, Lynox. Not at all." That was as close to the truth as Deborah was going to get.

"Oh yeah?" He stood up. "Then why does it feel like you have an attitude with me, like you're mad at me?"

"I'm mad at myself," Deborah said. "I'm disgusted with myself. I'm disappointed in myself." The more she spoke, the louder and more emotional she got. "I hate myself, and as I sat in that nasty jail cell all night long, all I could think about was how I wished I was dead."

"Oh, no, baby," Lynox said. "We are not going to start talking like that." He walked over to Deborah.

"But it's how I feel," Deborah said, trying her best to keep her tears at bay. "You have no idea what I'm going through. It's like a war is going on, and my mind is the battlefield. I'm both the enemy and the ally. It's me against my own self." Deborah looked Lynox in his eyes. "I have tried everything to get right, but I can't."

"Why don't you try counseling again?" Lynox suggested.

"I did, several months ago." Deborah turned her back to Lynox and faced the dresser. Unable to look at herself in the mirror attached to the dresser, she simply closed her eyes.

"What? When? For how long? Why did you stop?" Lynox had an array of questions. Why hadn't he known about his wife starting up counseling again? Had he been that involved in writing and book signings that she felt she couldn't even stop him long enough to tell him what was going on? Or had she been telling him? Showing him? The signs were all there, now that he knew what the signs were.

When he and Deborah had hooked up again, Deborah hadn't hidden from him the fact that she'd had a meltdown/breakdown period, though she hadn't used those exact words. She'd decided to get help by going to counseling. Lynox hadn't had a problem with that. In his unprofessional opinion, more people needed to see counselors, just because. It was like preventative maintenance, as far as he was concerned. If a person had a nice vehicle, they should make sure they did all the right things to take care of it and keep it in tip-top shape. Take it to the shop to get oil changes, tire rotations, tune-ups. Regular maintenance would keep the vehicle up and running. Why wait until the CHECK ENGINE light had been on for a year and the car had completely broken down before taking it in for service? Most people with good sense wanted to get the most out of their vehicles and didn't wait until that happened, so why shouldn't people show the same consideration with their mind?

Deborah was a little overwhelmed by all the questions Lynox was shooting at her. She took a deep breath and attempted to answer them one at a time. "A few months ago, when I started to feel like my old self again . . . the not so good old self, I decided to give counseling a try again."

"Okay. And you didn't tell me, because . . ."

"Because I didn't want you to be disappointed in me." Deborah turned to face Lynox. "Or leave me."

"Why would I leave you or even be disappointed in you?"

"Because I told you I was fixed," Deborah snapped. "I told everybody I was fixed." Tears began to flow from Deborah's eyes. "I stood at that church altar and told everybody how God had delivered me and healed my mind." Deborah was referring to the Sunday she'd gone to visit Cinnamon's church. "If people found out that I really wasn't, everyone would think I was a joke."

Deborah turned back away from Lynox and began to weep as she thought back to that Sunday at the altar. When Cinnamon had invited Deborah to attend her church that time in Persia's basement, Deborah had kept her word and gone.

"Deborah, I'm so glad you made it," Cinnamon had said when Deborah walked through the church doors. She'd promised Deborah in a text message that she'd wait for her before going into the sanctuary.

Deborah was glad about that, because she wasn't comfortable visiting other churches. New Day had been her church home for as long as she could remember. The only times she ever stepped foot inside another church were when Pastor Margie was a guest preacher somewhere and asked New Day members to come out and support her, or when she was attending a church wedding at a different church. Not all churches operated the same way. Deborah was a creature of planning and habit. She had to know what was going on and what to do next at all times. She was almost neurotic when it came to such matters. She hated feeling like she stood out. Even worse, she didn't want people to think she wasn't a seasoned Christian who attended church on the regular. Looking like a fish out of water was too overwhelming for her. She wouldn't be able to enjoy a service just because of that.

The only reason she'd even agreed to visit this church was that, ironically, she wanted to prove that she was a Christian. She wanted Cinnamon to know that she was more than a weed head. It wouldn't be the first time she had gone to church not for God, but for reasons of her own.

"Thanks for inviting me," Deborah had said and then had hugged Cinnamon.

"Well, we better head inside. Service is about to start." Cinnamon turned toward the sanctuary doors.

"Wait a minute," Deborah said. "Where's Klarke? I thought she was supposed to be coming too." Deborah looked around, hoping to spot Klarke. It would be nice not to be the only fish out of water.

"Oh, she can't make it," Cinnamon said. She leaned in and whispered in Deborah's ear. "She got a bad batch of you know what . . . homegrown. She has a mad headache."

Deborah looked confused. She hadn't been a weed smoker long enough to know the different kinds of weeds and the different effects they had. Cinnamon could see that Deborah was confused, so she shooed her hand and led her on into the sanctuary.

Now Deborah was more nervous than ever. Klarke wasn't there to take some of the attention away from her. Besides that, Cinnamon wasn't even her friend per se. She knew her only through Klarke. Now Deborah really didn't want

to be there. It was too late for her to cry headache too, though, as they had already entered
the sanctuary.

"Hi, Sister Ethel," Cinnamon said to one of
the ushers. "How are you?"

"Blessed and highly favored," Sister Ethel
responded.

As Sister Ethel led them to their seats,
Cinnamon spoke to several of her other fellow
church members. She'd say good morning to
them, and they'd reply, "Joy comes in the morning, indeed." She'd ask them how they were, and
they'd reply, "Blessed," or "It's not how I am. It's
who am I, and I am a child of the king."

Deborah noticed that out of the five or six
people Cinnamon had greeted or asked how
they were, not a single person had replied with
a simple "Hello" or an "I'm fine. How are you?"
Deborah could tell right off the bat that half
of these people were going to be too heavenly
religious to be earthly good at all.

A couple of minutes after they were seated, a
church elder took the pulpit and began exhorting. Even though she had smiled during her
entire trek to the pulpit, once she got to talking,
she sounded mad at the world.

"I don't know what you came to do, but I came
to praise Him," she shouted. "How can you sit

there, sit down on God, after all He's done for
you?"

Deborah hadn't been led by the spirit to stand,
but this lady seemed to be glaring right at everyone who hadn't stood to their feet at the sound of
her voice. That was the only reason why Deborah
eventually stood.

Standing wasn't enough for this woman.
She scolded the congregation for not clapping
hard enough. "How y'all gon' pity pat God? He
deserves more than an old pity pat clap!"

Nothing the congregation did seemed to
please this woman. If Deborah wasn't mistaken,
their mission, though, wasn't to please man, but
to please God. *Oh well.*

"Some of you got the nerve to straggle in late
and then sit down on God," the woman continued. "I bet y'all don't be late for that nine-to-five,
for the man who didn't hang, bleed, and die for
you, yet you have no problem showing up to the
house of the Lord late." She shook her head.

And just when Deborah thought the Holy
Spirit was the only one with the power to convict
folks, this exhorter proved her wrong. This
woman was making half the people wish they
hadn't bothered to come to church at all, and
Deborah was one of them.

Sure, once upon a time Deborah had had that same attitude about being late for church. But then she had had that crazy morning when everything that could go wrong had. Her family had arrived at church late, but at least they'd gotten there. It was safe to say that the person in the pulpit didn't always know the hell it took for some folks to get to church . . . late or alive!

After the woman finally got finished using the pulpit to fuss everybody out, she introduced one of the deacons to open up the service with prayer.

"Come on, saints. Let everyone please come down to the altar and pray," the deacon told them.

Cinnamon and some of the other members of the congregation headed to the altar, and Deborah followed suit. There were some who remained in their seats, however, either because it had gotten too crowded down at the altar or because they were older and had a hard enough time sitting on a pew, let alone standing up. Some just plain ole didn't feel like making the trip. Fifteen minutes into the prayer, Deborah wished she'd been one of those who had remained in their seat.

And I thought Elder Ross was bad, Deborah thought to herself. She'd take an Elder Ross prayer over this deacon's anytime.

Once the prayer had finally ended everyone went back to their seats. Scriptures were read, from both the Old Testament and the New Testament. Next, someone came and made announcements, and then the woman who had fussed everybody out returned to the pulpit, this time to tell folks about themselves when it came to paying their tithes. She did everything from accusing folks of stealing from God by not paying their tithes to charging them with using God's money to buy pizza and fast food.

"Even if you have to give your last gas money to pay your tithes, then that's what you are commanded to do," the woman said. "So what if you have to walk to work? Jesus did all His work on foot for His entire life."

Deborah looked around at the faces in the sanctuary. The older saints agreed 100 percent, as evidenced by their nods and amens. That was probably because they were true and faithful tithers, so they didn't have to worry about struggling down the road with canes and walkers. Some of the younger folks had their noses turned up and were rolling their eyes. Young people had to give their last gas money to the church offering basket? Some of them wouldn't even catch the bus, let alone walk. Deborah had seen a Facebook post once about someone's child who had called off work because he or she didn't have a ride. These young folks with a spirit of entitlement were too much.

Deborah was so glad when the church choir entered the stands. She was definitely ready to be taken to the throne. She said a silent prayer that they would usher in the spirit, set the atmosphere so that the house could be prepared to receive the Word of the Lord from the pastor.

"You all right?" Cinnamon whispered to Deborah. "You enjoying yourself?"

Deborah nodded and then smiled. The nod was to confirm that she was all right. The smile was because her grandmother had always told her that if she didn't have something good to say, then she shouldn't say anything at all.

Deborah turned her attention back to the choir as the musicians began to play. From the first note, Deborah knew these people could *sang*, but within seconds she realized that they were not singing for the Lord, but rather for the choir director.

Although the choir director was rather short, he wasn't so short where he needed to stand on a chair to direct, but that was exactly what he was doing. He had his director's stick and was just a-flapping and swinging those arms as he stood on that chair. The members of the choir never took their eyes off of him, for fear they might miss a beat and be reprimanded.

The choir sounded good, but it was pure entertainment. The choir director was serious, too, as he pointed that stick and mean mugged anyone who he thought even looked like they were about to sing a wrong note. The choir members were sweating bullets. The director was sweating too. Deborah was so glad when they finally sang a song with a slower tempo. One more fast song, and she was sure he was going to flap them arms until he flew right out of one of the stained-glass windows.

"Our choir be jamming, don't they?" Cinnamon asked Deborah, elbowing her.

"Oh, they be jamming," Deborah agreed. They were definitely treating those songs as if they were the jam.

Praise and worship finished up their show. Right when Deborah thought she was finally going to get to the Word of God, the first lady of the church was introduced, and she welcomed all the first-time visitors. Deborah closed her eyes and bowed her head. This was too much. It became even more to bear when the first-time visitors were asked to stand. The first lady welcomed them one by one and asked them to introduce themselves.

When it was her turn, Deborah said, "I'm Deborah Chase. I'm a member of New Day Temple of Faith, where Pastor Margie Hill is the shepherd of the house."

"Pastor Margie," the first lady said. "She that white woman, right?"

Deborah was stunned. What the fact that Pastor Margie was white had to do with anything, Deborah had no idea. Still, she nodded out of respect, even though she felt nothing but complete disrespect.

Luckily for Deborah, the first lady moved on. When the next visitor introduced herself, the pastor asked her if she attended a church or if she was looking for a home church.

"I belong to a church," the woman said.

"What church?" the first lady asked.

"Victorious Life Christian Center."

"Who is the pastor?"

Deborah couldn't believe the first lady was drilling that poor woman, trying to catch her in a lie. It was a known fact that visitors to a church often made up lies about which church they belonged to. Either they didn't want the church they were visiting to hound them about joining, or they didn't want to appear to be unchurched heathens, so they lied. Usually, the unchurched heathens, when asked which

church they were a member of, named one of
the popular or larger churches in town. They
might know the name of the church, but nine
times out of ten they had no idea who the pastor was. It was clear that the first lady's intentions were to catch someone in a lie. After
watching the way she drilled this poor woman,
the remaining visitors knew better than to lie.

The pastor couldn't have mounted that pulpit
any sooner than he did. Deborah looked down at
her watch. This church service had started at the
same time that New Day's had. Pastor Margie
would be about to close out her sermon by now,
yet this pastor was just getting started.

The pastor had named the sermon, had even
based it on a scripture, but what he talked
about for the next half hour did not relate to
the title of the sermon or to the scripture at all.
By the time the pastor had altar call, Deborah
wanted to run down there and prostrate herself
on the altar, to express her thanks to the Lord
that she could finally see the light at the end of
the tunnel.

"Won't you come?" the pastor said as the
musicians began to play a soft melody behind
his pleas. "God is calling you. If you have a
need, bring it to the altar. God already knows
your need. He wants you to come lay it on
Daddy's lap."

A couple of members made their way to the altar.

"If you need a healing, won't you come?" the pastor said. "If you need a healing in your body or mind, I declare that today is the day God has set aside for you to get your healing. It's no coincidence or accident that you are here today."

Deborah's ears perked up. The pastor's words were starting to penetrate her soul. She had a need. She needed to get her mind right. She needed to be healed. She needed her mind to be healed. And maybe it wasn't a coincidence or an accident that of all the churches she could have attended today, she was at this one.

"You probably woke up this morning and didn't even feel like coming to church today," the pastor continued. "That was the devil trying to keep you from your healing. Ha. *Ba ta rah cha.*" He began to speak in unknown tongues.

Before Deborah knew it, she was on her feet. That pastor was definitely talking about her now. Lord knows, she did not want to come to this church today. Five minutes ago, she still hadn't wanted to be there.

"Don't walk out of here the same way you walked in," he declared. "If you do, you have no one to blame but yourself, because your promise is right here at this altar. Come meet God at the promise."

A tear rolled down Deborah's cheek. She really did feel led to walk down to that altar, but her feet were like cement. For the past three hours nothing that had been done, said, or sung had touched Deborah. If she could have, she would have walked out two and a half hours ago. But she'd stayed. Her blessing might not have been in the exhorting, the scripture reading, the prayer, the announcements, the welcome, the praise and worship, or the sermon, but she strongly believed it was right now. And she would have missed it, had she listened to her flesh.

This reminded Deborah of Pastor Margie once telling the saints that they didn't know where in a service God had placed what He had for them. It could be all the way in the benediction, but what God had for you, He had for you. Well, today God had something for Deborah, and she was going to miss it if she didn't make her way down to that altar.

One slow step at a time, Deborah was drawn to the altar for the second time during this service. Only this time she was responding to a tugging in her spirit, which was urging her to go, and not to a request made by an individual. Her yellow dress was like a beaming light as she walked down the aisle. In her spiritual mind

still might mean you need to utilize other
ources in staying delivered, such as doctors
d medicine."

But—"

No buts, Deb," Lynox said. "Some things in
are about wisdom, as well as that feeling
there in your gut." He pointed to her stom-
"Now, you went back to see a doctor, you
to take your pills again—even though
idn't follow the instructions properly—but
ave you ever thought that these are things
od is leading you to do, but you are fight-

orah thought for a minute. She nodded,
e everything Lynox was saying was true
de sense. That superwoman syndrome
d her wanting to do God's job. "You might
," Deborah said. "I'm really going to get
gether and get back in God's face to hear
vhat He has to say about this. I don't
v easy it's going to be to clear my head
court date coming up and . . ." Deborah
hand on her forehead. She was already
side herself just thinking about tomor-
les and worries.

own. Relax." Lynox hugged her. "I'm
u. We are going to get through this
'm not going anywhere. You hear

she was running down the aisle to get to that altar, but she knew better than to try that in her heels. So she bent over, and with one step, she removed one pump, and with the next step, she removed the other. Now, with bare feet, she felt like she was suspended in air and was floating down to the altar.

"That's right, daughter. Come," the pastor said to Deborah, who was the only one making her way to the altar at that very moment.

At first tears were flowing from her eyes, but as she approached the altar and stood in front of the podium, Deborah was weeping. Her chest was rising up and down, and her shoulders were going up and down.

"Bring it to the altar and leave it," the pastor ordered as a couple more people made their way to the altar. "Tell your Heavenly Father what you want. Begin to call it out."

What Deborah was feeling was familiar to her. She'd felt this way once before, only not at a church, but right in her very own living room. That was the day she'd been delivered from the guilt and shame of having had a late-term abortion. She'd never looked back after that day. She'd repented, let go, and let God. God had truly delivered her, and she'd walked in it. Well, if God had delivered her before for one thing, He could do it again for something else. This time she didn't need Him just to touch things that had affected her mind. She needed Him to keep her mind altogether.

"Lord, you are a mind keeper," she cried out. Having already been delivered of shame, she had none when calling out what she wanted from God. "Lord, I need you to keep my mind. Touch my mind, O God. Renew it in you. Protect my mind, O God, so that nothing that is not like you infiltrates it."

"Yes. Make it clear," the pastor said, encouraging Deborah. "God wants to restore your soul. Your soul is your mind, your will, and your emotions."

Deborah heard what the pastor was saying as she continued her communication with God. "Lord, forget about the doctors, the medication, happy pills, or any other drug, legal or illegal," Deborah declared. "I need you to be the cure, your Word to be what helps gets me through."

"That's right! You don't need drugs," the pastor said as he put his hand on Deborah's forehead. "You don't need no head doctor. You need *the* doctor. The number one physician. All you need is Jesus!"

The congregation began shouting and praising. The musicians played an upbeat tempo that

incited some Holy Ghost dancing a altar and out in the congregation.

"Your soul is what the enemy co tries to destroy," the pastor told I knows where your brokenness i you ask God to restore your sou Twenty-three, and God will ma When our Father in heaven re makes you better than you ever

Deborah continued crying until her body became wea attempted to come to her aid, them to let her be. Deborah and used one hand to balan wooden podium. She tried but slowly slid to the floor drained. She felt as if a b At this point all she cou to God for once again he mind was right, what co

But so much had g at Cinnamon's chur bedroom at this mom with Lynox, was a su

Lynox put his arr thinks you are a i strongly believe day at church, th

Deborah didn't respond.

Lynox pulled away and looked Deborah in the eyes. "Do you hear me?"

She stared into Lynox's eyes for a few seconds; then she nodded. "I hear you."

Lynox pulled her back in for one more hug and then released her. "Now, you go get a bath so you can get Tyson from the bus stop. I'm sure he'll be happy to see you."

Deborah nodded her agreement and then headed to the bathroom. She closed the door and then leaned against it. "I hear you, Lynox," she said in reference to him telling her that he wasn't going anywhere. As a tear slid down Deborah's face, she said softly, "I just don't believe you."

Chapter 18

"Mommy," Tyson yelled when he got off the bus and saw Deborah standing at his bus stop, waiting on him. "You're alive! You're alive!" He ran into her arms and gave her the biggest hug ever.

Deborah let out a chuckle as she waved at Charles, who was at the bus stop, waiting for CJ and Tyson to get off. She'd already thanked Charles for caring for Tyson last night.

Deborah looked at Tyson. "Of course I'm alive, silly boy." She bent over and kissed him on the forehead.

He looked up at her and smiled. Deborah smiled back, but within seconds she noticed the wide, huge grin on her son's face vanish, as if he'd seen a ghost.

"What is it, baby?" Deborah asked, his emotions rubbing off on her. "What's wrong?"

"Where's Daddy? Did he have to go to jail for hurting you?"

Deborah exhaled. "No, Tyson. Daddy didn't go to jail, and Daddy didn't hurt me."

"Yes he did!" Tyson exclaimed. "He pushed you. You fell and bleeded. I saw it. Daddy tried to kill you!"

A couple of the children who rode the bus with Tyson and were heading to their own domiciles turned to look back at them and see what all the commotion was about. Deborah looked at the children, smiled, and nodded, hoping they took that as a sign that everything was okay and would move along.

"My mom said his dad beats them," Deborah heard one of the older elementary kids say to another child as they walked away from her and Tyson. "Said the police were there last night and everything, and that the property value, or something like that, is going to go down if we have hoodlums for neighbors."

If things were like they used to be when Deborah was coming up, she'd get that kid straight, take him to his doorstep by his ear, and get his mother straight too. But she'd already had the people called on her before when it came to her own son. And she'd already gone to jail for a quarrel with her own husband. They'd probably put her under the jail if she dealt with someone who wasn't even kinfolk. So instead, she focused on calming Tyson down.

"Let's take a walk to the park real quick, okay?" Deborah said to Tyson.

Even though she and Lynox had decided they would have a talk together with Tyson about everything that was going on, right now Tyson saw Lynox as the bad guy. Deborah could tell by the fear in his voice and the look in his eyes when he asked if Lynox was home. She never wanted Tyson to be afraid to walk into his own home. She felt that if she told him that Lynox was in fact at the house without first having a one-on-one with him, it might be harmful to him.

At the idea of a quick trip to the neighborhood park, Tyson's eyes lit up. Just that fast he forgot all about his proverbial evil stepfather. "Ooh, yay! The park." Tyson took off running.

"No, no. Wait up," Deborah said. "We're going to *walk* to the park." Even though the path to the park was right up the next block, Deborah wanted to take advantage of all the time they spent getting to the park.

"Oh, Mom." Tyson stopped, turned around, and frowned. "It's right there." He pointed. "You'll see if a stranger gets me."

"Boy, just get back here and walk with me."

Tyson stomped the entire few steps back to Deborah with his shoulders slumped.

"You better straighten up, or there won't be no park." Deborah gave Tyson a stern look. The fact that she was mortified about what he'd been exposed to last night didn't take away from the fact that he needed to act like he had some sense. Still, Deborah lightened the mood. "So how was school today?"

"Not good. I was sad a lot," Tyson replied.

"Why?" Deborah asked, even though she could have bet the farm on her idea about why he'd been sad.

"Because you were bleeding and dying and stuff. And Daddy's mean."

"Yes, I was bleeding, but like I said before, I'm not dead. I wasn't dying," Deborah said. "And, honey, you have a very kind, loving father who would do anything in the world for you. He's not mean."

"Uh-uh. He is. He was mean that time in the basement, and he was mean last night. He makes you sad. I see your face, and it looks like mine when you made me sad."

"When?" Deborah asked, wondering how the focus of this conversation had shifted to her.

"When you used to be mean too. Remember?"

Deborah remembered, all right. That was back when she had first realized that she needed some help when it came to her anger and her snapping off. Poor Tyson had had to bear the brunt of her mess. Now there was Lynox, and that had led to Deborah having to have this conversation in the first place. If only she'd kept up with her meds, the counseling, or something, all this could have been prevented. If only she had been a better Christian and had kept up with God. If she was stronger in the Lord, she bet she wouldn't be dealing with this situation right now. Seemed like things had gotten worse. Once upon a time Deborah had considered herself a Sunday only Christian, now Sundays were even too much for her.

"Mommy does remember when she used to be mean to you," Deborah admitted. "And lately, Mommy hasn't been so nice."

"Yes, you have. You let me eat ice cream for dinner the other day," Tyson reminded her as they turned off the street they'd been walking on and headed up the trail to the park.

Deborah smiled. She'd let Tyson eat ice cream for dinner that evening because she'd felt so awful for shooing him away all day. There was a manuscript that she had been editing, and she had told herself that she would get at least twenty-five pages done a day until it was complete. She had been on the cusp of meeting her goal for the day when Tyson started coming down to her home office what seemed like every five minutes.

"Mommy?" he'd said the first time.

"Yes, Tyson?" Deborah had replied, not taking her eyes off the computer screen.

"Can I have a peanut butter and jelly sandwich?"

"Just a second, Tyson. Go on upstairs, and I'll be up."

When she told him she'd be just a second, he took it literally, as less than a minute later the little tyke was right back down at her desk again.

"Mommy, I want a peanut butter and jelly sandwich, and don't tell me to wait a minute. I'm hungry. And some water with it too." Tyson wasn't a milk drinker. If he couldn't get juice or a soda, he'd take water over milk any day.

"Hold on, Tyson. I'll be up. Mommy has work she has to get done, so you have to be patient."

He sighed, creating a huge gust of wind, slumped his shoulders, and walked away with his head down.

"And lift that big head up so you can see where you're going."

He sucked his teeth and stomped hard up the steps.

"Boys don't suck their teeth, and stop stomping," Deborah told him.

The door slammed closed as she got to her final few words. If she hadn't been so entrenched in her work, she probably would have jumped up from her seat and yoked him up. She'd contemplated it as her blood boiled over this sign of disrespect, which, she knew, needed to be nipped in the bud. Instead, she continued editing away.

She had two more paragraphs to go, and her creativity was at its peak. Her adrenaline was pumping, and then the door opened again. She didn't hear Tyson stomping down the steps. She figured that maybe he'd just opened the door to feel her out, and she thought that he was waiting up there for the moment when she did decide to get up. Whatever it was that was keeping him at the top of the steps instead of at the foot, she took as a blessing.

Right when Deborah reached her last paragraph, she realized that some things were too good to be true. At that moment Tyson, who had tiptoed down the steps without her hearing him, popped up beside her desk.

"Mom?"

"What?" Deborah yelled. His little voice had set her off. Why was he being so hardheaded? All he had to do was sit upstairs in the television room and watch cartoons. She had turned on his favorite show and had even left him her iPad to play with. When she had asked him if he wanted something to eat before she retreated back down

to her work space, where she'd been all day—
except when she had to feed the baby and tend to
him—why hadn't he said something then and let
her fix him something? *Why? Why? Why?*

She'd been up and down those stairs all day,
shifting from working on her laptop to working
on her PC. When she had to be in the same room
with the baby, she was on her laptop. When he
was in his swing, she worked on her laptop. But
once he dozed off, she'd go do work that she
preferred doing on her PC. She kept a play gym
down in the home office area, so sometimes she
would even work with the baby right next to her
there.

This day in particular had been so overwhelming. It seemed like whenever Deborah had
a deadline, all these mini projects would pop
up and take time away from the main one she
wanted to focus on. So even though at one point
in the week she might find herself a day ahead
of schedule, sure enough issues and distractions
would pop up, and she would fall her two days
behind.

One time recently her mother had needed her
to accompany her to the repair shop to drop her
car off. Another time Lynox had asked her to
read over real quick something he was working
on. A couple of times it had been a field trip or a

class party she'd volunteered for a long time ago, and those obligations had crept up on her during the busiest workweeks possible. But today it was Tyson wanting a peanut butter and jelly sandwich.

The sound of his voice, which was usually a melody to her ears, as he sang the anthem of precious motherhood, was like nails down a chalkboard today.

"What, Tyson?" she yelled at the top of her lungs again. "Don't you see me working? Didn't I tell you that I would come up when I was finished?"

"Yes, but I just wanted—" Tyson continuously tried to get a word in edgewise during Deborah's rant, but he couldn't. She'd popped her hood, and all kinds of smoke was coming out of the engine.

"You have to learn to be patient," Deborah continued. "When somebody tells you to wait a minute, you have to go sit your butt down somewhere and wait a minute. You understand me? Now, get on upstairs and wait, like I told you to do in the first place."

A broken Tyson walked away, beat down and shattered. Deborah immediately felt so bad. She wanted to drop everything and go after him, but what was one more paragraph? To make up for it, she later told Tyson he could have whatever he wanted for dinner. She then apologized to him over dinner, which was a bowl of ice cream. After Deborah apologized, they talked and laughed while he finished up.

That event was like a double-edged sword. Tyson remembered the experience of having dessert for dinner. But, unfortunately, he also remembered the reason why he'd been given the special treat—because Mommy was being mean. She wondered which side of the sword he'd recall when telling his own kids tales about his childhood with their grandma. Deborah cringed at the possibility of it being the latter.

But right now the conversation she had to have with her son wasn't about her being mean, but about trying to convince him that Lynox was not. It was safe to say, though, that in these past few months, Deborah had been pushing Lynox emotionally. Ironically, it was Lynox pushing her physically that she had to explain to Tyson.

"Baby, let's go to the swings. I'll push you," Deborah said once she got a good look at all the playground equipment at the park. This time when Tyson ran off, she didn't stop him, since his final destination was clearly in view.

"I want to go high, until my stomach laughs," Tyson said, hopping on a vacant swing. Actually, all the swings were vacant. Since the kids had just gotten out of school, most of them were home, eating after-school snacks and doing homework.

"High, it is," Deborah said as she stepped behind Tyson and began pushing him. After four pushes, he was already screaming that this was high enough. Deborah giggled and then went and sat on the swing next to him. "Tyson, you know your father loves you, right?" she asked him.

"Yes, but he's still been acting mean," he said as he pumped his feet to make himself go higher on his own. He had yet to figure out the rhythm needed to do so, so he wasn't going any higher.

"He's not mean. He's never yelled at you. He's never hit you or anything like that, right?"

"No," Tyson said. "But he was mean to you. He made you bleed and stuff. I was scared. I was crying. When you hurt other people, you are mean."

"That can be true," Deborah said, "if you hurt them on purpose."

Tyson looked over at his mother. "Did Daddy hurt you on purpose?"

"No. That's the thing I'm trying to explain," Deborah said. "Your father loves me. He loves all of us. He would never do anything to hurt us on purpose. Actually, it was Mommy who was doing some mean things to Daddy. I was really, really, really upset. Daddy was trying to calm me down, and he accidentally pushed me while he was doing it."

"But the police had him, not you. Police get the bad guy."

Deborah sighed. "Son, the police *did* get me. They let me go get my head fixed first, though."

"Oh," Tyson said as his swinging slowed down.

Deborah could tell he was a little confused. If the police took her, then why was she sitting there with him? Even though Deborah could see all the questions swirling around in her son's little head, she decided she'd answer them later. The day would come when she'd have to tell her son she'd been in jail. She didn't want to dump it all on him at once. One thing at a time, and right now she had to get his father back on his good side. After all, if anything was ever to happen to her, Lynox was all he'd have besides her mother. But even she was getting up there in age. And with that court date still pending, something really could happen to Deborah, something that could make it so that it was just Tyson, Lynox, and Tatum.

"Mommy isn't mad at Daddy for the accident, and you shouldn't be, either," Deborah said.

"So you're not going to be mad and fight him?" Tyson said. He stopped the swing himself with his feet.

"No, I'm not going to fight Daddy," Deborah said, shocked he'd even ask her something like that. He'd never witnessed her getting physical with Lynox.

"Well, you were fighting him last night. I heard you fighting him."

Deborah was horrified. Her heart just about stopped beating. There was no way Tyson could have seen her swinging at Lynox. Hadn't the door been closed? Deborah couldn't remember. She had to figure out how to ask Tyson what all he'd seen without leading him with her line of questioning.

"Are you sure you saw us fighting?" Deborah said.

"Yep." Tyson hopped off the swing. "I'm going to go get on the slide now." He ran over to the slide, leaving Deborah with a sick feeling in her stomach.

Deborah gathered her bearings after being knocked out by Tyson's words and then went over to the sliding board.

"Weee," Tyson said as he came breezing down the slide. "That was fun, Mommy. Can I do it again?" He jumped up and down.

"Sure, baby." Deborah watched as Tyson went to climb up the steps again. "So, Tyson, tell Mommy what you saw as far as the fight goes."

"I heard it. I heard you yelling at Daddy. You guys were fighting with your words."

Deborah felt some relief as Tyson reached the top of the slide and came floating back down again. Thank God he hadn't seen her windmilling Lynox, not that it was much better that he'd heard her viciously attacking him verbally.

"Yes, Mommy was fighting Daddy with her words," Deborah confirmed.

"And that's why I thought he hurt you with his hands, because you hurt him with your mouth."

Deborah shook her head. "No, that's not what happened, but just so you know, even if someone does hurt you with their words, it's never, ever okay to hurt them with your hands. Do you understand?"

"Yep." He nodded. "One more time on the slide." He ran to go down the slide again before Deborah even gave him the okay.

"This is the last time, Ty. Then we have to go home."

"Okay," he agreed, without putting up a fight. He knew better.

As promised, Deborah let Tyson do the slide one last time before they headed out of the park.

"That was fun," Tyson said. "Can we do it again tomorrow?"

"We'll see," Deborah said.

They were exiting the park when Deborah decided, for good measure, to make sure that her conversation with Tyson had cleared up things. There was already a wedge in her and Lynox's relationship. She didn't want there to be one between Tyson and Lynox.

"So, I want to tell you again that Daddy isn't mean. He didn't hurt Mommy, so you don't have to be afraid or worried. Everything was an accident, and we're going to be careful so that it never happens again, okay?"

"Okay," Tyson said. "I'll tell my teacher, 'Never mind,' tomorrow, when I go to school."

Deborah stopped in her tracks. She had to; her legs had just about given out on her. She balanced herself with the little bit of strength she had. Her mouth dried up. It was a toss between whether she had sand in her mouth or peanut butter. Or both. No saliva to swallow, to lubricate her throat, to keep her from choking on her words if she dared to speak. It was as if something had her mouth jammed shut, and she couldn't speak if she wanted to.

Why in the world would Tyson have to tell his teacher, "Never mind"? *Never mind about what?* Lord, what had he told her that he would have to recant?

"Ty . . . Tyson." Deborah forced out the words, at the same time forcing her feet to step one in front of the other. It was a very hard and slow process. "Just what do you have to tell your teacher, 'Never mind,' about?" Deborah held her breath.

"About you and Daddy fighting and him hurting you, the police, and everything."

A gasp erupted out of Deborah's mouth. It was so loud that Tyson turned to look at his mother.

"You okay, Mommy? Did the swing hurt your belly?" Tyson walked back and put his hand on his mother's abdomen. "You look like you are going to throw up, like CJ did that day Mr. Charles made him eat spinach. Mr. Charles told him he would like the creamy spinach, but CJ still threw up. Mr. Charles said he wished he'd listened when he had to clean it up."

Usually, Deborah liked Tyson's cute little stories, but now every word he said went over her head. It was his earlier words that had landed smack-dab in her face. "Tyson, you told your teacher about last night? Why?" Deborah was oblivious to the fact that she'd raised her voice, enough to make Tyson draw back.

"I was sad. She asked what was wrong." Tyson began backpedaling toward their home.

"But you shouldn't have told her that. It was family business. You don't discuss what goes on in our house with other people."

"I'm sorry," Tyson said. "But I didn't want to lie. At first, I was going to tell her nothing was wrong, but something was wrong, so that would have been a lie."

Noticing how afraid Tyson was starting to look, she changed her demeanor. She didn't want to scare him. She wanted to get to the bottom of what he'd told his teacher and then figure out how to undo it.

"You're right, Tyson. You shouldn't lie, but it's okay to tell people you don't want to talk about things, especially things that go on in our home."

"I didn't know," Tyson said sadly. "You and Daddy said I could always tell you anything. You said I can talk to Pastor and tell adults when something is wrong. I thought my teacher was a grown-up." He put his head down, turned, and began walking home as if he'd just witnessed his dog get run over by a car.

"Tyson, honey, wait a minute." Tyson stopped, and Deborah caught up with him. "Mommy didn't mean to make you sad or make you feel like you did something wrong, okay?"

He shrugged. "Okay."

"I do want you to be able to tell Daddy and me and adults anything," Deborah said, really wanting to add the word *almost* in front of the word *anything*. But now was not the time to be a hypocrite. Either she wanted Tyson to have open lines of communication or she didn't. She never wanted him to feel as though his voice didn't matter and couldn't be heard. She wished his teacher hadn't heard his voice on this particular matter. "So it's okay that you talked to your teacher, and you don't have to tell her, 'Never mind.'"

The last thing Deborah wanted was for him to try to correct the story he'd told the teacher. She could hear him now. *My mommy said* . . . The teacher would for sure think Deborah had put him up to recanting the story in order to cover up the truth, not knowing that the truth wasn't exactly what Tyson had relayed.

"Okay," Tyson said, his spirits lifting somewhat.

"Got any homework?"

"I have words to learn and sounds to make in a minute, Mrs. Riker said."

"Okay. I'll help you."

"Yeah. Because you're good at words," Tyson said. "You and Daddy, right?"

"Yep, me and Daddy."

Deborah watched as Tyson went into the house before her. She grabbed the screen door real quick before it slammed in her face. She made a mental note that she'd have to talk to Lynox about teaching him to hold the door open for a lady. For now, though, they had bigger fish to fry, and she was none the wiser that it was the cook who was about to get burned by the hot grease.

Chapter 19

"Dinner was so good, Mommy," Tyson said as he wiped the spaghetti off his mouth. "Can I have some cookies now?"

Lynox jumped in and spoke for Deborah. "How about you eat a couple more bites of that salad?"

"Aw, salad is yucky," Tyson complained.

"But cookies are yummy, and sometimes you have to go through the yucky to get to the yummy," Lynox said.

"Well put," Deborah told her husband, having watched him interact with Tyson.

She was so relieved that when Tyson walked through the door after school today, he went and gave Lynox a hug and a kiss on the cheek, like he'd done any other time he'd come home and Lynox was there. Her little talk with him had worked. After he had his after-school snack and did his homework, Lynox had had a little talk with him as well. Deborah had been present,

but she'd let Lynox do all the talking. He had
basically reiterated most of the things Deborah
had already told Tyson.

Tyson appeared to be good. As the family of
four sat around the table, Tatum in his bouncer
seat, they all appeared to be good. But there was
still a great number of issues that Deborah and
Lynox had to work out. Unfortunately, before
they could even get to the middle of what was
already on their plate, seconds would be piled
on.

"Okay, just two more bites." Tyson held up
two fingers. He then used those two fingers to
pinch his nose closed while he gobbled down a
bite of salad.

"Boy, you are so silly." Deborah laughed.

The ringing doorbell interrupted her laughter.

"Who in the heck?" Lynox asked with furrowed eyebrows. He wiped his mouth and finished chewing as he stood up and walked over to
the front door. He looked out the peephole.

"Who is it?" Deborah asked, coming around
the corner.

Lynox shrugged. "I don't know. Some lady.
I don't recognize her. Maybe it's for you . . .
someone from church or something."

Deborah approached the door as Lynox
opened it. It took her a few seconds to recall

how she knew the familiar face on her porch, but once it registered, she thought all the spaghetti she'd eaten was going to come back up.

The woman began to speak. "Ms. Lucas, I'm not sure if you remember me. . . ."

"It's Mrs. Chase," Lynox said, correcting the woman in a not so pleasant tone. He hadn't yet been able to ascertain exactly who the woman was, but he had a feeling she hadn't come in peace.

"Pardon me. Mrs. Chase," she replied, correcting herself. "I'm Pricilla Folins with—"

"Franklin County Children Services," Deborah and Lynox said in unison. This wasn't the first time either of them had come in contact with Ms. Folins.

The last time she showed up on Deborah's doorstep, Lynox had also been present. It was the time Pastor Margie had overheard Deborah interacting with Tyson in a very disturbing manner. She'd honestly felt that Tyson might be in trouble, so she'd reported the incident to Franklin County Children Services. Although initially Deborah felt as if Pastor Margie had betrayed her, she ultimately realized that God had used Pastor Margie to bring her destructive behavior to her attention. That was what had compelled Deborah to seek mental help. Had

Franklin County Children Services not gotten
involved and not threatened to take Tyson away
from her, Deborah might not have ever gotten
help and experienced the peace that came with
it. Was God using the same tactic He'd used
the last time to force Deborah to get help now?
Why did He have to keep going through all
that? Why couldn't He help her Himself and get
it over with?

"I remember exactly who you are," Deborah
said. "But if someone reported an incident of
alleged abuse against my son again, I will fight it
tooth and nail, because no one in this home has
been verbally or physically abusing either of my
boys."

"That may very well be the case," Ms. Folins
said, "but this complaint deals with a more
indirect form of abuse."

Lynox chimed in. "Indirect?"

"Either a kid is getting abused or they're not,"
Deborah noted.

"A child living in a violent setting, one where
there is domestic violence, fighting, physical
and verbal abuse going on, experiences a form
of abuse. Children should not be subjected to
that type of environment. It's endangering
a child. Children should be raised in healthy,
safe homes."

"And that's where both of our children are being raised," Lynox countered.

Ms. Folins shook her head and looked down at the clipboard she was holding. "Not according to this police report."

At the mention of the word *police*, a squad car driven by a female police officer pulled up to the house. There was a male officer on the passenger side.

Fear took over Deborah's face. "Lynox." She grabbed his arm and held on for dear life.

"What's going on here?" Lynox asked Ms. Folins. "Why are the police here?"

"I simply didn't want any trouble while I did my interview," she replied.

"Interview?" Deborah asked, puzzled.

"It's routine procedure that if abuse is suspected and reported, we do interviews and investigate. We interview the parents and the children separately. If it's determined that there is cause to remove the children from the home—" Ms. Folins said before Deborah cut her off.

"Remove the children?" That was the only thing Deborah had heard, and that was all it took to set her off. Deborah charged toward Ms. Folins, who took a step back.

Lynox grabbed hold of Deborah to hold her back. "I don't understand, Ms. Folins." Lynox tried to remain as cordial as possible, even though his blood was starting to boil. "Our boys are fine. I'm not sure why you're here." Lynox looked over Ms. Folins's shoulder and saw the officers getting out of the car.

"We got a report from your oldest boy's school today," Ms. Folins replied.

"Oh, Jesus!" Deborah smacked her hand against her forehead. "Tyson's teacher." She shook her head.

"What about Tyson's teacher?" Lynox asked.

"I told her about you and Mommy's fight, her bleeding, and the police and stuff."

Everyone turned and looked at a spaghetti-covered Tyson.

The police approached the door. A look of dread came over Tyson's face at the sight of the police.

"Oh, no. The police again." Tyson immediately began crying and was on the verge of becoming hysterical.

Tyson's behavior was very disturbing to Ms. Folins, not to mention Deborah's behavior. After all, the woman had lunged at her. Initially, she'd been there for a simple interview and investigation, but it looked as though that was about to change.

Lynox raced over and comforted his son. "It's okay, Tyson. Daddy is here. Everything is going to be fine."

"No, no, no." Tyson shook his head. "Who was mean this time?"

"Nobody was mean, Tyson," Deborah assured him.

"Uh-huh," Tyson insisted. "The police come when somebody is being mean. Please stop being mean. No more mean. Please." Tyson balled his eyes out.

This was all Ms. Folins needed to see. No way was she going to leave that poor kid in this home. She'd left him with Deborah before, and now he seemed worse. If she left this boy and something bad happened to him, she'd never forgive herself. She turned and began mumbling something to the officers.

Lynox bent down and wrapped his arms around his son. He held him and allowed him to get it all out. "Deb, why don't you go check on the baby?" Lynox suggested.

Deborah didn't oblige. She stood watching, with her mouth open. In that moment she couldn't do anything but agree with the words Ms. Folins had spoken. She had honestly never considered the effect her actions and behavior were having on her children. Back in the day her actions had directly affected Tyson. She simply had not stopped to think of the damage being done indirectly. But that still didn't mean she wanted her children to be taken from her.

It was too late for that, though, as Ms. Folins said, "Would you like to pack your children some things?" She addressed both Deborah and Lynox.

Lynox shot up, horrified. "Pack them clothes? But you said you were here merely to conduct an interview."

"I was . . . at first," Ms. Folins said. "But after witnessing what I've witnessed, I'm sorry, but I can't leave them here."

"No. You can't take my children away," Deborah said to Ms. Folins. She then looked at the officers. "Can she? Can she do this?"

The female police officer spoke. "They can if they deem the environment in which the children are living dangerous, unhealthy, or unsafe."

"But . . ." Deborah looked from Tyson to the officers. She felt so helpless. She honestly didn't know what to say. "Lynox, they can't do this."

Lynox looked at Ms. Folins. "Please, what can we do here? We've done nothing to harm our children."

"Maybe *you* haven't, Mr. Chase," Ms. Folins said, "but the verdict is still out on your wife. And this is the second time we've been called concerning your wife's behavior." She looked at Deborah. "Mrs. Chase, do your children a favor. Be a good mother and get yourself some help."

Deborah instantly saw red. Did this woman, in so many words, tell her that she was a bad mother?

"If you have an issue and are stressed with one child," Ms. Folins said, pouring salt on the wound, "you don't turn around and have another one. I don't get women like you." She tsk-tsked and began shaking her head.

Lynox couldn't get to Deborah in time once he saw her lunging at Ms. Folins. But, thank goodness, the officers were there to keep her from putting her hands on the caseworker.

"You stinking, judgmental . . ." Deborah called that poor woman everything but a child of the king as the officers attempted to restrain her.

Watching Deborah behave like a wild animal, Ms. Folins was now convinced she was making the right call.

"Deborah," Lynox said, trying to shush Deborah up. It was to no avail. With the officers holding her back, Deborah continued flailing her arms and cussing that woman a new butt hole.

"If you don't control yourself right now," the male officer warned Deborah, "we are going to take you right back downtown again and add this charge to your already existing case."

The words that officer was speaking might as well have been Chinese, because Deborah didn't understand any of it. She wasn't receiving any of it, and she continued to go off, trying to get at Ms. Folins.

"And this is why we are removing the children from your home," Ms. Folins declared, continuing to antagonize Deborah.

"Deborah, stop it!" Lynox shouted. He was getting angry at his wife for acting this way. It wasn't even like this was *his* wife standing there, acting like that. She honestly did look like one of them hood rats from reality television.

The more Deborah clowned, the harder Tyson cried, and the angrier Lynox got. It was so frustrating to Lynox to see Deborah risk their kids being taken from their home. At this point he honestly felt that she was too far gone even to care anymore. So if she didn't care about herself, then why should he care about her? But what he did care about was his boys.

Lynox walked over to the caseworker in the midst of all the ruckus and asked, "Ms. Folins, what do I have to do to keep my children? I'm their father. It's my job to protect them. I have thus far and will continue to do so. Just tell me what I need to do at this very moment."

Ms. Folins looked over at Deborah, whom the police had managed to calm down somewhat. "Well, right now, I will be taking the children, because there is no way I can leave them in the home with this woman without jeopardizing my job."

"*This woman*?" Deborah yelled. "I'm their effing mother, you witch!"

"Deborah, please!" Lynox yelled so loudly at his wife that the house shook. He then turned his attention back to Ms. Folins. Tears were resting in his eyes. This situation was a matter of life and death right now. "Ms. Folins?" His eyes pleaded with her to tell him everything he needed to do for the sake of his children. A tear managed to escape Lynox's eye and drip down onto his cheek.

Ms. Folins choked back her own tears as she watched this large, manly man try to keep it together. She sniffed. "Like I said, I do have to remove them from the home, but I will not put them in the system to be placed in foster care. I will give you two hours to have her removed from this home if you want them to stay here."

"I wish I might leave my home," Deborah yelled. "This house is in my name, and I ain't going nowhere."

Deborah was right. The home was solely in her name. At the time the two of them went house hunting for a family home, Lynox had owned his own home and a rental property. His tenant had been three months behind on the rent, then had upped and left without even letting Lynox know. Deborah's home, which had initially had a fifteen-year mortgage, had been practically paid off. They succeeded in finding a new home together, but they decided not to bring all his financial drama to the closing table and to place the family house solely in her name. It had seemed like a good idea, until now. The last thing he wanted was for it to seem like he was putting Deborah out of her own home. But the first thing he wanted to do was make sure his children resided in a safe one, in keeping with children's services' standards.

"If she doesn't want to leave the home, then what other choices do I have?" Lynox asked Ms. Folins.

Ms. Folins looked at Deborah and then looked at Lynox. "If she's not willing to leave the home, then you can leave the home . . . and take the children with you."

"Ha!" Deborah spat. She let out a laugh, as if Ms. Folins had just told the funniest joke ever.

Ms. Folins ignored Deborah and spoke to Lynox. "I know this is hard, but believe me when I say that my job is not to break up families, but to try to help keep them together."

"Yeah, right!" Deborah exclaimed, continuing on with her antics.

By now Lynox had totally tuned his wife out. His only concern was for his children. He looked at Tyson. "Son, go in the other room and make sure your brother is okay." He figured it was useless asking Deborah to do it, since she hadn't done it that last time he'd asked. And the last thing he was going to do was leave Deborah alone in that room. No telling what would transpire in the little bit of time he was gone.

Tyson did as he was told.

Lynox turned his attention back to Ms. Folins. "So explain to me how this works."

"I'll remove the children temporarily, and like I said, I will not place them in a home as long as you come down and prove you have a safe place for you and the children to stay in, a place that Mrs. Chase is not a resident of."

That didn't sound too hard. Lynox would get a hotel room if he had to. Fleeing to a hotel with his children . . . Now he really was starting to sound like a battered spouse.

Ms. Folins gave Lynox a stern look. "I'm telling you, Mr. Chase, if you break the conditions
under which your children will be released to
you by allowing her to be around them, all bets
are off. And if, God forbid, anything happens to
the children, then you will be held responsible."

"You can forget it, Ms. Help Keep Families
Together," Deborah said.

Both Lynox and Ms. Folins continued to tune
Deborah out. Their complete and entire focus
was all about the children. Besides, Ms. Folins
felt safe that Deborah couldn't get at her with the
two officers keeping her at bay.

"Can I at least explain to my oldest boy what is
going on?" Lynox asked Ms. Folins.

"Of course," she replied. "If you don't mind,
I'd like to come with you."

"You don't have to worry about me trying to
sneak them out the back door, Ms. Folins."

"I know," she assured Lynox. "I can see you
really want to do what's best for your boys. I
think if I'm there for you to introduce me to
them, then they won't be as scared when I, you
know . . ." She nodded to the door.

Lynox agreed. "Fine. Right this way."

Deborah couldn't believe what she was hearing, what she was seeing. She watched Lynox
escort Ms. Folins to the dining room, where
they'd all been having dinner.

"Lynox!" she called out. "Lynox, get her away from my children. Don't you dare take her around my babies!"

"Ma'am, this is the last time I'm going to ask you to get it together," the female officer said. "Even though this may not be easy for you, you can make it a whole lot easier for your children by cooperating. After all, isn't this supposed to be about both the physical and mental welfare of your children?"

Deborah couldn't argue with the officer. Well, she could have, but she didn't. She couldn't make this about her. Right now it had to be all about the children. But there was still a selfish part of her that wanted to keep on fighting, especially when she watched Lynox come around the corner with Tatum in his seat and saw Tyson holding Ms. Folins's hand.

"I can't believe this is happening," Deborah said under her breath. She wanted to yell it to the moon but didn't want to make this any tougher for her children.

"Mommy, why don't you help get Tatum a bag packed and get Tyson some toys?" Lynox said to Deborah. He tried to sound as chipper as possible. He wanted Tyson to know both his parents were in agreement about what was going on. He needed to know that there would be no more fighting, and that they were working together to make things right. Lynox stared at Deborah, urging her to play along.

She wanted to kick, scream, fight, and bite, with Lynox the object of her fury now for going along with this so willingly. But that would only make things worse. She trusted her husband, so she had to believe that he had a secret plan, one he'd clue her in on once the authorities were gone.

"Mrs. Chase, can we let you go so that you can help your children?" the male officer asked Deborah.

She breathed in and then breathed out. She nodded. "Yes. Yes, you can."

The officers stepped to the side and allowed Deborah to help Lynox get some things together for the boys. Deborah got Tatum's diaper bag together, while Lynox helped Tyson pack a couple of his favorite toys in his backpack.

"I'll be there to pick you up in a little bit, buddy," Lynox told Tyson fifteen minutes later, as he stood at the front door, handing the boys over to Ms. Folins and the police. "I'll see you in a little bit, okay?"

Tyson nodded sadly. He then looked at Deborah. "And you too, Mommy? I'll see you in a little bit too?"

Deborah held back her tears and simply smiled. For the first time in a long time, she was able to keep her emotions together. In her head she was watching the eight-millimeter film of herself losing it and going off, but repeating that would be so detrimental to the current situation. She watched Lynox help Ms. Folins and the officers load the boys up in Ms. Folins's car. Five minutes later, Lynox came back inside the house, closing the door behind him. He exhaled, trying to keep it together.

"So what's the plan?" Deborah asked enthusiastically. "How are we going to pull this off?"

Lynox looked at Deborah, dumbfounded. "Pull what off?"

"This!" She raised her hands and then allowed them to drop to her sides. "This whole 'you pretending to leave' thing."

"Deborah, this isn't pretend. This is something we have to do, and the sooner we do it, the sooner I can get the boys, and we'll at least know they are safe with me, instead of downtown with some strangers."

"Safe with you? You mean safe with *us*." Deborah stepped toward Lynox.

"No, I meant safe with *me*. You heard what Ms. Folins said. And I'm not messing this up." Lynox walked past Deborah and headed toward the steps.

"Wait!" she cried out, watching Lynox walk away. "What's going on? Where are you going? What are you doing, Lynox?"

Lynox stopped and turned to face Deborah. "What do you think I'm doing? I'm going to pack some things for me and the boys, and then I'm leaving."

Chapter 20

"You can't leave me!" Deborah yelled at Lynox, spittle flying from her mouth. She looked like a madwoman. She felt like a madwoman. Her hair was in disarray, and perspiration had beaded up on her forehead. It was no wonder she didn't have foam caked up in the corners of her mouth. She was acting rabid.

For the past fifteen minutes she'd been in disbelief that Lynox was really planning on obliging Ms. Folins. She'd watched him pack some of Tyson's and Tatum's clothing and things in a suitcase, and now she watched him pack his own. This was a nightmare, one that was coming true, and one she'd never even had. This was something she had never even thought would happen to her and her family. Yet lightning had struck twice as far as children's services stepping in to disrupt her life was concerned, and this time it had hit a tree, and the tree had fallen on their home and destroyed it.

"I can leave you, I am leaving you, and I'm taking the kids with me." Lynox tried to remain neutral. He didn't want to set Deborah off any more than she already had been. He'd tried to explain to her that this wasn't about her, that it was about the kids. She could fend for herself, but they couldn't. So if leaving her meant protecting them, then so be it. Sure it was tough, but it was a no-brainer.

Deborah stood blocking the closed door. She'd already told Lynox that he was leaving over her dead body.

"I promise I'll be better," Deborah pleaded, looking into her man's eyes. "I'll do whatever you want me to do." Deborah bounced up and down, like a child begging her parents to buy her something from the ice-cream truck.

Lynox rested his hands on Deborah's shoulders. The gesture was both to comfort her and to make her stop bouncing. He could see that his leaving was eating her up. He was afraid. He really didn't know what his wife would do after he walked out that door, but he was more afraid of what might happen if he didn't.

Deborah knew deep down inside that Lynox was leaving to protect the children, but a part of her still didn't want to believe that was the only reason. The voice in her head told her that he'd been waiting for a reason to leave her so that he could go be with someone else, so of course, she went as far as to voice that concern to Lynox. Lynox didn't even go on that ride with her. Instead, he opened their bedroom door to leave.

He should have thought twice about turning his back on Deborah. The Beats Pill box crashing against the door, missing Lynox's head by inches, was proof of that. Lynox held the door-knob. He gripped it tightly, causing the palm of his hand to turn red. The veins in his hand were pulsating. He squeezed his eyes shut so hard that he got an instant headache.

Deborah reminded Lynox of the vows he'd taken. He'd vowed that only death would part them, and not him walking out on her.

"The death of what, though, Debbie? The death of being in love? The death of trust? Given where our marriage is headed, the death of one of us? How many things have to die, things that are supposed to be the foundation of our marriage, before the marriage itself dies?"

Deborah had no reply for her husband. Sure, the vows they'd each read from the Bible and exchanged included the words "till death do us part." But Lynox was right. Their vows didn't specifically say that this death was the physical death of the husband or the wife. So many things had already died, some that probably couldn't even be resuscitated. Deborah was willing to ride this thing out, though, until the wheels fell off. That was easy for her to say, considering she was the one wearing them down until they did.

How had things gotten this bad? Why was God punishing her by taking her kids away? Taking her husband away? They were at the point of no return. And now she feared that once Lynox walked out that door, he wouldn't return, either. She wouldn't be able to live with herself knowing that she was the cause of her marriage being over, the cause of her family being split. She couldn't live like that. She couldn't live without Lynox. She couldn't live without her family together as one. She couldn't live. She wouldn't. So allowing Lynox to walk out that door and go on with his own life, leaving her on her own to bear such devastation, wasn't an option. So Deborah did what she had to do to stop the pain before it ever hit.

When Deborah opened her eyes, she saw nothing but white. White walls, white ceiling, and a white light shining in her eyes.

What? I can't believe I went to heaven, anyway, was all Deborah could think. Suicide supposedly was the ultimate abomination. There was no getting that right or repenting for that. So even though she'd taken every last happy pill that was left in her bottle, God had still allowed her to pass through the gates of . . .

"Heaven." The word fell off of Deborah's lips, and she felt such peace.

"Well, if that's where you're trying to go, looks like the Heavenly Father gave you one more chance."

Deborah didn't recognize the voice. Suddenly the white light was no more. She saw spots, and then the blurry image before her began to transform into a clear image. Deborah looked to the left and then looked to the right. She saw machines. She saw IV bags pumping something into her arms. She looked down and realized she was in a hospital bed. She went to sit up but then realized she was being restrained.

Oh, Lord. Had she been arrested again? The last time she'd been restrained in a hospital bed was the night she had to get stitches put in her head.

Deborah tried to move her arms. When she looked down, she realized that this time it wasn't handcuffs that were restraining her, but instead some pockets attached to the bed through which her arms had been weaved.

"Relax," said the woman who had been shining a white light in her eyes. "These are so that when you woke up, you didn't freak out and try to pull the IVs out or anything. Okay? Plus, we didn't want you to try to hurt yourself again. Okay?"

Deborah looked at the smiling nurse. She looked like she was really there to help Deborah, not like that Ms. Folins. Deborah nodded.

"Good," the nurse said. "Now, let me finish taking your vitals, and then I'll go get the doctor to come talk to you, okay, Deborah? You don't mind if I call you Deborah, do you? It's such a pretty name. Comes from the Bible, right? She was the first judge or first female judge?"

Deborah nodded again.

"Yay. I was right." She then leaned down and said to Deborah, "I don't know a whole lot about church and the Bible, but what I do know is that taking a bottle of pills is not the way to get to heaven." The nurse winked, then left the room.

Deborah lay there, feeling really surreal at that moment. Then embarrassment took over. What in the world was she going to tell people when they learned that she'd tried to end her own life? What would Lynox say? Dear God, what would her kids say? How would she explain to them that she didn't try to kill herself because they weren't enough for her to live for, but because she couldn't live without them?

Watching Lynox leave that bedroom, hearing that front door slam shut, and seeing him drive out of the driveway had pushed Deborah over the edge. She had lost everything, not just her mind, but her husband and her children too. Those were the only people she'd lived for, and since they were gone, she had no reason to live.

Perhaps going back to counseling and taking pills would have ultimately helped Deborah, but she hadn't thought she'd be able to bear the process of doing it without her family by her side. She'd been in mental pain, which had turned into physical pain. Her mind had hurt; her body had hurt. She'd just wanted the pain to end. So she'd ended it, or so she'd thought.

"Mrs. Chase. It's good to see you awake," the doctor said as she entered the room. "You had us worried there for a minute."

"Us?" Deborah questioned.

"Of course," the doctor said as she began removing the restraints from Deborah's arms. "There are a lot of people who love you and care about you. You scared quite a few people. But everyone is glad you are okay."

Deborah watched the doctor free one arm and then the other. She rubbed her arms, and then she spoke. "Who? Who found me?" Deborah asked.

The doctor pulled Deborah's folder from where she had it tucked under her arm. She opened it and then read through it. "Margie. Your pastor, I believe. She's actually waiting to see you, if that's all right."

"Lynox? My husband. Is he here?"

"Um, I'm not sure," the doctor said. "But why don't we worry about that in a minute? Let me ask you a few questions, chat with you a second, and then I'll let you see a familiar face. How's that sound?"

Deborah agreed, and for the next few minutes the doctor asked her questions about both her physical and mental health. Not wanting to bombard Deborah, she then told her she'd allow her a few minutes of visits, and she'd be back to check on her later.

About five minutes after the doctor left, Pastor Margie entered the room. When Deborah looked into her pastor's eyes, she couldn't do anything but burst out crying. "I'm sorry. I'm so sorry, Pastor Margie."

Pastor Margie immediately went to Deborah's bedside and took her member's hand in hers. She began praying in the spirit while Deborah cried. This went on for a couple of minutes

before Deborah stopped crying and was ready
to talk.

"I'm so sorry," Deborah said, apologizing
again to her pastor.

"You don't have to apologize to me, Deborah.
I'm so glad Lynox had called me and asked me to
go see about you. Otherwise, you wouldn't even
be here for us to have this conversation."

"Lynox? Where is he?" Deborah asked. "Is he
out there?"

Pastor Margie shook her head. "No, but I
did call him. Considering the whole thing with
children's services, he can't leave the boys right
now."

"Where are they?"

"Staying with a friend of his. Rock. Rico.
Larrock. Or something like that." Pastor Margie
couldn't recall clearly.

"Reo Laroque?"

"Yes, that's it," Pastor Margie said. "They
have a guesthouse or something they are letting
them stay in. I could tell when I was talking
to him on the phone that it took everything in
him not to break down. But he was with the
boys. He has to be strong for them." She petted
Deborah's hand. "And you have to live for them."
She smiled. "As badly as he wants to be here,
he didn't think it would be a good idea for him

to leave the boys. I promised him I'd come see about you and call to update him."

Deborah found some comfort in her pastor's words. She'd figured that Lynox and the boys would go to a hotel or something. The last thing she wanted was for her boys to have to live out of a hotel. She figured if she was gone, they could all go back to the house and live happily ever after . . . without her.

"Lynox was tore up when I had to call him. I prayed for him. Told him to keep the faith," Pastor Margie said. "He'll be up in the morning, once he gets Tyson to school."

"Okay," Deborah replied, already getting nervous about seeing Lynox face-to-face. She was worried about what Lynox would think about her now.

Pastor Margie could see the worry in Deborah's eyes. "But don't think about that right now." She petted Deborah's hand again.

"Can you call him? I want to talk to him and the boys."

"I wasn't allowed to bring a cell phone in here with me," Pastor Margie said. "But there is someone else here who I think you'd love to see."

Deborah couldn't fathom who else besides Jesus or her family she wanted to see more than anything right now. Then a person popped into her head. "Is it my mother?"

Pastor Margie shook her head. She then thought for a moment. "Well, kind of, sorta." She stood. "But I'll let you see for yourself." She headed over to the door. "I'm going to keep praying for you."

Deborah smiled and watched her pastor exit the room. No sooner had Pastor Margie left the room than someone else entered it.

"Well, if you wanted me to come all the way from Kentucky to see you, the only thing you had to do was call me. But leave it to you to be so dramatic."

Deborah immediately broke out crying when she saw the woman standing in the doorway. It wasn't Deborah's biological mother, who in fact had been in Deborah's room before Deborah had come to. Ms. Lucas was now in the cafeteria, grabbing a bite to eat and some coffee. But the woman standing in Deborah's room was her spiritual mother, the one assigned to mother and nurture her by God Himself.

"Mother Doreen!" Deborah cried out in between tears.

Mother Doreen walked over to Deborah, who couldn't even look Mother Doreen in the eyes. Instead, she was weeping into her hands. Mother Doreen took Deborah's head and pulled it right to her bosom. She then wasted no time doing what she'd come to do.

She planted her hand on top of Deborah's
head and began to pray as if she had an all-con-
suming fire on her tongue. "Lord, I bind up
that spirit of suicide right now, in the name of
Jesus. We're not going to play with it today,
O God. I'm coming straight to the throne with
Holy Ghost boldness, demanding that you hear
my prayer and act on it. God, your Word says
that the prayers of the righteous availeth much.
Well, I haven't been righteous all my life, but
you changed me, Lord. You picked me up and
cleaned me up with the very blood of your Son,
who is blameless, spotless, blemish free, and
sinless. I've lived it, and I've walked in it. I'm not
perfect, but, dear Lord, I stand here before you
today holy and righteous. I can honestly say that
I present this body to you holy and acceptable.
So, Father God, I trust that your Word will not
come back void and that you will hear my prayer
and it shall avail."

"Thank you, Jesus," Deborah said between
tears.

"God, I ask that from this point on, Deborah is
about your business. Let her not be like the man
in the field that was left behind. Yes, he was busy,
but not about your business. The man next to
him that you took, Lord, the man you welcomed
into the Kingdom, was busy with the business

of the spirit. Let her not be so overwhelmed in life with things that bear no witness or fruit to you, dear God. Let her not operate out of fear of poverty, for financial gain, but consume her with the works of you, God. Take her mind back to when she first was on fire for you, Lord. Take her mind back to when she was a child, for we know that it's easier to train a child than to fix a broken man. But we know you can do it all, Lord."

"Yes, Lord, do it," Deborah cried out. "Train me. Fix me. Have your way." This was the closest to, and the most focused on, God that Deborah had been in a long time. Too bad it had taken getting her into a hospital psych ward to achieve such a feat. But God would break a person all the way down to get them to see that they needed fixing and that Jesus was the answer.

"God, I know with this prayer you are going to have to shut off some things in Deborah's life. But don't let her fret. Don't let her lose her mind over the stuff you are going to shut off, God, because she is going to need her mind for the stuff you turn on."

"Keep my mind." Deborah wanted God to know that she was a part of the prayer. She was cosigning everything Mother Doreen had to say on her behalf.

"God, I know Deborah is going through a storm right now and has gone through one. Give her the patience of Job to wait on you, God. Let her know that even if you don't take her out of the storm right now, you will give her the power and the resources to get through it. And, God, we know your resources never run dry."

Deborah raised her hands and continued sobbing.

"Right now, God, you have asked the woman of God to sacrifice her children unto you. But let her see that like with Abraham, you only want to see how far she is willing to go in your obedience and sacrifice."

"Yes, Jesus, my babies." That last part of Mother Doreen's prayer really stirred up something in Deborah. She was no longer looking at children's services removing her children from her home as a punishment from God, but instead as her sacrificing them to God. She had to look at this thing from the spiritual perspective. And the same way God had allowed Abraham to keep his son, she would be able to keep hers and would give them the peaceful life they deserved.

"Let this time be a time for Deborah to separate herself from the world while she saturates herself with your Word. The success of the devil is based on the ignorance of your Word, O God, so fill her up," Mother Doreen continued. "Lord, fill her with the spirit of the fruit of temperance, which is self-control. Increase her power, because you have to have power to have patience to wait on the Lord. Whatever man serves will control Him, so let her serve only you, God."

Deborah nodded.

"So we rebuke that jezebel spirit of control right now in the name of Jesus," Mother Doreen said. "Father God, we know that everything we are praying for will come to pass, because as long as we pray according to your Word, we are praying according to your will. So, Lord, we say this prayer in the name of your Son and our Savior, Jesus Christ. Amen."

"Amen," Deborah said, closing her eyes as tears seeped out.

There was such a peace in the room that Mother Doreen began to pray softly in tongues. Deborah joined in. Being of one accord, the two women ceased their prayers.

Deborah opened her eyes. "You're like my Superwoman," Deborah told Mother Doreen. "Every time Lois Lane is in trouble, there you are."

Mother Doreen laughed. "I'm not Superwoman, but I am a woman of God who is always on assignment to do God's will."

"Well, I'm sorry I keep making you have to come all the way from your home in Kentucky to see about me."

"Well, don't feel too bad," Mother Doreen said. "I was actually already headed to Malvonia."

"Really?" Deborah asked. "What brought you here?"

"Oh, that pastor of yours," Mother Doreen said. "I can't speak on it right now, but, oh, you'll find out about it soon enough . . . you and the rest of the world."

By the way Mother Doreen was talking, it sounded like something juicy was going down. But the last thing Deborah needed to concern herself with was somebody else's business. Nope, she was going to be all about her own and God's.

"Thank you so much for your prayers, Mother Doreen," Deborah said. She looked downward as tears began to fall from her eyes.

Mother Doreen handed her a tissue.

"I truly feel as if my mind is renewed and that God will heal me." Deborah began wiping her eyes.

"God has already healed you, daughter. He told me that on my drive here," Mother Doreen said, believing her very words to the fullest. "You need to walk in it. Walk in your healing and walk in your deliverance. Need I remind you that Second Corinthians five-seventeen says, 'Therefore if any man be in Christ, he is a new creature: old things are passed away; behold, all things are become new.'" Mother Doreen pointed at Deborah. "The spirit in you is renewed. It's re-created in Christ. Retrain yourself according to your spirit of Christ instead of your old self and traits."

Deborah nodded. "Thank you for helping me see that."

"Your help will always cometh from the Lord, but the Lord puts people and sources right here on earth to help us." Mother Doreen put her hands on her hips and said in her sister girlfriend voice, "Now, walk in that healing and deliverance by going and finding yourself a good shrink."

Deborah's mouth dropped. "What?"

"You heard me," Mother Doreen said. "Black folks and church folks better recognize something." She rolled her eyes and sucked her teeth. "There is nothing wrong with prayer, fasting, and speaking healing over one's life, and there is also nothing wrong with therapy."

"I hear you," Deborah agreed.

"And relax a little and enjoy life," Mother Doreen said to Deborah. "Nobody ever makes it out alive, anyway."

Deborah smiled.

"But let God be the one who decides when it's time for you to go out. You hear me?"

Deborah exhaled and nodded. "Yes, Mother Doreen. I hear you. But sometimes I feel like I'm going to lose control."

"Good!" Mother Doreen exclaimed. "Because when you finally lose control, maybe God can finally take control."

"You just preached right there," Deborah said, putting up her hand and shaking her head.

"Good. Now, let me get on out of here so that your mother can get back in here to see you now that you're awake," Mother Doreen said. "She was in here earlier, you know."

Deborah didn't know. She'd been too out of it.

"I have faith that you can do this, Deborah," Mother Doreen said. "But I have more faith that God is going to help you do it."

"I believe your words, and I receive them, Mother Doreen," Deborah said. "But I'd be lying if I said I wasn't afraid of failing again."

"God will never set you up for failure. But He will set you up to learn from your failure. Have you learned from your failure?" Mother Doreen asked.

"I have." And Deborah meant that.

"Then you already know what failure looks like. Now go get the victory."

"I've already got it," Deborah declared, pumping a fist in the air. "I've got the victory!"

Epilogue

It had been two weeks since Deborah's suicide attempt. The hospital had suggested, and the courts and children's services had ordered, that Deborah seek counseling as well as attend anger management classes. She'd hoped that when Lynox refused to be a state witness, her domestic violence case would be dismissed. It wasn't, not completely, anyway. She ended up being charged with battery. She didn't have to serve jail time, but she did receive one year's probation and one hundred hours of community service, and she had to pay court and attorneys' fees.

Realizing that it was more convenient for Deborah to stay at the Laroques' than for Lynox and the kids to remain there, she and Lynox switched up. Lynox and the boys returned home. Both Ms. Lucas and the Perkins pitched in to help Lynox care for the boys.

Deborah now stood in the bathroom mirror, getting prepared for her first visit with Dr.

Vanderdale since being released from the hospital. As she stood there, with lipstick, foundation, blush, mascara, eyeliner, and lip liner at her fingertips, she couldn't help thinking about the question she'd posed to Dr. Vanderdale during her only visit with him. "I can't help but wonder if I'm looking crazy right in the eyes," she said aloud. What was the definition of *crazy*? What did crazy feel like? Could some of the feelings Deborah had experienced be categorize as crazy? Crazy couldn't just be let go to run free. Crazy needed to be treated.

Well, she was about to find out officially if she was crazy or not. And this time she wouldn't jump up and exit the courtroom without getting the verdict.

Deborah finished getting herself together, and an hour later she was thirty-five minutes into her session with Dr. Vanderdale. In speaking with Dr. Vanderdale, Deborah learned that Klarke's layman's assessment about her had been right. More than likely, postpartum depression had triggered Deborah's mental condition.

"You should have talked to someone, Deborah," Dr. Vanderdale said. "Told someone what was going on with you."

Deborah sighed. "I've always told Tyson that what goes on in our home stays in our home, that it's nobody's business. I guess I followed that same rule for whatever was going on in my head."

"Yeah," Dr. Vanderdale said, "I hear that a lot, and there is nothing worse you can tell a child to stifle his or her voice. Do you know how many children are molested and/or abused right there in their own home and don't tell because that's been embedded in their brains?"

"I never thought about that," Deborah said.

"Most people don't. My take on it is that if there is something going on in the home, you know, adult business, that you don't want children to tell anyone about, then don't do it or say it in front of them. I believe that a lot of parents tell their children to keep silent because it makes them less accountable for the things they do in the home. Knowing that your children are watching and could tell someone makes adults more accountable, so it verges on cowardice to ask children to obey such a rule. Like I said, telling a child that can really be detrimental in some cases."

"In other words, we should act like our children are Jesus and not do anything in front of them that we wouldn't do in front of Him?"

Dr. Vanderdale laughed. "Um, not quite, but I love the analogy." Dr. Vanderdale tapped his pen against his tablet. "So how are things going?

Have you been back to church?" Dr. Vanderdale recalled Deborah telling him how Sundays had been hard for her mentally.

"Sundays always have been and still are sort of the worst days for me and my depression," Deborah admitted. "I'm glad to be back on my happy pills, but I still have my moments. With Sundays being my day of Sabbath, for some reason, all my demons like to show their faces. Depression, anxiety, low self-esteem, even suicide. On occasion I still feel like death is easier than fighting."

"But you know that's not true, don't you?"

"I know it, but the voices in my head won't let up on trying to convince me otherwise."

Dr. Vanderdale took some notes.

"For a while I had mastered hiding things from both my family and my church family. To the outside world, I appeared to be so well put together." She chuckled. "Especially on Sundays. I had considered myself to be nothing more than a Sunday only Christian. The other six days were pure hell."

"Well, you know what, Deborah?" Dr. Vanderdale said. "I'm glad you're back and willing to do the work."

"Me too," Deborah said. "God gave me another chance at life. I can't let Him down. I can't let

Lynox down, and I can't let my children down.
But more importantly, I can't let me down."

"Amen to that," Dr. Vanderdale said, giving
Deborah a high five.

The following Sunday, Deborah enjoyed her
time in the Lord at New Day Temple of Faith.
After Dr. Vanderdale and the counselor who
worked on behalf of children's services filed
reports, Deborah was approved to attend church
with Lynox and the children. Deborah didn't
even take the boys to children's church. The
family that prayed together stayed together, so
she insisted that they all stay together in order
to pray together in the sanctuary. Lynox had
no problem with that. He loved every moment
he could get with his family under one roof,
unsupervised.

After service, Deborah kissed Lynox and the
children good-bye and watched them head out
of the sanctuary. She stayed behind for the counseling session she had scheduled with Pastor
Margie. No longer was Deborah's motto "What
goes on in my home stays in my home." She had
to begin to look at this thing from a spiritual
standpoint. Her home was her body, the Lord's
temple. Whatever was going on in her body and

mind, she was going to share it. For now, she felt the people she had been assigned to share things with were her counselor, Dr. Vanderdale, her pastor, and, of course, Mother Doreen, who was also now her prayer partner and who held her accountable for walking in her healing and deliverance.

As Deborah stood in the sanctuary, waiting for Pastor Margie to finish up greeting folks, she saw someone. She felt led in her spirit to go over and say a word to him. By the time Deborah headed his way, someone else had already stopped to greet him. Deborah waited patiently off to the side until they were finished conversing.

"Sister Deborah. God bless you," Elder Ross said, then shook Deborah's hand.

"Hi, Elder Ross," Deborah said, placing her other hand on top of Elder Ross's. She looked him in the eyes. "I just wanted to say something to you before I left church today."

"Oh?" Elder Ross said, wondering what Deborah could possibly have to say.

Deborah stared the older gentleman in the eyes and said, "Sometimes it does take all that." Deborah gave him a hug before walking away. She figured Elder Ross was standing back there with a puzzled look on his face, but that was all right. It really wasn't about him understanding. It was about her finally getting it.

Sometimes healing and deliverance were more than just knowing God had done it for a person. They entailed a person doing it for themselves and taking all the necessary steps to walk in that healing. Deborah looked up at the beautiful sky, the sun shining down brightly. "I got it, God. I finally got it."

It wasn't going to be easy, but Deborah was willing to put in the work, rather than trying to rush things and looking for an easy fix. Even though God could perform a miracle in the blink of an eye, she didn't expect hers to happen overnight. She'd take it one Sunday at a time.

Reader Discussion Questions

1. Do you feel the author did a good job of putting the reader inside Deborah's head to experience her thoughts, feelings, and emotions?
2. Can you relate to Deborah feeling overwhelmed in life?
3. Deborah had reservations about befriending Klarke because Klarke wasn't a practicing Christian who attended church regularly. How do you feel about that?
4. Klarke wasn't into church and introduced Deborah to drugs. Would you advise Deborah to break her ties with Klarke? Support your answer.
5. Reo was equally yoked with his wife, Klarke. Would you give Lynox the same advice about befriending Reo as you would Deborah when it comes to Klarke?
6. Do you believe Deborah should have gone to jail for hitting Lynox? Do you think Lynox

should have gone to jail, even though the injury Deborah sustained at his hands was an accident? Support your response.

7. How do you feel about Ms. Folins removing the children from the home?

8. Did Lynox do the right thing when he left Deborah in order to keep the children out of the children's services system?

9. What is your opinion of what Dr. Vanderdale had to say about teaching children that what goes on in the home stays in the home?

10. How do you feel about an act of suicide being attempted in a Christian fiction book?

Reo and Klarke are characters from the secular novels *The Root of All Evil* and *When Souls Mate*, which E. N. Joy wrote under the name of Joylynn M. Jossel, before she became a Christian fiction author. Would you like to see their story continued? E-mail the author at enjoywrites@aol.com to tell her why or why not.

Joylynn M. Ross is now writing as

**BLESSEDselling author
E. N. Joy (Everybody Needs Joy)**

BLESSEDselling author E. N. Joy is the writer behind the five-book series "New Day Divas," the three-book series "Still Divas," the three-book series "Always Divas," and the forthcoming three-book series "Forever Divas," all of which have been coined "Soap Operas in Print." She is an *Essence* magazine bestselling author and has written secular books under the names Joylynn M. Jossel and JOY.

After thirteen years as a paralegal in the insurance industry, E. N. Joy finally divorced her career and married her mistress and her passion: writing. In 2000 she formed her own publishing company, where she self-published her books until landing a book deal with a major publisher. Her company has published *New York Times* and *Essence* magazine bestselling authors in the "Sinner Series." In 2004 E. N. Joy branched off into the business of literary consulting, providing one-on-one consultations and other literary services, such as ghostwriting, editing, professional read-throughs, and write behinds. Her clients include first-time authors, *Essence* magazine bestselling authors, *New York Times* bestselling authors, and entertainers. This award-winning author has also been sharing her literary expertise on conference panels in her hometown of Columbus, Ohio, as well as in cities across the country.

E. N. Joy has not forsaken her love of poetry. Her latest poetic project is an eBook of poetry entitled *Flower in My Hair*. "But my spirit has moved in another direction," she says. Needless to say, she no longer pens street lit. (Two of her titles, *If I Ruled the World* and *Dollar Bill*, made the *Essence* magazine best sellers' list. *Dollar Bill* was mentioned in *Newsweek* and has been translated into Japanese.) She no longer writes erotica or adult contemporary fiction, either. (*An All Night Man*, a collection of novellas to which she and three other authors, including *New York Times* bestselling author Brenda Jackson, contributed, earned the Borders Bestselling African American Romance Award.)

You can find this author's children's book *The Secret Olivia Told Me*, written under the name N. Joy, in bookstores now. *The Secret Olivia Told Me* received a Coretta Scott King Honor from the American Library Association. The book was also acquired by Scholastic Books and has sold over one hundred thousand copies. E. N. Joy has also penned a tween/young adult eBook entitled *Operation Get Rid of Mom's New Boyfriend* and a children's fairy-tale eBook entitled *Sabella and the Castle Belonging to the Troll*. Elementary and middle school children have fallen in love with reading and creative writing as a result of the readings and workshops E. N. Joy gives in schools nationwide.

E. N. Joy is the acquisitions editor for Urban Christian, an imprint of Urban Books, the titles of which are distributed by Kensington Publishing Corporation. In addition, she is the artistic developer for a young girls' group called DJHK Gurls. She pens original songs, drama skits, and monologues for the group that deal with issues that affect today's youth, such as bullying.

You can visit BLESSEDselling author E. N. Joy at www.enjoywrites.com, or e-mail her at enjoywrites@aol.com.

Keep up with the Divas by liking the "New Day Divas Fan Page" on Facebook.